## …RAISES
## *NE*… …LING AUTHOR
## …H!

"Bobbi Smith is a terrific storyteller whose wonderful characters, good dialogue and compelling plot will keep you up all night."

"Ms. Smith's memorable cast of characters and secondary plot lines are what make her a truly wonderful storyteller."

**AWARDS:**

*Romantic Times* Storyteller of the Year
*Romantic Times* Career Achievement

**CRITICS RAVE FOR *HAVEN*!**

"*Haven* is a wonderful book. The story is multifaceted and gripping. It delivers a powerful message of God's love and care to each one of us no matter where we are in our walk with Him."

—Bestselling Author Debbie Macomber

"*Haven* is, by far, one of the best Inspirational novels I have read this year. The story starts out running and doesn't stop until the very last word, leaving you with feelings of peace and contentment and basking in God's glow. *Haven* is a guaranteed one-of-a-kind novel that will stand out in your memory for years and is the perfect addition to your keeper shelf to read again and again."

—Romance Reviews Today (A Perfect 10)

"The author delivers a thoroughly enjoyable read, with high stakes for the appealing characters."

—*Romantic Times*

"*Haven* is an in-depth look at human emotion. I could not put this story down."

—Writers Unlimited

Other books by Bobbi Smith:

**HALFBREED WARRIOR**
**BRAZEN**
**BAYOU BRIDE**
**HUNTER'S MOON**
**FOREVER AUTUMN**
**LONE WARRIOR**
**EDEN**
**WANTON SPLENDOR**
**SWEET SILKEN BONDAGE**
**THE HALF-BREED (SECRET FIRES)**
**WESTON'S LADY**
**HALF-BREED'S LADY**
**OUTLAW'S LADY**
**FORBIDDEN FIRES**
**RAPTURE'S RAGE**
**THE LADY & THE TEXAN**
**RENEGADE'S LADY**
**KISS ME FOREVER**
**THE LADY'S HAND**
**LADY DECEPTION**

The *Brides of Durango* series:

**ELISE**
**TESSA**
**JENNY**

As Julie Marshall:

**HAVEN**

# BOBBI SMITH

writing as JULIE MARSHALL

# MIRACLES

LEISURE BOOKS

NEW YORK CITY

A LEISURE BOOK®

February 2006

Published by

Dorchester Publishing Co., Inc.
200 Madison Avenue
New York, NY 10016



ISBN 0-8439-5647-X



Printed in the United States of America.

*This book is dedicated to Carter David.*
*You're the perfect grandson!*

*My thanks to handsome Harry Spiller, ex-sheriff and current Associate Professor of Criminal Justice at John A. Logan College in Carterville, IL, and at SIU-Carbondale and author of the* Murder in the Heartland *book series (as seen on* Forensic Files*) for his help with law enforcement research.*

*Thanks, too, to Leann and her handsome husband, Sam Orrico, and Amy Templer and her handsome husband, Michael Williams, for their help with Harley-Davidson research.*

*Thanks to Betty Murr of the St. Charles City-County Library District. You're wonderful!*

# MIRACLES

THE TERROR GROWS
THREE DEAD IN THREE WEEKS
POLICE STILL BAFFLED IN SEARCH FOR
DEADLY HIGHWAY SNIPER

The main headline of *The Daily Sun* and the article that followed criticized the police and their lack of success in arresting the killer. The sniper read the article and smiled. He enjoyed learning that the authorities were no closer to identifying him.

He knew they would never catch him.

He was too smart for them.

Satisfied that all was well in the world, he carefully folded the paper so as not to crease the headline, and then set it aside. He would read it again later.

# *Chapter One*

*The Lord Be With You . . .*

Seventy-two-year-old George Taylor quietly entered Holy Family Church and slipped into a pew halfway up the main aisle. The beauty of the old church never failed to move him. The statues and the altar were glorious to behold, and at this early-morning hour, the sun shining through the stained-glass windows bathed the interior in a rainbow of vibrant colors. It was heavenly there, truly peaceful, and just now George needed some peace.

Kneeling down, George bowed his head in prayer. The week before, he hadn't been feeling well and had gone in to see his doctor. He'd thought he had just a virus or something that was going around, but after checking him over, Dr. Murray had ordered several tests to be done. And tomorrow the results would be back. George hoped they would show he was fine, but he had his doubts. He'd been feeling so poorly these last few days.

George finished praying and sat back in the pew. He glanced around to see who else had come for the seven a.m. Mass. It wasn't very crowded, maybe thirty-five or forty people, but then, that was normal for an early weekday Mass like this one. He noticed Lydia Chandler, a friend from his prayer group, sitting across the aisle a few pews ahead of him. She was an attractive young woman who worked at one of the newspapers in town. He liked Lydia a lot, and he knew he'd seek her out and say hello when Mass was over.

"Please stand," Father Richards announced, drawing everyone's attention, "and let's sing the Entrance Antiphon together, Number 224 in the hymnal, 'God Is Calling Me.' "

George stood and joined in the singing as the pastor made his way down the main aisle to the altar.

Lydia watched Father Richards pass by, but she didn't bother trying to sing. When she was in sixth grade, her teacher had convinced her she had no talent for singing by telling her she was off-key right in front of the whole class. The embarrassment had stayed with her through the years and kept her very humble where her singing ability was concerned.

But singing wasn't even on Lydia's mind as she concentrated on the Mass and listened to the readings and Father's homily. She had come to Mass because she needed God's help to cope with everything that was going on in her life. The newspaper she worked for as a reporter, *The Daily Sun*, had been sold the year before.

The new owners had brought in Gary Newman as the managing editor, and under Gary's management, things had really changed—and not for the better. Gary was concerned only with the bottom line. He'd cut jobs and laid longtime employees off without warning. When one of their best reporters, a man who'd been with the paper for years, confronted Gary one day, he had fired him on the spot.

It was an ugly time at *The Daily Sun*, but Lydia was determined to stick it out. She loved her job as a reporter. She loved searching for the truth, digging up the facts and covering breaking stories. The scary part was, she was twenty-nine and single, and had no one to look out for her. That was why she was at Mass this morning, praying for the strength and wisdom she needed to deal with the uncertain situation at the office.

"Let us offer each other the sign of peace," Father Richards said.

*Peace is just what I need*, Lydia thought as she shook hands with the people in the pews close to her and then looked around to smile at the others in attendance. It was then she spotted George. He nodded to her in greeting, and her smile broadened. He was a dear, dear man, and she loved him a lot. She hadn't seen him for a while, and she was looking forward to saying hello after Mass.

It came time for Communion, and everyone filed forward to receive the sacrament. Returning to her pew, Lydia knelt down and bowed her head. Again, she prayed for the strength and wisdom she needed to get through the challenging times ahead.

When Mass was over, Lydia found George waiting for her in the greeting area.

"How are you?" she asked, giving George a warm hug and a kiss on the cheek.

"Fine, now that I've had a kiss from a pretty girl," he told her with a grin as they started to walk out to the parking lot together. "What a wonderful way to start my day!"

"You are such a charmer."

"I just tell the truth, that's all."

"Are you ready for prayer group tonight?"

"I'm looking forward to it. It'll be fun to see everybody again." He enjoyed the social aspect of their prayer meetings.

"What's the topic for this session?"

"I believe we're covering the Ten Commandments."

"That should be interesting."

"I'll see you tonight," George told her as they reached her car.

"You stay out of trouble today," she said with a laugh.

He laughed with her. "I'll try, but as wild as I am, sometimes it's not easy."

George stood back and waited as Lydia got in her car and started up the engine. He waved when she drove off, then headed for his own car. He thought about going out for breakfast somewhere, but he was feeling a little tired already this morning so he decided to just go home.

Lydia drove toward the newspaper office, as ready as she would ever be for another day working for Gary. She knew she would be early, but she was hoping to have some quiet time to get caught up on her work before everyone else came in. She was surprised when she discovered Gary was already at work in his office.

Gary looked up from his desk when he saw Lydia come in. He immediately went out to speak with her.

"I just got word that Captain Donovan is going to hold a press conference about the sniper shootings at ten o'clock this morning down at police headquarters," he informed her.

"Have they learned anything new?"

"Not that I could get out of him. I want you to cover it. Find out why they haven't caught this guy yet. This murderer has killed three people in three weeks, and the police still don't have any idea who he is! What kind of police work is that? Ask the tough questions. Find out what they know and what they don't know. Surely there are tips coming in on that sniper hot line they set up. See if you can learn if there have been any reliable leads. The public needs to know what the police are doing to stop this menace."

"I'll see what I can find out."

"You do that."

Gary turned and walked away without another word.

It wasn't far to police headquarters from the newspaper office, so Lydia was able to work at her desk for a little longer before she had to leave for the press conference. When she arrived at headquarters she found the room designated for the conference crowded with reporters from all the different media in town. Everyone was waiting anxiously for Captain Donovan to come in and address them. When the captain finally made his entrance, he went to stand at the lectern. All the lights, cameras and microphones were turned on and ready for him.

"Ladies and gentlemen, I'd like to read a statement first, and then I'll take your questions. Our investigation into the three unsolved murders is ongoing. As you know, the same weapon was used in all three shootings. Two witnesses of the second shooting reported seeing a dark green, four-door sedan in the area around the same time, but they were unable to identify the make or model of the vehicle, and they had no license plate information. Our hot line here at police headquarters is open twenty-four hours a day, and we are following up on every lead phoned in. We are doing everything we can to make an arrest as quickly as possible." Captain Donovan paused and looked out at the sea of reporters. "Now I'll take your questions—"

Everyone started shouting at once. The captain held up his hands to try to slow down the verbal barrage aimed at him.

"One at a time, please. Miss Chandler—"

"Are any of the leads that have been phoned in promising?"

"As I said, people have been calling in," he repeated, refusing to elaborate, "and we are following up on all calls. If anything does develop, the press will be notified."

He called on another reporter.

"Do you have any likely suspects?"

"Not at this time."

"What are you doing regarding the car? Have you taken any action to follow up on that tip?"

"We are looking into it."

" 'Looking into it' is great," the reporter from one radio station said sarcastically, "but what steps are you actually taking, Chief? Are you pulling over all the dark green, four-door sedans in town and checking them out?"

The captain began to look irritated. "If that's what it ultimately takes to find this killer, then that's what we'll do. We'll check every green sedan. Our job is to keep the public safe."

"Were the victims connected in any way? Did they have anything in common?" Lydia asked without waiting to be called on.

"So far, the only thing we've found that the victims have in common, is that they had nothing in common."

"So these are totally random acts of violence like the D.C. sniper?" a reporter from the other local paper, *The Evening News*, asked.

"I'm afraid so."

"If you're afraid, Chief, what hope do the rest of us have?" Lydia challenged pointedly.

Captain Donovan glared at her, his growing irritation obvious. "Our police force is one of the finest in the state. Our officers work hard, twenty-four hours a day, seven days a week to protect the citizens of this town, and they do a fine job of it."

"Tell that to the families of the three victims!" a reporter from one of the television stations shouted out, deliberately trying to provoke him to get his reaction on camera.

It worked.

Captain Donovan turned a hate-filled glare on the newsman and abruptly ended the press conference. "That's all for today. You'll be notified of any new developments."

He turned and walked out of the room, ignoring all the other questions being shouted at him as he went.

Lydia wasted no time. She hurried back to the office to fill Gary in on what had transpired. She just wished there had been more concrete information available, so *The Daily Sun* could get the word out to the public. If the leads were really that few, though, it was no wonder the captain had been so short-tempered and walked out on the press.

Gary was watching for Lydia and confronted her the moment she walked into the office.

"What did you find out?" he demanded.

"Captain Donovan was not a happy man this morning."

"Who cares about Donovan! What have you got on the sniper?" he snapped.

"The only real clue they're willing to talk about is a car." She told him what little the investigators knew about the suspected vehicle. "But no one really knows for sure that the dark green sedan is actually involved."

"So, basically, you're telling me that our headline from yesterday was right on target: *Police Still Baffled in Search for Deadly Highway Sniper.*"

"It looks that way for right now. Captain Donovan walked out on us."

"A little irritated, was he?"

"Yes, but I have faith in the department."

"You're probably the only one in town who does, right now," Gary derided.

"They're going to catch the shooter."

"But how many more dead bodies are going to be littering the city streets before they do?"

"The sniper is bound to make a mistake," Lydia argued, "and when he does, the cops will be ready and waiting for him."

"We hope."

Lydia didn't bother to respond as Gary turned away and went back in his office. She sat down at her desk and got to work. She had another meeting to cover at two o'clock; she had to get her notes from the press conference written up and on Gary's desk before it was time to go.

# *Chapter Two*

Detective Steve Mason and his partner Charlie Tucker were frustrated and angry as Steve drove them back to police headquarters in their unmarked police car. There had been three cold-blooded murders in their town in recent weeks, and though they'd worked endless hours on the case, they were no closer to catching the killer now than they had been on day one.

The first murder victim had been an elderly man on his way to a doctor's appointment. The second shooting had been four days later. The victim was a school bus driver on his way back to the district's parking area after dropping the kids off at school, and the third victim was a young woman driving to work early one morning in the midtown area. All three shootings had occurred on the interstate, along a ten-mile section within the city limits, and the bullets had been fired from the same rifle.

Despite their best efforts, the only thing Steve and Charlie had turned up were two witnesses in the area of the second shooting who'd reported seeing an unfamiliar dark green sedan in the neighborhood around the time of the shooting. That was it. They had no license plate numbers, no description of the driver, no make or model on the car. Just a dark green sedan. Nothing else.

Steve and Charlie kept investigating every possible angle. So far they'd learned that none of the dead had had any known enemies. The elderly man had been beloved by his family and friends. The second victim, the school bus driver, had been admired by all and adored by the children he'd served every day, and the young woman had been newly engaged and a secretary at a local business.

The detectives were on their way back from questioning Bob Gray, an ex-con who'd just returned to the area after serving time downstate. After speaking with him, they were more convinced than ever that the murders were random acts of violence committed by someone imitating the D.C. serial sniper.

"Interviewing Bob Gray was a real waste of our time," Steve said in disgust.

"I'll say. When I first heard he was back in the area, I thought we had our man," Charlie remarked.

"So did I."

Bob Gray had vowed to get even with the cops when he'd been sent off to prison some years before. As much as Steve and Charlie had believed and hoped he was the perp, Gray's alibis for the times of the shootings were airtight. He was not their man.

*"Attention all units. We have a 10-56—"* The call came in over their police band radio.

Steve scowled darkly at the news. A 10-56 was a drunk driver, and Steve had no use for drunk drivers. Some five years before while he'd been on patrol with his close friend and partner, Drew Barton, they'd been broadsided by a drunk. Steve's injuries had been minor, but Drew's back had been broken and he'd been left paralyzed from the waist down. Steve had always known drunk drivers were trouble, but ever since that day he'd become even more determined to get them off the road.

The dispatcher continued, *"The citizen who called it in said the car is a late model red Chevrolet Camaro, traveling erratically at a high rate of speed on Castle Avenue near Broadway."*

"That's just two blocks over. Tell them we're on it," Steve ordered Charlie, and he immediately turned right at the next corner. He didn't want anyone getting hurt.

Charlie quickly radioed the dispatcher that they would be following up.

As they reached Castle Avenue, the Camaro raced through the intersection right in front of them. Steve put the red light on the roof of their unmarked car, turned on the siren and gave chase. Charlie called in the plates, while Steve concentrated fully on his driving.

"Slow down, Jim!" seventeen-year-old Tom Lewis shouted as Jim Hunt drove his Camaro wildly through the streets of town.

"Slow down? A few minutes ago you were dissing my car, saying it wasn't fast, and now you're telling me to slow down?" Jim was still angry over the insults, and he was glad he'd called Tom's bluff. "Changed your mind, did you?"

"Yeah, yeah, I changed my mind." Tom was disgusted and couldn't wait to get away from Jim. He'd only invited Jim over to his house today because he had been hanging out in the school hall with several of Tom's other friends. Whenever he got the chance, Tom and his buddies would go to his house after school. His parents usually worked late, making it easy for Tom to sneak a few beers from the ample supply his father kept on hand. They'd been having a good time that afternoon until Jim had gotten insulted over some comment about the Camaro.

"I told you this is one hot machine," Jim bragged, giving the engine even more gas.

"You proved your point! Now quit driving like an idiot!"

"Who's an idiot?" Jim demanded as he glanced over at Tom.

Tom and his friends were varsity athletes, and Jim thought they always acted like they were better than everyone else. The invitation to Tom's house had surprised him that day. He'd gone along, wanting to fit in, and he thought he had. When the other guys started drinking, he'd joined in, and he'd outdrunk them. Now he was determined to show Tom how well he could handle his car.

"*You* are if you don't slow down! Do you want to get pulled over? Do you want to get a ticket?"

The words were barely out of Tom's mouth when they both heard the sound of a siren over the music blasting from the radio.

Jim glanced into his rearview mirror and swore loudly at the sight of the police car pursuing them.

Tom cursed aloud, too. This was what he'd been afraid of when Jim had started driving like a wild man. He panicked, though, when Jim hit the brakes and started to pull over.

"What are you doing?"

"It's the cops, man!"

"You think I don't know that?" Tom was incredulous.

"I gotta pull over!"

"Don't! We've been drinking! Get the hell out of here!" Tom hollered. He realized all too well what would happen if his parents found out what he and his friends had been doing at the house. "Show me how fast this car really is!"

Jim floored it again and took the next corner at a breakneck speed that scared even him.

Earlier Tom had thought Jim was a wuss for buckling up, but now he regretted not doing it himself. He made a grab for his seat belt, but there was no way he could reach it with the wild way they were tearing through the streets.

Jim had hoped to lose the cops with his fast turn, but they stayed right with him. When he saw the stop sign at the corner ahead, he knew what he had to do. It was scary, but he had no choice. He was desperate. He'd let the cops worry about stopping at the intersection. He wasn't going to.

Jim kept the pedal to the metal, and the Camaro roared on.

The intersection looked clear.

He thought he could make it.

But as they reached the corner, a large gray sedan with the right of way pulled into the intersection.

Shocked and suddenly frantic, Jim shouted an obscenity as he drunkenly fought to avoid hitting the other car. He braked as hard as he could and struggled for control, but the speeding Camaro careened wildly about. It barely missed the sedan before it crashed into a lamp post.

The impact jolted Jim and Tom, and both their air bags inflated. Tom's door flew open and he was thrown from the car. Jim was left slumped behind the wheel.

"Oh, my God!" Charlie shouted in horror as he and Steve witnessed the crash.

"Forget about God!" Steve ordered harshly as memories of the wreck with Drew haunted him. "Call it in!"

Steve slammed on the brakes and pulled to a stop close to the wreck. He could see the passenger lying on the ground beside the damaged sports car and rushed to get out of the patrol car so he could go to his aid.

"And tell them we're going to need an ambulance!" Steve called back to Charlie.

* * *

Lydia was a few miles away on her way back to the office after covering the two-o'clock meeting that had been on her schedule. She was listening to the police band radio as she drove. Good reporter that she was, she always wanted to stay on top of any breaking news stories.

When she heard the call go out about the speeding Camaro, she realized the drunk driver was heading in her direction. Her Ford Focus was no match for a speeding sports car or a police car in pursuit, but if the cops managed to pull the driver over, she could be at the scene in time to see what happened.

Lydia knew it was worth a try. She had a feeling that Gary would be glad for any kind of excitement in the newsroom on such a slow day.

Lydia hadn't gone far when her police band radio picked up another call to police headquarters.

*"This is Tucker and Mason. There's been a wreck at Jefferson and Lennox. We need an ambulance right away!"*

Lydia hurried to the scene.

"You all right?" Steve shouted to the driver of the gray sedan, who'd braked to a stop at the curb.

The elderly man looked stunned and shaken by his close call, but he waved to Steve in response.

Satisfied that the driver hadn't been injured, Steve ran to check on the youth who'd been ejected from the car. He knelt down beside him and was relieved to find he was conscious, though obviously in pain.

"We've called it in. An ambulance will be here soon," he assured the boy.

"My leg hurts." Tom groaned, writhing in agony.

Charlie came running up to join Steve. "The ambulance is on the way, and there's another squad car coming."

"Good."

"How is he?"

"Lucky—real lucky. He may have a broken leg, but I don't think his injuries are life-threatening." Steve glanced over at the wrecked car to see the driver trying to force his door open. He wasn't about to let the fool get away. "Charlie, stay with him while I take care of the driver."

Though his head was aching, Jim was worried about Tom. He struggled to get out of the car, wanting to go help him, but his door was jammed. He glanced back in Tom's direction and was relieved to see he was conscious and talking to one of the cops. His relief was short-lived, though, for then he saw the other cop heading his way.

Sudden terror filled him as he realized what he'd done. What were his parents going to say when they found out he'd been drinking and had wrecked his car? What had he been thinking? Impressing Tom and his friends wasn't worth all this! Frantic, he gave a final, violent shove, and the car door opened far enough for him to get out. Jim climbed out of the car, ready to make his escape.

Steve eyed the teenage driver warily as he approached him. He always expected trouble at moments like this, and, in all his years of law enforcement, he'd rarely been disappointed.

"Sir, I need to see your driver's license, please," Steve said. He deliberately kept his tone calm and disciplined.

Jim glanced nervously around. He was in trouble—big, big trouble. Drunk as he was, his only thought was to get away. He pretended to reach for his wallet, hoping to catch the cop off guard when he made a break for it.

Steve wanted to make the arrest without violence, but he could smell the liquor on the kid, see his eyes darting about. Steve had a feeling this wasn't going to be an easy arrest.

And, as usual, he was right.

The driver took off at a dead run.

"Stop now!" Steve shouted.

Jim heard the cop's order, but he didn't pause or look back. He kept running as fast as he could.

Disgusted, Steve went after him and managed to tackle him before he'd gotten very far. They fell to the street and grappled violently on the ground.

There was no sense or reason in Jim's thinking, only drunken fear and desperation. He swung out at the cop, hoping to break the hold he had on him.

When the teen landed a punch, Steve had had enough. It was bad enough that the kid had made the choice to get behind the wheel of a car after drinking, but his attempt to resist arrest showed just how drunk he really was. Steve hit the youth square in the jaw and felt some satisfaction when the teen collapsed to the pavement, groaning.

"You need any help over there, partner?" Charlie called from where he was stationed beside the injured passenger.

"No, I got him." Steve made short order of handcuffing the now-moaning driver.

"Are you all right?" The driver of the sedan rushed over to Steve's side.

"I'm fine. Thanks."

"He's just a kid." The older man sounded incredulous as he watched Steve get up and drag the unsteady driver to his feet. "It's so sad."

"I know," Steve agreed. "I'm going to put him in the car. If you'll wait here for a moment, I'll need to get a statement from you about the accident."

"Fine. I'll do whatever I can to help you, Detective."

"Thanks."

Steve dragged the drunken teen forcefully toward the unmarked car. "What's your name?"

"Jim Hunt."

"Where's your ID?"

"In my wallet," Jim muttered, humiliated and angry.

Steve checked the teen's license and gave him a cold, condemning look as he began to read him his rights. "Mr. Hunt, you have the right to remain silent—"

Steve finished just as the ambulance pulled up.

Charlie turned the care of the injured passenger over to the paramedics and went to join his partner and their prisoner by the car.

"You want to make him blow now?" Charlie asked.

"I don't think there's any chance he's going to sober up before we reach the station. He can do the Breathalyzer there," Steve replied, pushing Jim down into the back seat.

"We've got quite an audience." Charlie nodded toward the crowd that had gathered to watch.

"That's just what we didn't need," Steve answered.

"The excitement is over, folks," Charlie called out. "Go on about your business."

As Steve shut the car's back door he caught sight of Lydia Chandler, a reporter from *The Daily Sun*, taking pictures of the accident scene.

It was hard to miss Lydia. She was one lovely woman. Steve had met her several times when she'd been covering cases he'd been working on. He'd found her to be not only darned good-looking, but a decent, honest reporter. He couldn't imagine why she'd be interested in covering a routine drunk-driving arrest.

"Any idea what she's doing here?"

Charlie had noticed her, too. "Why don't you go find out, while I get a statement from the other driver?"

Steve strode over to where Lydia was standing with the other onlookers. "Can I help you?"

"Detective Mason, it's good to see you again," she said.

"Miss Chandler," he responded. "Is there something I can do for you?"

Lydia had met Detective Mason and knew his reputation. He was a man who took his job seriously. He never gave up on a case, and she could see that grim determination in him now as he dealt with the wreck and the injured passenger.

"I heard the call over the police band about the speeding car. I was nearby, so I thought I'd check it out. Is the injured boy going to be all right?"

"His injuries do not appear to be life-threatening. The driver and the passenger are both minors, so if you want more information, you'll have to follow up with headquarters."

Lydia quickly jotted down the information he'd given her. "Was this a simple DUI?"

Steve tensed at her question.

"There's nothing simple about drunk drivers," he answered tersely.

"I'm sorry. I didn't mean to imply that," she said, quick to make amends.

Steve relaxed a little. "In answer to your question, it does appear liquor was involved, but we'll have to do the Breathalyzer test at headquarters to confirm that."

"Thanks for taking the time to speak with me."

"No problem. Now, if you'll excuse me—" He started to move off.

"Oh—and Detective Mason?"

Steve looked back at her questioningly.

"That was a nice tackle you just made."

Steve managed a half-grin at her remark. "Thanks."

Lydia had never seen him smile before. She'd always thought he was a nice-looking man, but she discovered now that when he smiled, Steve Mason was downright handsome. "See you around, Detective."

He nodded and walked back to the wrecked car.

With her final deadline rapidly approaching, time was of the essence to Lydia. She would talk with the ambulance crew and then contact police headquarters. She wasn't sure if her editor would run an article about the accident and the arrest, but it was worth a try. There certainly wasn't anything new on the sniper shootings to report.

Steve was glad when the other patrol car finally arrived. He and Charlie could leave the accident scene for the reinforcements to clean up while they took the driver to headquarters.

As he climbed behind the wheel of their car, Steve felt some satisfaction with his job for the first time in days. They might not have tracked down the sniper yet, but at least they'd gotten a dangerous drunk driver off the road.

# *Chapter Three*

Jim was miserable as he rode in silence in the back seat of the unmarked police car with his hands cuffed behind him. He ached all over from the car crash and his fight with the detective. The officer who'd hit him was driving, and his partner was sitting next to him in the back seat. Neither detective had had anything to say to him since they'd started driving, so Jim just sat there staring out the window. He was nervous about what was to come. This was the first time he'd ridden in a police car, and he'd never been inside the police station before. He wondered what they were going to do to him.

Steve glanced up in his rearview mirror to see the teen staring sullenly out the side window. It still infuriated him that the kid had been stupid enough to drink and drive. He just hoped the boy was smart enough to learn from this experience.

When they reached police headquarters, Steve parked near the main entrance.

"Get out," Charlie ordered, as he opened the door and climbed out of the back seat.

Jim did as he was told. He felt awkward and very self-conscious as they roughly led him, still handcuffed, into the building.

"What have you got here?" Sergeant Edwards asked when they walked up to the desk.

"DUI suspect," Steve told him. "We need to make him blow."

"Young man, would you like to call an attorney?" the sergeant asked.

"No," Jim answered tersely.

"Fine. Take him on back," he directed Steve and Charlie.

"If you'll turn around, please?" Steve requested.

Jim did as he was asked, and he was relieved when the detective unfastened the handcuffs.

"All right, let's go," Steve told him, pointing the way.

"Where are you taking me?" Jim balked, suddenly even more scared than he had been. He was afraid they were about to lock him up in a jail cell.

"To a holding room. We have to process your arrest and write up the reports."

Jim was very aware of the condemning, curious looks the other people in the main office were giving him as the two detectives escorted him from the room. He cloaked the fear that was threatening to overwhelm him with a look of defiance and stared straight back at them. He displayed no semblance of remorse or concern.

Steve was aware of the boy's attitude, and it irritated him. The kid didn't look like he was stupid, but the way he was acting sure was.

"You might want to wipe that smirk off your face," he ordered. "It wouldn't bother me at all to put the cuffs back on you."

Jim dropped his gaze to the floor and continued to follow the two detectives down the long, narrow hall.

"You got it from here, Steve?" Charlie asked, pausing in front of the entrance to a small holding room.

"Yeah, no problem."

Charlie left Steve to finish up the work on the DUI.

Steve led the way into a room that was furnished with only a desk and two chairs. Jim followed him and stood in the middle of the room, uncertain what to do.

"I need you to take the Breathalyzer test first," Steve said.

"All right." Jim knew that if he refused, it would only make matters worse.

The test was administered, and Jim was shocked to learn that even though several hours had passed since he'd had the beers at Tom's house, he was still registering .8 on the scale—and .8 meant he was drunk.

Steve was not surprised by the test's results, considering the way the teen had acted at the accident scene.

"I need fingerprints from you now."

Jim was humiliated when the detective fingerprinted him five different times.

"Just sit back down until I finish writing up the incident report. I have to issue your tickets, and then I'll contact your parents to see if they'll come down and post bond for you," Steve instructed.

"What's going to happen after they post my bond?" Jim asked.

Steve's expression remained grim as he looked up at the teenager. "*If* they show up and post your bond, you'll be released into their custody."

Jim knew a moment of panic as he imagined his parents refusing to bail him out. He knew they were going to be furious, but he prayed they wouldn't leave him in jail. He nervously sat down in the chair to wait for the detective to complete the paperwork. He thought of Tom and hoped he was doing all right at the hospital.

Steve finished filling out the forms and stood up to leave the room. "Wait here. There will be an officer outside the door if you need anything."

Jim watched the detective leave the room, locking the door behind him. Alone and terrified, he waited for what was to come.

Almost an hour passed before Jim heard voices outside in the hallway. He'd been slowly sobering up as he sat there all alone, and with each passing moment, he was more and more conscious of the damage he'd done. No one had told him how Tom was doing, and he was worried about him. He'd never intended for anyone to be hurt. When the door opened, he quickly turned in his seat to see the detective standing there.

"Your parents are here and they've posted your bond," Steve told him. "Let's go."

Jim got to his feet, and that simple movement made him realize just how badly he was hurting. He ached all over, and though he tried, he couldn't stifle the groan that escaped him.

Steve showed no reaction to his misery. He simply motioned for Jim to follow him down the hall to the main office where his parents were waiting.

Paul and Belinda Hunt were in shock as they stood at the main desk waiting to see their son. When the door opened behind them, they turned quickly and Jim walked in.

Belinda loved her son, and at the first sight of him so battered and bruised, she wanted to run to him and hug him and reassure herself that he was all right. But she didn't. She couldn't. True, she was thankful he hadn't been more grievously injured, but there were other issues they had to deal with—very serious issues.

Paul stared at his son, torn between rage and sorrow. He could tell the boy was hurting, but he was so furious over the choices he'd made that he didn't trust himself to speak.

"We'll be holding your license until your court date, which will be in thirty days," Steve explained to Jim. "You'll be notified by mail of the time. If you'll sign these papers, you'll be free to go with your parents."

His words jarred Jim to action. Jim went to the desk and signed the required documents. Then he looked at his mother and father.

"I'm ready," he told them, but he wasn't ready, not really. He could tell by his mother's anxious, stricken expression what she was feeling, and his father's stony regard spoke volumes.

"We're parked out front," his father said in a cold tone as he turned to open the door. He held the door for his wife, then waited for his son.

Jim walked out ahead of his father and followed his mother to the car. He climbed in the back seat without saying a word and waited for what was to come. His mother got in the front, and his father finally entered on the driver's side. His father turned to look at him, and Jim felt the chill of his condemning stare to the depths of his soul.

"We're going to go to the hospital first to check on your friend and to have the doctors take a look at you. Then we'll go home," Paul told him in a voice that brooked no dissension. He slammed the door and turned on the ignition. "Buckle up."

Jim realized then that he hadn't, and quickly did as he was told. He said nothing as they drove off. He just stared out the side window at the city streets, his head aching, his thoughts confused.

"I've got one question for you before we get to the hospital," Paul said.

"Yes, sir."

"Where did you get the liquor? Who bought it for you?"

"A whole bunch of us went over to Tom Lewis's house after school. His dad always has beer around."

"And he lets his son have it?" Paul was shocked.

"That's what Tom said," Jim offered. "He said his father didn't care."

Paul said no more, but he intended to speak with Tom's parents about what had happened that afternoon. When they reached the hospital, Paul led the way into the ER. He and Belinda went to the admissions desk to explain the situation, while Jim hung back. His parents had only started to speak with the admitting nurse when someone started shouting at them from down the hall.

"You! How dare you show up here?" Tom's mother, Diane Lewis, came storming up the hall to confront Jim. "Tom could have been killed because of you!"

"Mrs. Lewis—how is Tom?" Jim managed to ask as he turned to face her.

"It's a little late for you to start worrying about that, isn't it?" she raged.

"Mrs. Lewis? I'm Paul Hunt, Jim's father, and this is my wife, Belinda." Paul went to stand at his son's side. "How is Tom? We came here to find out how he was doing."

Diane turned her hate-filled gaze upon him.

"Tom suffered only a broken leg, but you can be sure you'll be hearing from my lawyer!"

Paul understood her fury, but he had issues of his own over what had happened. He didn't hesitate to bring them up. "Mrs. Lewis, we are relieved and thankful Tom's injuries weren't more serious, but there's something you need to know."

"What?" She glared at him.

"Have you spoken to your son about what happened?"

"Of course. Tom told me everything. He said Jim was speeding and driving like a maniac, and lost control of his car."

"Yes, Jim was speeding," Paul agreed, "but before they got in the car, the boys had been at your house—drinking."

"You're wrong," Diane snapped. She was absolutely certain in her denial.

Paul would have felt some sympathy for her if she hadn't been so arrogant in refusing to hear the truth. "No, Mrs. Lewis. I'm right. Why don't you go check with Tom again, and ask him?"

"I'll do just that." She turned her back on them and stalked off down the hall to her son's room.

Paul looked over at Jim. "Go sit down."

Jim nodded and took a seat in the waiting area. He was unsure what Tom would tell his mother about the events leading up to the crash. Based on the reputation Tom had around school, Jim seriously doubted he'd own up to the truth.

Completely sober now, he waited in misery to see what would happen next.

Gary looked up at Lydia from where he was sitting at his desk in his office at *The Daily Sun*. He pinned her with a thoroughly disgusted look.

"This is the best you could do? You wasted your time covering a drunk-driving arrest? How do you expect me to sell newspapers with stories like this?" He threw her copy and photos down on his desktop. "I want information leading to the arrest and conviction of the sniper—not this crap!"

"We both know it was a slow news day, and considering the trauma the town's been through lately, we should be glad things were quiet," she said defensively.

"You're a reporter. You're supposed to be out there digging up good stories. I need explosive, exciting news. If you want to keep your job, you'll remember that! Now get out of here," he dismissed her curtly.

Lydia turned and walked out of his office. She was beginning to believe that Gary had missed his calling. He would have fit in much better as an editor for one of the tabloids sold at the grocery stores. She particularly thought he'd do well at the tabloid that always proclaimed headlines like "*Aliens from Outer Space Are Already Here Among Us!*" or "*Adam and Eve Are Found Alive and Well in the Middle East!*"

Lydia glanced at the clock in the outer office. It was after seven, and her prayer-group meeting had already started. For a moment, she thought about skipping, but then decided to go, even though she would be late. She enjoyed getting together with her friends from church, and always found the church-sponsored sessions interesting and educational.

Paul and Belinda were seated in the waiting room while Jim was being examined. It was there that Diane Lewis sought them out.

"I need to speak with you," Diane said coldly as she came to stand before them. The news her son had given her had been horrific, but that still didn't excuse what Jim had done.

"Have a seat," Paul invited, as ready as he would

ever be to hear what she had to say. This wasn't a good situation for any of them, and there was no way to make it easy.

Diane sat down across from them, her hands clenched tightly in her lap. She was glad the waiting room wasn't crowded; no one else would hear what she had to say. "Tom admitted to me that the boys had been drinking at our house."

It didn't change a thing, but Paul and Belinda felt some satisfaction at her admission.

"And I can assure you that it will never happen again."

"Good."

"But from now on, I don't want your son anywhere near Tom. Do I make myself clear?"

"Perfectly. How is Tom?" Paul asked.

"Is he going to be all right?" Belinda worried.

"Yes, they'll be releasing him to go home in the next hour or so."

Relief flooded through Belinda and Paul.

"That's good news," Belinda offered.

"Yes, it is." Diane stood up to leave. "I called my husband. He's out of town on business this week, but I told him what's happened, and he said there was no need for lawyers to get involved in any of this. He said he would speak with you about what happened when he gets home—if that's all right with you?"

"Of course."

"Fine. I've got to get back to Tom."

"Tell him we're glad he's going to be all right."

She nodded and walked away.

When she'd gone, Belinda glanced at her husband. "I'll be back in a few minutes."

"Where are you going?"

"To the chapel," she answered, her heart heavy. "I need some quiet time."

He only nodded as he continued his vigil, waiting to hear from the ER doctor about Jim's condition.

It took Belinda a few minutes to find the chapel. She had to wind her way through the myriad of halls in the hospital, but she finally located it and went in. Slipping into a pew, she knelt down to pray.

In the silence of her heart, she pleaded, "Oh, God, please let Jim and Tom be all right—"

After a few moments, Belinda sat back in the pew to meditate on all that had happened that afternoon—from the terror of that first horrible phone call to the moment when she saw Jim at the police headquarters. She knew from what the police had told them that Jim had been very lucky that day. Both boys could have been seriously injured in the wreck or even killed. Belinda lingered on in the chapel before heading back to check on Jim. It wasn't going to be easy to keep peace in the family, but she knew that with God's help, anything was possible.

Gary Newman was aggravated as he tried to figure out which article to use for the lead story the following morning. He'd wanted something connected with the sniper, something to titillate the public, but there was nothing new to report.

There was no hint that the cops were closing in on anyone.

There was no hint that they were even after anyone in particular.

There was no additional, detailed information on the dark green sedan.

There was nothing.

Gary knew he needed a hook, something exciting that would make readers pick up *The Daily Sun*. Sorting through the articles he had spread out before him on his desktop, he looked for anything that might cause a stir or get some talk going around town.

His gaze fell back to Lydia's story about the car wreck and the drunken teenage driver. He scowled. A drunk-driving arrest wasn't much, but he was beginning to think he might be able to turn it into something more intriguing. He picked up the photos she'd taken and studied them carefully, hoping to come up with an angle . . . .

# *Chapter Four*

Lydia drove to Holy Family and parked out front where the other members of the prayer group had left their cars. She hurried inside to the meeting room off the main greeting area.

"Here's Lydia now," announced Mary Sherman, the leader of the prayer group, when Lydia appeared in the doorway. "Come on in."

"You're late!" George Taylor looked up and smiled at her from where he was seated at the table with the others in the group.

"No, I'm not," Lydia replied, going to join them. "You all just showed up real early."

Everyone laughed. They were glad she'd finally managed to make it to the meeting.

Lydia noticed that George looked a little paler than usual tonight, but said nothing of it as she took the chair next to him.

"We were missing you," George told her.

"Things ran late at work."

"Were you busy working on a big story? Have the cops caught that sniper yet?"

"No, there's no new information about the sniper at all. I just had the usual deadline hassle."

"Well, we're glad you finally made it," Mary assured her with a warm smile.

"That we are," George agreed.

"I'm glad I made it, too," Lydia said, smiling and relaxing now that she was with them.

The prayer group was sponsored by Holy Family Church. Mary had been the leader for the last several sessions. During the weeks when they met twice, everyone had gotten to know one another, and they'd become friends.

It was an interesting, eclectic group. Phyllis Logan was a forty-something high school teacher. She was married, but her husband didn't come to the prayer meetings. There were the Wymans, Ed and Cindy. Ed was a fireman, and Cindy stayed home with their two-year-old daughter. Keith and Lori Hudson were the parents of three teenage boys, who were running them ragged, and then there was Frank, Mary's husband. Lydia and George, both single, rounded out the group.

"Shall we get back to tonight's lesson?" Mary directed, now that Lydia had settled in. "Phyllis, I believe it was your turn to read."

They turned their attention back to their real reason for being together—exploring their faith.

It was half an hour later when they finished their discussion of the evening's topic—the Ten Commandments. Then, as they always did, they prayed together, offering up prayers for one another and for their own personal intentions.

When Lydia heard Mary offer up a prayer for George's health, she grew worried and knew she'd have to ask him what was wrong when the meeting ended. He hadn't said anything to her that morning, but she still was concerned.

Lydia offered up a prayer of her own for the teenagers who'd been involved in the wreck that day. She prayed the injured boy would fully recover and the boy who'd been driving drunk would learn from his mistakes.

They prayed for soldiers on active duty, and George even added a prayer that the cold-blooded murderer haunting their town would be caught and brought to justice. Mary concluded the meeting with a final blessing.

The group broke up then. Most headed home, but a few stayed on to visit and partake of the refreshments Mary had provided this week.

"So there's been no news about that sniper?" George asked Lydia when he joined her at the side table where Mary had put out a plate of her delicious homemade chocolate chip cookies.

"Nothing at all."

"That worries me," Frank Sherman said as he came to stand with them.

"The sniper worries everybody," George agreed.

"How can anyone do something like that? Just shoot complete strangers for no reason?" Lydia was still at a loss to understand the killer's motivation. "I've been trying to get inside his head, but I don't think there's any understanding this kind of insanity."

"Neither do I. It's at times like these I wish St. Michael would show up and take charge. He'd clean things up real fast." George chuckled, thinking about how his favorite saint would handle things.

"The police department probably feels the same way. It looks like they could use all the help they can get," Frank agreed.

"It's not the department's fault. There are no clues and no witnesses, so they've got absolutely nothing to go on," Lydia said in defense of the police investigation.

"If you say so." Frank was less than believing. "Who were the boys you prayed for tonight?"

"They were in a bad wreck this afternoon. The driver had been drinking."

"Kids can be so stupid sometimes," Frank remarked, saddened that the teenagers hadn't had enough sense not to drink, let alone not to get behind the wheel of a car in that condition.

"The car was totaled when the driver tried to outrun the cops. It was a miracle he and the friend weren't killed."

"Their guardian angels must have been working overtime," Mary put in.

"I'll say."

"They're going to be all right, though, aren't they?" George asked, sounding concerned.

"I hope so. The passenger was thrown out of the vehicle and injured, but not too seriously. From what I could find out, he suffered a broken leg. The driver tried to run from the scene, but one of the detectives caught him."

"Good."

"Thank God the cops stopped them before anything more terrible happened," Mary said.

They talked for a little while longer, then Lydia got ready to leave.

"I've got to call it a night. Good luck with the doctor tomorrow, George." Lydia gave him a warm hug. Still worrying about him, she asked, "It's not anything serious, is it?"

"No, no, just the usual 'getting old' stuff," he answered, smiling at her.

"You're not old! You're just real grown-up!" she teased, knowing that laughter could sometimes be the best medicine.

Her ploy worked. She got a good laugh out of him. It made her feel good to see him light up, since he'd been a little quieter than usual tonight.

"I like the way you think, Lydia."

Everyone joined in their laughter.

"You take care, all right?" she told him, growing more serious.

"I will." George was touched by Lydia's thoughtfulness. He'd been trying to convince himself all day that he was just feeling bad because he was old and, no doubt, the warranty on his body parts was up. "I'll see you next week."

"Yes, you will," she assured him. "Good night, everybody."

* * *

Usually, Jim was glad to get home, but not tonight. When his father pulled the car into the garage and parked, Jim was almost too scared to get out. He sat there waiting.

Paul opened his car door and got out. He stood there watching and waiting until Jim finally climbed out of the back seat.

"Go to your room and stay there," Paul ordered. "I can't talk to you tonight."

Jim quickly did as he'd been told. The farther away he got from his father right then, the better.

Once he was safely in his room, Jim got into his pajamas and went to bed. Try as he might, though, he couldn't sleep. There was no rest for him as he kept reliving the events of the day in his mind, and getting angrier and angrier with himself.

He'd wrecked his car!

His Camaro was totaled.

How could he have been so stupid?

Jim was devastated. He bit back a sob. He realized too late now all that he'd done wrong that day, and he felt like an idiot. He'd had all kinds of counseling at school about not drinking or doing drugs, and he'd never drunk liquor before today. He'd never seen any reason to, yet when he'd been at Tom's house, he'd wanted to show the guys he could keep up with them. The school counselors had warned students about peer pressure. They'd warned them that there could be a terrible price to pay for that kind of behavior, but Jim hadn't listened. Now he'd found out the hard way they'd been right. He'd paid the price.

What troubled him even more deeply was that his mistakes weren't going to disappear. He would have to face up to what he'd done tomorrow. His father would see to that.

And then there would be dealing with the kids at school—

Jim rolled over and pulled his pillow over his head to try to hide from the reality of what was to come. He felt as if his life was over, and it was all his own fault.

Steve sat alone in his living room, clicking between channels to check on the local news. Just as he'd suspected, the lead story on each news broadcast was about the police department's efforts to find the highway sniper. He settled on the highest-rated channel to see what was being reported.

"We're here with Captain Donovan of the Metropolitan Police Department," reporter Edmund Foley said, looking straight into the camera. He turned and thrust his microphone at the captain. "Captain, what can you tell us about the status of your investigation into the highway shootings?"

"As I mentioned earlier today at the press conference, our investigation is continuing," Captain Donovan answered calmly. "We're following up on all leads, and doing everything possible to find the killer."

"But what do you know about this killer? Is there anything you can tell the viewing public to reassure them that this won't happen again? I mean, we've had three cold-blooded murders in three weeks. This is a terrifying situation."

The police captain tensed as he answered, "We have not made an arrest yet, but we believe we are closing in on a suspect."

"It's been reported that a dark green sedan may have been involved; have you learned anything more regarding the car?"

"No."

"Is there any information you'd like to share with the public? Do you have a description of the shooter?"

"Not at this time."

*We are closing in on a suspect—*

Steve couldn't believe what he'd just heard. He cursed his boss and changed the channel. The other channels were reporting the same thing, so he turned the television off in disgust and tossed the remote aside. If the department had a serious suspect, this was the first he'd heard about it, and he was the lead investigator on the case.

Getting up, Steve went to stand before his open window.

He looked out across the neighborhood.

It was dark and quiet.

No sirens sounded in the distance.

It seemed a peaceful night.

He only hoped it really was.

The sniper stared at the television screen as he listened to the police captain's comments. His expression was dark. He wondered if the cops really knew anything about him, or if the arrogant captain was just covering up for his inept underlings. He preferred to believe the latter, but he would continue to be careful—very careful. He couldn't afford to get too confident, no matter how inept the cops were.

When the news ended, he got up and went to the closet. He took out his rifle and caressed it with loving hands. He thrilled to the sense of power that holding the weapon gave him. He was God when he was armed, for he had the power of life and death. The tension he'd been feeling eased, and after one last, loving caress, he put the weapon back in its hiding place.

He would strike again, but not just yet. He wanted to let the cops worry for a while. He wanted to let the tension build before he went hunting for his next victim. He found it entertaining to watch the police squirm when they faced the demanding reporters and the terrified public.

Feeling in complete control, he smiled.

# *Chapter Five*

It was just after seven when Steve made his way into headquarters the following morning. He was ready to settle in and get some paperwork done, but that plan didn't last long.

"Mason! Get in here!" Captain Donovan shouted from his office when he spotted Steve at his desk.

Steve couldn't imagine what the trouble was. As he headed the captain's way, one of the patrol officers standing nearby gave him a sympathetic look.

"What the hell is the meaning of this?" the captain demanded, shoving the front page of *The Daily Sun* at Steve as he came through the office door.

Steve took the newspaper and stared at the headline, which boldly proclaimed, "*Police Brutality!*" Beneath it, centered on the page for all the world to see, was a picture of him hitting the seemingly helpless teenager the previous afternoon—and the byline was Lydia Chandler's.

Steve grew angry as he looked down at the paper. Up

until now, he'd trusted and respected Lydia. He'd thought she was a skilled and decent reporter, but now he had his doubts. The last thing he needed was this kind of grief when the sniper was still at large.

"The department is taking a lot of heat for not having made an arrest in the sniper investigation, and now, thanks to you, I have to deal with this!" the captain raged. He didn't care that his office door was open and everyone in the outer office could hear him.

"I was defending myself," Steve said.

"Tell that to the people who get a look at this front page this morning," Captain Donovan snarled, scowling blackly. "They're going to see that picture and wonder why you're beating up some defenseless kid when there's a madman running around loose killing innocent people!"

"That 'defenseless kid' was driving drunk, and I got him off the street!" Steve countered.

The captain fixed him with a fierce glare. "Good, now go get the damned sniper off the street."

"I heard your press conference last night. You said we were closing in on somebody."

"That's right."

"Who is this suspect we're supposedly closing in on?" As one of the lead investigators, Steve was angry that he hadn't been kept informed of the new development.

"It's not 'who' the suspect is. It's who he's not. You and Charlie ruled out Bob Gray yesterday. That narrows down the number of suspects, doesn't it?" the captain demanded sarcastically.

Steve was disgusted. He glanced at the picture Lydia had taken once more, then tossed the paper down on the captain's desk and walked out. If this was any indication of what the rest of the day held in store, it was going to be a long one.

Lydia was up early, but she wasn't due into work until ten a.m. She retrieved her wrapped newspaper from the middle of her driveway and settled in on a stool at her kitchen counter to enjoy a cup of coffee and check out the morning news. She unwrapped the paper and spread it out on the counter before her. She was about to take a sip of coffee when she caught sight of the headline.

"*Police Brutality!*"

Lydia stared down at the article in disbelief, shocked by Gary's decision to use the drunk-driving arrest as the lead story. She abruptly set her coffee aside and almost scalded herself when it sloshed over the rim. After scanning the caption beneath the picture and then reading the article, her mood improved a little. Everything in print was as she'd written it, but, that still didn't make up for her editor's misleading headline. As a reporter covering the city beat, she couldn't afford to get on the bad side of anyone in the police department. She needed to stay in the detectives' good graces, so she would have the contacts necessary to get the latest information on breaking stories.

Determination filled Lydia as she faced the day to come. Somehow, she was going to have to find a way to meet with Detective Mason and apologize for the headline. She only hoped he would take her phone call and give her the chance to explain.

"There he is now!"

Jim heard the girl squeal as he entered the school building the following morning. He stopped where he was, suddenly aware that the other students who'd been milling around the main-floor hall had all turned to look at him. Most of them were grinning slyly at him, but there were a few, he could tell, who were looking at him like he was the lowest creature on the face of the earth.

It was obvious the news of his arrest had traveled fast through the school. He ducked his head and started toward his home room. He didn't want anyone to get a look at the bruise on his jaw where the detective had hit him.

Sam Orrico was one of the varsity football players who'd been at Tom's house the previous afternoon. When he saw Jim walking down the hall, a taunting grin spread over his face.

"Hey, Jimmy boy!" Sam called out sarcastically from where he was standing with several of his friends. "That was some ride you took Tom on last night. Guess you really showed him what a great car you had, didn't you? How fast is your car going this morning?"

Jim tried to ignore him as he kept on walking.

"Bet you didn't know you were going to be front-page news, did you, Jim?" added Mike Williams, another varsity athlete who was standing with Sam.

"What are you talking about?" Jim stopped and turned to face them.

Mike waved the front page of the morning newspaper at him. "You mean you haven't seen it yet? You're the big news today."

Jim's parents didn't get *The Daily Sun* delivered at home.

"Here, take a look." Mike handed him the paper, smiling slyly. "Get a load of this headline—'*Police Brutality!*' You're famous!"

Jim stared down at the picture of himself in disbelief. The worst moment of his entire life was centered on the front page of the local newpaper for everyone to see.

Jim had wanted to just go to his homeroom and mind his own business. He'd wanted to avoid people today, but he knew now that wasn't going to happen—not after seeing the paper.

"That was stupid, trying to outrun the cops," Mike jeered.

Jim thought about speaking up and telling him it had been Tom's idea to try to get away, but he remained silent. There was no point. No one would have believed him anyway.

Sam was smirking. "Yeah, that was real stupid, and it looks like you didn't get very far."

"Hey! That detective did a pretty good job on you, didn't he?" Mike noticed the ugly bruise on his jaw. "Or did you get that when you totaled your car? I guess your car did go real fast, just like you told Tom it would. But he found that out the hard way, didn't he?"

"Shut up," Jim ground out, humiliated and angered by Mike's sarcasm.

"Why? What are you going to do to me? Wrap me around a light post? Or fight me like you did the cop?"

The other teens who'd gathered around them started laughing derisively.

"What's going on here?"

The rowdy students were suddenly silenced when the known-to-be-strict English teacher, Mrs. Logan, appeared in the doorway of her nearby classroom. She'd overheard some of the comments being made and knew something bad had happened.

"Nothing."

Sam and Mike gave Jim one last taunting look before they moved away.

"Loser," someone else muttered as they followed their lead.

Mike stopped and turned back. "Hey, Jim—you can keep the paper. Why don't you show it to Mrs. Logan? She might be interested in knowing you're front-page news today."

Mrs. Logan frowned at his words and went to stand beside Jim. She'd had Jim in her English class the year before and knew he was a good student.

"Jim, what's this all about? Are you all right?" It was then that she noticed the bruise on his cheek. "Your face—"

"I'm fine," he mumbled, quickly trying to fold up the page so she couldn't get a look at it.

"Let me see what it is you're trying to hide from me." She reached out and took the paper from him.

Having worked with teenagers for many years, she knew how vicious they could be to each other. She always made it a point to work hard to stop the hatefulness between students whenever she could.

Jim was nervous as he watched Mrs. Logan unfold the paper and get her first look at the picture.

"Jim—this is terrible." Phyllis Logan gasped. Then she went quiet as she quickly scanned the article. When she'd finished reading, she looked up at him again, shocked. The byline was Lydia's, so she realized Jim had been one of the boys they'd prayed for at the prayer meeting the night before. She guessed the headline was an exaggeration of what had happened, but there was no denying it had been a dangerous situation. "I heard about the wreck last night, but I had no idea you were involved. Thank heaven you and Tom weren't killed! How is Tom?"

"He broke his leg."

"Is he still in the hospital?"

"No, they sent him home."

"What about you? How do you feel?"

He'd been expecting a lecture on how stupid he'd been, and he was surprised by her concern. "I'm okay," he muttered.

"Are you sure?" she pressed him.

Jim shrugged. "I'll be all right."

"Good."

The bell rang just then, announcing the start of the school day. As students began rushing down the hallway to their homerooms, Jim started to move away, too.

"Jim—" Mrs. Logan called to him.

He stopped and turned to face her again.

"I know your car was totaled, but cars can be replaced. You couldn't be. I'm glad nothing serious happened to you." Her words were heartfelt, and she gave him a reassuring smile.

"Thanks," he said. Her words had touched him deeply.

As Phyllis Logan watched Jim move off into the crowd of students, she offered up a quick silent prayer that he would have the strength he needed to get through these difficult times.

It was just past eleven a.m. when George stepped out of the medical building into the sunshine. He drew a ragged breath and paused for a moment to look numbly around.

It seemed strange that nothing appeared to have changed since he'd gone inside an hour earlier.

The sun was still shining.

The temperature was perfect—not too hot, not too cold.

The sky was a pure, vibrant blue, dotted with only a few light, wispy, high-flying clouds.

But, though everything looked the same, George knew it wasn't.

In fact, George knew that nothing was ever going to be the same again.

Spotting a concrete bench nearby, he walked over and sat down weakly upon it. He clasped his hands together in front of him to stop them from trembling. Shock radiated through him as he contemplated what he'd just been told. He lifted his gaze to stare off in the distance as he relived those fateful moments in the doctor's office.

"*George—*" *Dr. Murray had said when he'd come into the examining room with his chart in hand, his tone unusually solemn.* "*The results of your tests have come back and . . .*"

"*And?*"

"*Well, the results are not good.*"

"*I flunked the tests?*" *he had quipped, trying to ignore the fear that shot through him. He'd sensed that something wasn't right, but he'd never suspected it was anything too serious. He'd expected his longtime physician to just give him a prescription for some antibiotics or painkillers and send him on his way.*

"*George—*" *Dr. Murray hadn't responded to his humor.*

"*What is it? What's wrong?*" *George's mood had sobered instantly at the doctor's strained demeanor.*

*Dr. Murray had met his gaze straight on as he'd answered,* "*Your condition is very serious.*"

"*How serious?*"

*The physician had drawn a deep, steadying breath as he gave him the bad news.* "*You have only a few months to live.*"

George shook his head again in disbelief as he relived that horrible moment in his mind.

He was going to die.

There was no doubt about it.

And it would be soon.

*"We can start chemo and radiation—"* Dr. Murray *had begun.*

"No."

*"You might want to think about it before you reject any treatment outright."*

"No."

*"But treatment might prolong your life—"*

*"For how long? A few months? And the whole time I'll be too sick and weak to do anything," he had argued. "No. Right now—put 'no extraordinary measures and do not resuscitate' in my file."*

*"George," the doctor counseled him again, "take time to think about this. Don't make any rash decisions."*

*"The decision's already been made for me," he'd answered simply. "You just said I only have a few months left to live. If that's the truth, then I want to enjoy them."*

The rest of what had happened in the doctor's office was only a blur now. Nothing else the doctor said had stayed with him. He had a prescription for painkillers in his pocket, and he had the rest of his life to live—the way he wanted to live it.

Fighting for control of his runaway emotions, George lifted his gaze heavenward.

The sky was blue.

The sunshine was bright.

Nothing had changed.

And yet, everything had changed.

George got to his feet and headed out to the parking lot to his car.

He needed to get away from the doctor's office.

He needed time to think.

Almost as if on autopilot, George got in his car and drove straight to Holy Family. The church was always open, and he was never more thankful for that than today.

George parked out front and quietly went in.

The afternoon sun shone through the stained-glass windows, bathing the interior in rich, vibrant hues. The church provided a glorious haven from the harsh ugliness of the real world.

George was glad to find that no one else was there. He needed a place of privacy to deal with his turbulent emotions. He needed to be alone.

Entering a pew close to the back, he knelt down and bowed his head in prayer.

He drew a ragged breath as his tears fell unheeded.

Only God could help him now.

# Chapter Six

*Lord Have Mercy . . .*

Father Richards, the pastor of Holy Family, was busy working in his office in the rectory when someone knocked on the door. He got up to answer it and found longtime parishioner George Taylor standing in the hallway.

"George! It's good to see you. Come on in."

"Thanks, Father." He followed him inside the office.

"What brings you here today?" Father Richards asked, delighted to see him. He glanced at his old friend, and when their gazes met he realized immediately this wasn't just a casual visit. George looked deeply troubled. "George—is something wrong?"

"I need to talk."

"Of course," he answered, moving to close the door behind them for privacy. "Have a seat."

George sat down in the chair in front of the desk. After spending almost an hour alone in church, George had realized he needed to confide in someone. Since he had no close family, he'd decided to speak with Father Richards. They'd known and respected each other for years. He knew he could trust his pastor.

The priest took his seat at his desk. He could see the strain in George's expression and wondered what was causing him so much pain. "How can I help you, George?"

Drawing a ragged breath, George looked straight at him and answered, "That's the problem, Father. I wish there was something you could do to help me, but there's not."

The priest frowned. "I don't understand."

"Earlier today I learned the results of some medical tests I had taken."

"And?" Father Richards encouraged.

"And the news wasn't good."

Father Richards said nothing as he waited to hear what George was about to reveal.

"Dr. Murray told me I'm dying."

"What?" The priest was shocked. George had always seemed a healthy man.

George could see the shock on his friend's face and managed a half-smile. "I know. I reacted the same way at first, but Dr. Murray said there was no denying the results. He'd already checked them over twice. The tests show I only have a few months to live."

"Isn't there something they can do for you? Some kind of chemo or radiation?"

"No," George replied quickly, shaking his head. "There's no point. I went over everything with the doctor. Why put off the inevitable? In just a few short months, I'm out of here."

Father Richards paused for a moment, uncertain about how to respond. "Is there anything you need? Anything I can do to help you? Do you need counseling?"

"Just pray for me, Father. I'm going to need all the prayers I can get."

"I will, and if you need me, call me, no matter what the hour."

"Thanks."

George stood up and so did Father Richards. They shared a long look of understanding as they shook hands; then George started toward the office door.

"Oh—and Father?" George paused and glanced back at him.

"Yes?"

"Don't tell anybody about this. I'm not going to say anything—at least, not for a while. There are some things I've got to put in order."

The priest nodded, signifying his agreement.

"See you later," George said. He went out and closed the office door quietly behind him.

Father Richards stared at the closed door, feeling saddened and confused. George was a good man. Whenever help was needed around the parish, George had always been one of the first to volunteer. And now he was dying—

Silently, he offered up a prayer for George, asking

God to give George the strength he would need to get through these next months in peace.

"Detective Mason, this is Lydia Chandler from *The Daily Sun*. If you could give me a call, I'd appreciate it. I wanted to speak with you about the article in the paper today." Lydia left her number on the detective's voice mail at police headquarters and hung up, a bit disappointed that she hadn't gotten through to him.

She wondered if they had Caller ID at the police station and he was screening his calls. With that headline today, she wouldn't blame him for not wanting to talk to her.

"Lydia, are you about ready to leave for the awards luncheon?" asked Sandy Wallace, another reporter at the paper, as she stopped by Lydia's desk. "Gary and several of the others have already headed over to the hotel."

"Is it that late already?" Lydia was startled to find it was almost noon.

The Press Club Awards Luncheon was an important event in the city, and everybody who was anybody in local television, radio or newspaper reporting showed up.

"The program doesn't start until one, but they're going to serve the luncheon at twelve-thirty."

"Give me a minute to finish up here, and I'll be ready to go."

"I'll meet you by the elevators," Sandy told her. "You know, we both might win this year."

"If only," Lydia said with a wry grin. She'd been nominated twice before for her reporting, but had never won. She was used to losing, but still found being nominated an honor.

"Have a positive attitude, Lydia, and by positive, I don't mean 'I'm positive I'm going to lose,'" her friend laughed.

"All right. I'll try."

"With five of us from the paper nominated, surely at least one of us will win something," Sandy said hopefully.

"We'd better. I hate to think what Gary will do if *The Evening News* sweeps us—especially since he's been nominated for Best Editor. It'll be bad around here if we don't win, but if he doesn't win the Best Editor Award it'll be—"

"Don't even go there," Sandy interrupted her, not wanting to think about that possibility. "Let's hope we all win, but especially Gary."

"You got it."

Lydia finished what she was working on, then checked her makeup. Certain she was as ready as she would ever be, she met Sandy, and they hurried toward the Radisson Hotel two blocks away where the ceremony was being held.

The plush Radisson dining room was crowded with members of the press.

Lydia and Sandy spotted the table reserved for *The Daily Sun* staff right in front of the podium. Leave it to Gary to get the best table. They joined their coworkers there.

Tension was in the air. No one paid much attention to the food when it was served. They were all waiting anxiously for the program to begin and this year's winners to be announced.

"I expect big things from you," Gary said, glancing around the table at his staff as the master of ceremonies made his way to the podium.

They all managed to smile back at him.

"Good afternoon, everyone. Welcome to the Fiftieth Annual Press Club Awards Luncheon. It's our pleasure to be here today to honor the best and the brightest among us," began John Dunn, the president of the Press Club. "Our first presentations today will be the television awards for excellence."

All at *The Daily Sun's* table sat quietly as the television reporting awards were presented.

"And now for the print media. We have many distinguished newspaper men and women among us, and it's an honor to present these awards to them." John went on to announce the first category, sports writing.

Matt Clark, *The Daily Sun's* best sports reporter, won, and a roar of approval went up from the table as he was called forward to receive his plaque.

The presentations continued.

Seated next to Lydia, Sandy waited nervously for the winner in her category—local interest reporting—to be called. Disappointment wracked her when the reporter from *The Evening News* won.

"And now for best investigative reporting," John Dunn continued, "our nominees are Lydia Chandler of *The Daily Sun*, Chad Wells of *The Evening News* and Ken Rockwell of *The Evening News*. And our winner is—"

There was a dramatic pause as he looked out across the crowded dining room.

"Lydia Chandler of *The Daily Sun* for her comprehensive coverage of the murder of Faye Reynolds."

Cheers erupted again from their table.

"I won?" Lydia gasped, honestly surprised by the honor.

"Get up there!" Sandy encouraged, smiling in delight at her friend's success.

Thrilled and still a bit in shock, Lydia rose from her chair and made her way to the podium. She was gracious in her acceptance of the award, thanking her coworkers and, as much as it irked her, Gary, for all their support.

When she'd returned to her seat, John Dunn announced the nominees in the last reporting category and awarded the prize to the reporter from *The Evening News*. Then it was time for the final category—best editing.

Lydia glanced toward Gary as the emcee got ready to announce the editors who'd been nominated. Gary was looking very confident as the emcee called his name. A loud round of applause followed. He smiled and nodded in regal acknowledgment to those seated at nearby tables. Gary had won the year before, and Lydia had no doubt he fully expected to win again.

"Well, here we go," Sandy whispered to Lydia as they waited for the final announcement.

"And this year's winner is"—the emcee paused for effect before continuing—"Justin Lawrence of *The Evening News*."

The people from *The Evening News* cheered as Justin Lawrence went up to get his award.

Everyone at *The Daily Sun*'s table was shocked, and no one more than Gary. It had been tense at the table before, but now a new kind of tension fell over them. They were all relieved when the radio awards had been given out and it was finally time to go.

"And that concludes our ceremony for this year. Keep up the good work, ladies and gentlemen! Our community needs you!"

Lydia and Sandy were more than ready to head back to the office.

"Congratulations, Lydia, Matt," Gary offered as he looked over at the two reporters who had won.

"Thanks, Gary. Too bad you lost, but there's always next year," Matt told him.

"That's right," Gary said calmly as they left the banquet room. "We'll just keep reporting the news and selling papers. That's what it's all about."

They returned to work.

Once Gary had gotten settled in, he summoned Lydia into his office.

"The annual 'Above and Beyond' police fund-raiser is this Friday night."

"I know. I'm going with a friend," she told him.

"The event is going to get coverage in the paper, but I want you to do some background research for me."

"What do you need?"

"Find out which families of officers killed in the line of duty are being helped by the fund-raiser, and which injured officers are being helped. Follow the money trail."

"You're making it sound like something bad is going on there. I've been to the fund-raiser several times in the past, and I've always been impressed with it. It's a wonderful way for our community to give back to the officers who put their lives on the line every day, protecting all of us."

"Whatever," Gary blew her off, bored. Fuzzy, heartwarming, happy-ending stories were not his forte.

Lydia realized she shouldn't have been surprised by Gary's indifferent attitude toward the good things that came out of the fund-raiser. She had no doubt he was looking for a way to twist and exploit the event to his liking. Losing the best editor award to Justin Lawrence at *The Evening News* was going to be a driving force for Gary for some time to come.

"I'll see what I can find out," she told him.

"Get on it," he ordered. He had already planned the headline he was going to run about how the police were partying the night away while a killer was on the loose and the town was in a state of panic. He smiled slightly, thinking how the headline would get everyone riled up and sell a lot of papers. "I want this to be the lead story for the Sunday edition."

Summarily dismissed, Lydia returned to her desk to get to work. When she glanced at the clock and saw how late it was, George slipped into her thoughts. She remembered that he'd been planning to see the doctor that day and she wondered what the test results showed. She hoped the news had been good.

# *Chapter Seven*

"Is anybody working here?" a man bellowed.

Bonnie Zimmerman, the director of the Saving Grace Animal Shelter, heard the man's call and went into the main office to meet him. "Yes, sir. Can I help you?"

"Here." The unshaven, unwashed man dumped a three-legged, filthy beagle on the floor in front of her. "He's all yours. He ain't good for nothing no more."

Bonnie noticed how weak and pitiful the dog looked as it lay sprawled before her and knew it had been badly neglected. "We'll be glad to help you with your dog, sir, if you'll just fill out the necessary paperwork for me—"

"I ain't got time for that," he snarled, and he was out the door before she could say any more.

"But, sir," Bonnie called out as she went after him. "We need to know if—"

Before she could catch up with him in the parking lot to find out if the dog had had his shots, the man had jumped in his car and started to drive away.

"What's his name?" she shouted after him.

But the man never bothered to look back.

Bonnie was used to dealing with his kind, so she wasn't surprised by his fast exit. She went into the office again to find the dog lying where she'd left him. The beagle looked up at her, his big brown eyes wary and fearful. Though he was obviously frightened, he was too weak to try to escape.

"It's all right, little guy," she crooned, wanting to ease his terror. She got a dog treat from the jar on a nearby counter and knelt down beside the animal to offer it to him.

The beagle watched her warily, but the scent of the treat was more powerful than his fear. It had been a long time since he'd had anything to eat. He took the proffered treat with less than perfect manners and scarfed it down.

"A little hungry, were you?" Bonnie spoke to him in calm, even tones as she reached out to pet him.

Unused to affectionate petting, he ducked his head to try to dodge her hand and avoid what he expected to be a punishing blow. Her gentle caress puzzled him. He relaxed a bit as she scratched him behind his ears. He looked up at her with big, brown, questioning eyes.

"That's a good boy," she crooned. "I know you're scared. Why don't we get you cleaned up and fed, and then see how you feel? What do you say?"

The beagle was collarless, so she got a collar and leash from the office and put them on him. She was glad he didn't resist. She hoped he was strong enough to walk to the back of the shelter so she wouldn't have to pick him up, but when she encouraged him to get to his feet, he only whined and looked even more pitiful.

Bonnie was a sucker for pitiful.

"All right. You win."

She bent down and gathered the filthy beagle in her arms. She expected him to resist the intimacy of such close contact, but to her surprise, he looked up at her adoringly and gave her a big, sloppy lick on the cheek.

"I love you, too," she said, laughing and smiling now as she carried him back to have a bath.

Dogs like this one were the reason she'd opened the shelter five years before. She'd witnessed the treatment of some abused and abandoned dogs and wanted to help them. She'd had a little money from an inheritance left by her parents, and she knew they would have appreciated her efforts. Her parents had had a mutt named Grace they'd gotten off of death row at the dog pound. Old and blind in one eye, Grace had turned out to be just what her parents needed in their later years. Grace had been their devoted, loving companion, and that was why she'd named the shelter "Saving Grace," in her honor.

"Who've you got there?" called out Larry Collins, an elderly man who'd been volunteering at the shelter for the past several years, as Bonnie entered the grooming area with her arms full of beagle.

"Our newest resident," Bonnie replied. "Have you got time to give him a bath, or should I?"

"I can take care of him. Where'd he come from?"

"A man just dropped him off and drove away."

"Typical." Larry nodded in understanding. "The good news is he brought him here."

"You're right. With only three legs, he wouldn't have lasted long if he'd been dumped out in the country." Bonnie gently put the beagle in one of the bathtubs and took the leash off of him.

"Or worse."

She didn't want to think about what might have happened to the poor animal. He was there, safe and sound now. "I have no record of his inoculations, so we'll have to see if he's chipped."

"I'll take care of it."

"Thanks." She reached down and petted their new guest to reassure him. "I don't even know his name."

"If he was a girl, we could name him Eileen," Larry said, trying not to smile as he came over to join her.

"Eileen?" Bonnie frowned in confusion at his choice.

"You know—'I lean,'" he chuckled.

"You're bad." She groaned at his joke.

Larry just grinned.

She petted the beagle one last time, telling him, "I'll see you after your 'extreme makeover.'"

Someone rang the bell in the front office just then, so Bonnie hurried out front to see who needed help. She was surprised to find an officer from the sheriff's department standing there, looking very serious.

"Is there something I can help you with, Officer?" Bonnie asked, surprised by his presence and his demeanor.

"Yes, ma'am. Are you Miss Zimmerman?"

"I am."

He handed her an envelope.

"What's this?" Bonnie stared down at it and looked back up at the officer.

"It's an eviction notice, ma'am. If you have any questions, there's a contact number at the bottom of the notice."

The officer turned to go.

"But I've been trying to catch up on what I owe!"

"I'm sorry, Miss Zimmerman. It's the law," the officer said regretfully, then let himself out of the building.

Bonnie opened the envelope. She was heartsick as she stared at the eviction notice. She'd been trying not to think about the financial problems the shelter had been having, but now her worst fear had been realized.

She was going to have to shut the shelter down.

She'd hoped the recent publicity for Saving Grace in the newspaper would increase donations, but times were hard for everyone. There had been no calls or donations after the article ran.

And now it was too late.

She would have to close by the end of the month. Which meant she had ten days to find homes for the eighty-five animals the shelter was housing. The sad part was most of the dogs and cats were full-grown, and the public generally wanted to adopt cute little puppies and kittens. People always figured if a pet was grown up and at the shelter, there was something wrong with it.

Bonnie knew that way of thinking was wrong. Sometimes families had to relocate and couldn't take a pet with them. Other times the owner passed away and no one else could take the pet in. There were any number of reasons why mature pets ended up at Saving Grace, and many of them had nothing to do with bad behavior on the animal's part.

Walking into her office, she sank down in her chair and tossed the eviction notice on the desk before her. She stared at the document miserably and tried to figure out what to do next. The way things looked, it was going to take a miracle to save the shelter.

"It's time we talked," Paul began as he came to stand in Jim's bedroom door. He'd thought long and hard about how to handle the situation, and he knew what he had to do.

Jim looked up at his father. The moment he'd been dreading all day had finally come.

"Let's go down to the kitchen."

His father led the way downstairs. They walked in silence to the kitchen and took their usual seats at the table, where his mother was already waiting for them.

"What was last night all about?" Paul demanded harshly without hesitation. "Who were those kids you were hanging out with? And why on God's earth did you drink and drive?"

"Tom's one of the varsity football players. He invited me over to his house, so I went."

"And that's when the drinking started?"

"Yeah."

"Why did you drink? Haven't we taught you better than that?"

"I wanted to show them I could do it."

"Well, you sure showed them, didn't you?"

Jim wisely remained silent.

"Why did you drive if you'd been drinking?"

"Tom made fun of my car, so I wanted to show him how great it was."

Paul shook his head in disgust. "It's not so great anymore, son. I had the Camaro towed to the body shop. The mechanics there told me it's totaled."

Jim's heart sank at the news. He had feared as much, and it was all his fault. "I'm sorry, Dad."

"You should be," Paul said tightly. "I know today your mother drove you to school, but from this day on, you're back on the bus. And there are going to be a few other major changes around here."

Jim waited in silence, unsure of what was coming.

"The first thing you're going to do, young man, is get a job. You're going out after school tomorrow, and you're going to start putting in applications at all the stores around town. It seems to me if you've got enough time to go drinking and partying after school, you've got enough time to work."

"Yes, sir." Jim tried not to flinch before his father's cold-eyed regard.

"Once you start getting a paycheck, you're going to pay me and your mother back for any and all expenses and fines we incur on your court date. And one other thing."

Paul paused for effect. He waited until Jim was looking straight at him before he continued, "You're also going to pay us back for the Camaro. I want to make sure that every hour you're working, you're thinking about the wrong choices you made and why you ended up where you are. I believe you're smart enough to learn from what happened this time and never do anything like this again. Don't prove me wrong."

"And just because you'll be going to work, that doesn't mean you can let your grades fall," Belinda put in. "We expect the same hard work out of you at school."

"Exactly," Paul said sternly. "Do you understand us?"

"Yes, sir."

Paul still wasn't fully convinced that Jim was contrite. "I want to know you understand what we expect from you. What happened yesterday was horrible. I want you to reassure us right now while you're sitting here looking at us, that nothing like this will ever happen again."

Jim bravely met his father's gaze as he answered, "I won't do it again. I promise."

"You won't do *what* again?" Belinda deliberately pressed him.

"I won't drink any more or do anything stupid like that again."

"All right."

Paul and Belinda were satisfied for the time being.

Paul went on, "It's time for you to grow up and take full responsibility for your actions, Jim. You're sixteen.

You're almost a man. I expect you to start acting like one. Do I make myself clear?"

"Yes, sir."

"Go on up to your room now. We'll call you when dinner's ready. You might want to start thinking about where you'd like to apply for a job. You could work fast food or at the show or maybe at one of the stores around town."

Jim nodded and started to leave the kitchen. He was ready to hurry to his room, but his mother's call stopped him.

"Jim."

He stopped to look back and found his mother coming toward him.

She wrapped her arms around him and hugged him to her heart. No matter what, he was always her baby, her son, and she loved him.

"I don't know what we would have done if anything had happened to you." Belinda held him close, treasuring the fact that he was safe at home.

When she let him go, he went up to his room. She went back to Paul and embraced him.

"So this is why everyone says how hard it is to raise teenagers," she said.

"You got it. Let's just hope he's strong enough to stay away from those other kids."

"He will. I trust him," Belinda said, her faith in her son firm.

"I hope you're right," Paul said quietly.

# *Chapter Eight*

Bonnie went looking for the volunteer staff members to tell them there was to be a meeting in her office in ten minutes.

Larry showed up first. "Our new guy looks a lot better cleaned up," he told her.

"I'll check on him later."

Her tone sounded so serious, Larry knew something was wrong. "What happened?"

"Wait until the others get here, then I'll tell you."

A few minutes later, Leann, Fern and Ruth joined them.

"To what do we owe the pleasure of this meeting?" Ruth asked, her good humor always making everyone smile. She wondered why Bonnie didn't smile, and she soon found out.

"I've got some bad news." She stopped for a moment to gather her wits. She looked up at her staff to find them all watching her with great interest. "The sheriff's department just paid me a visit."

"The sheriff's department?" Larry asked in a shocked tone.

Bonnie nodded. "We've been served an eviction notice."

"No!" Leann's protest was immediate.

"They can't just shut us down!" Fern argued, thinking of all the poor, desperate animals they tended every day.

"I'm sorry to say, they can—and they will. Our donations have been down for quite a while now, and I'm several months behind on rent. The way things have been going, I don't see any change in the near future. We'll have to vacate the premises by the end of the month."

"But that's less than two weeks away!"

"It's not going to be easy, that's for sure, and that's why I called this meeting. I want you all to get on the phones and start calling the other shelters in the area to see if any of them can take some of our animals."

"We've got what—fifty dogs and thirty-five cats?" Larry asked.

"Eighty-six now with the beagle that was just brought in. I don't know much about him yet, but all the other animals have been either spayed or neutered, and they're all current on their shots. Get started and see what you can come up with."

"What if we can't find places for all of them? What will happen to them?" Ruth had grown attached to many of the dogs, and she wanted to make sure they would be safe. She couldn't bear the thought that they might have to be euthanized.

"We're going to find them all homes. Don't you worry, Ruth." Bonnie tried to sound positive. She wouldn't even allow herself to consider the horrible alternative. She loved them all too much.

They combed through the phone books for the numbers of the other shelters and then went to work making the calls. In less than half an hour, they were back standing in the doorway of her office.

"We called everybody within a fifty-mile radius," Larry announced, his expression grim.

"And?"

"And we didn't have much luck," Ruth told her, handing her the list they'd made. "Only three places had any room at all, and they could only take twenty animals all together—and mostly cats."

Bonnie had feared this would happen, but she tried not to appear too dejected. "Thanks for your help. I'll take it from here."

"If there's anything else we can do, just let us know."

"I will."

The volunteers returned to their work, leaving Bonnie alone. She remained in her office, trying to come up with a plan to save the shelter. She realized it was going to take a miracle to keep Saving Grace open, for she didn't have the necessary cash or the manpower to operate a fund-raising campaign.

Bonnie took one last look at the eviction notice, and then set it aside on her desk. She thought of the scene in *Gone With the Wind* when Scarlett O'Hara was in danger of losing Rhett Butler and whispered, "Tomorrow is another day." To quote a famous sportsman, Bonnie told herself—it wasn't over until it was over. She still had almost two weeks, and she wouldn't quit or give up.

"God, help me," she prayed as she began shutting down for the night.

It was late. George sat at his kitchen table staring down at the documents he had spread out on the table before him. Always a numbers man, he carefully entered the dollar amounts from his various savings and retirement accounts in his adding machine and then hit the total button. He smiled at the size of the digital readout.

"Looks like we did real good, Duchess," he said with some satisfaction, looking down at his dog, who lay sleeping contentedly on the floor beside his chair.

At the sound of George's voice, the black and white, short-haired, medium-sized mutt lifted her head to look at her master with an adoring gaze.

"Yes, my dear," George went on as he reached down to scratch her behind her ears, "we've got quite a goodly sum stashed away. I kept saving for a rainy day, and it looks like that day has finally come."

For a moment, George allowed himself to fantasize about cashing in all his accounts and taking the money and going on a wild and crazy road trip, but he knew that wasn't a possibility. He was too ill, and besides that, except for Duchess, he had no one to go with. What good would an adventurous road trip be if you didn't have someone to share it with?

"What do you think, Duchess? Should I leave all my money to you, so you can continue to live the life of luxury after I'm gone?"

He said it in such a teasing voice that Duchess barked at him playfully in response.

"All right, all right, I'll make sure I leave you in the style to which you've become accustomed." He laughed and petted her more.

George frowned, though, as he again thought about the reality of what his future really held. He had no close relatives. His only son, George Jr., had been born with a heart defect and had only lived until his late teens. His wife had died six years before from cancer, and he'd been alone ever since. He had no siblings. No family to speak of at all.

For many years, he'd owned a successful advertising business, but when a bigger conglomerate offered a very handsome buyout three years ago, he'd taken it. He'd kept busy since then by volunteering to help out at church whenever he could, so he'd never felt overwhelmed by his loneliness and by the emptiness of his life—until now.

George had always considered himself a strong man, but at that moment, the weight of the world came crashing down on him. He couldn't stop the tears that blurred his vision, or the deep, wracking sobs that tore from deep within him.

Duchess didn't know what was wrong, but she instinctively knew what to do. She sat up and leaned against his leg, offering him, by that gentle contact, solace and unconditional love.

George lifted her onto his lap and held her close as he continued to weep.

"Thank God, I had sense enough to take you from the shelter that day, Duchess," he managed, remembering the time when he'd claimed her from the pen at the animal shelter shortly after his wife had died.

Duchess licked his face, making him smile even as he wept.

As he held her close, an idea came to him. He had been wondering what to do with his money when he died, and now he knew. He put Duchess back on the floor and got up to go to the recycling bin where he kept old newspapers. He'd read an article recently about how the local animal shelter was in dire need of funds.

George saw this morning's paper on top of the stack and he noticed again Lydia's article and the accompanying picture on the front page. He remembered how she had mentioned on occasion that her editor at the paper favored sensationalism, and the "Police Brutality" headline proved it. He almost would have felt sorry for the kid pictured there if he hadn't been drinking and driving before the fight occurred. Drunk driving was a serious offense, and he didn't blame the detective at all for doing what was necessary to get the offender off the road.

Flipping through older papers, George finally located the article about the animal shelter and wrote down the name of the contact person. He was definitely going to see that Saving Grace got some funding.

"Well, sweetheart, I think we're going to get this done," he told Duchess.

She barked her approval and wagged her tail.

George smiled.

Bonnie was ready to call it a day. She locked the entrance after the staff had gone and went out back to visit with some of the dogs. She took them treats whenever she got the chance, so when they saw her coming, they immediately perked up and began barking in welcome.

Smiling, Bonnie stopped at the first pen to pet the German shepherd mix named Handsome. "Hello, Handsome. How are you doing?"

He barked and whined excitedly as he pressed up against the metal fence, wanting her to pet him. She was quick to oblige as she fed him a treat. Six months before, his owner had moved into a retirement center that didn't allow pets, and Handsome had been brought to the shelter in hopes he'd find a good home. It hadn't happened yet, but Bonnie still believed he would be adopted by another family. He was good-natured and healthy, and he was great around kids.

She moved on and found the beagle in a pen nearby.

"Well, don't you look nice now that you're all cleaned up? You're pretty agile even with your missing front leg," she complimented him as she reached in to pet him. "I wish I knew your name, but since your wonderful owner didn't have you chipped, I guess we'll just have to come up with a new name for you—something that fits you."

The beagle just kept wagging his tail as she continued to pet him.

"We could call you Tripod or maybe Bunny. You do have a tendency to hop around, you know. What do you think?"

Bonnie couldn't come up with the perfect name just then, but she knew she would keep thinking on it. Something would occur to her sooner or later.

After giving out the treats, she returned to the office. The night worker was there, so she handed over the keys and headed for home.

The stress of the day had left her exhausted, but even so, Bonnie knew she wouldn't get much sleep that night. She had to find a way to save her animals. She wouldn't rest until she did. She was certain Noah had been more confident of his ability to rescue all the animals on the earth as he loaded them on the Ark, than she was of saving her cats and dogs right then, but she wouldn't give up. She'd keep praying. In a situation like this, God was definitely in charge.

"How do you want me to handle this?" Martin Peters, George's lawyer, asked George the following day when they met in his office.

George had called him earlier that day and had asked him to purchase the building that housed the Saving Grace Animal Shelter. George then wanted to turn the ownership of the building over to the people running the shelter. Martin had made a few phone calls and had completed the deal before lunch at a price that suited both George and the building's owner.

"Anonymously. Do you have any idea how long it will take to finalize the whole thing? I'd like the shelter to be notified as quickly as possible."

"I can probably complete everything in a day or two, but since everyone is in agreement with your offer, there should be no problem notifying the people at the shelter today."

"I'd like that."

"I'll take care of it, and, just as you've instructed, George, I'll make sure that the documents are sealed so your identity will not be revealed."

George stood up and shook his lawyer's hand. "Thanks."

"If there's anything else you need, just let me know."

"I'll be in touch."

Martin Peters watched him go. He'd known George Taylor for a few years and had always believed he was a good man. His action today showed how generous he truly was.

Without hesitation, the lawyer picked up the phone and dialed the courier service. He had an important delivery that had to be made right away.

Bonnie was meeting in her office with Leann and Fern.

"I went online last night and checked out the other shelters around the state. I'm going to get in touch with them today, to see if they can take any of our animals."

Fern noticed how tired Bonnie looked. "Did you get any sleep at all last night?"

"Sleep? What's that?" Bonnie managed a weary half-laugh. "I'm probably not going to get any sleep until I know everything's been taken care of here."

"Just make sure you take care of yourself," Leann advised.

"I'll worry about me later. Right now, I've got to find homes for our animals."

They heard the front door open. Bonnie used to be excited when someone came in. She'd always believed the visitor was stopping by to adopt a pet. After the events of yesterday, though, her optimism had faded.

"I'll take care of this," Fern offered.

"Thanks."

Leann went on back to work with the animals, leaving Bonnie alone at her desk. She'd just gotten back to work when Fern appeared in the office doorway.

"Bonnie—"

When she looked up, Fern gestured to her.

"There's a courier here who needs your signature on a delivery."

Bonnie frowned, but got up to take care of it. She went into the front office to find the courier waiting for her, an envelope in hand.

"You're Bonnie Zimmerman?" he asked.

"Yes, that's me."

"If you'll sign here for me." He held out the clipboard with the form attached.

"What is it?"

"I have a letter for you."

Bonnie's spirits sank even lower as she signed her name to the delivery confirmation document. Probably the letter was a follow-up on the eviction notice.

The courier handed over the missive and left.

Bonnie stood there for a moment, more depressed than ever. She turned and walked wearily back into her office. She glanced down at the envelope, intending to toss it unopened on her desk. She'd had enough bad news for the day, and she didn't need any more.

It was then that she noticed the envelope was not an official one. There was no return address on it—neither from the county nor the landlord.

Puzzled, she sat down and opened the envelope.

Leann and Fern were working with the dogs when they heard Bonnie screaming their names. Fear filled them. They raced to the front office, dragging with them the dogs they'd been walking. From the frantic sound of her screams, they were deathly afraid something tragic had happened. They found Bonnie standing in the middle of the office, crying hysterically, and feared the worst.

"Bonnie! What is it?" Leann demanded.

"What happened?" Fern asked.

Bonnie looked up at them. She was unable to speak. She could only hold out the piece of paper that had come in the courier's letter.

Leann and Fern shared a tortured look. They could well imagine what was in the document.

Leann finally reached out and took it. She quickly read it.

Fern was watching her carefully and she saw how Leann's eyes widened in shock at the news contained there.

"How bad is it?" she asked sadly.

"Fern—look!" Leann's expression was wondrous as she passed her the letter.

Fern took it from her and quickly read it. "I don't believe it! This is a miracle!"

"It is—it truly is a miracle!" Bonnie said, looking up at Fern. "But who would do this? Who would buy the building and donate it to us just so we can continue to run the shelter?"

"It's someone who respects what you do here, Bonnie," Fern told her.

"But why do they want to remain anonymous?"

"Who knows?" Leann said. "And it really doesn't matter. What matters is that an unknown hero has saved us!"

"And thank God they did," Bonnie said. She felt as if the weight of the world had just been lifted from her shoulders. "I feel like doing the Snoopy dance. I've got to call the newspapers in town and let them know about our secret helper. Whoever it is, they're our guardian angel! Saving Grace has been saved!"

Leann and Fern hugged Bonnie, then each other. The dogs didn't know what all the shouting and merriment was about, but they grew just as excited as the ladies. They danced around, tangling Fern and Leann in the leashes and leaving everyone laughing in delight.

It was a glorious day at the Saving Grace Animal Shelter.

By the day's end, Bonnie had come up with the perfect name for the beagle.

He was now officially named Trinity.

# *Chapter Nine*

The posh ballroom in the luxury hotel was crowded with supporters of the police department attending the annual Above and Beyond police fund-raiser. Both active and retired officers were there with their families, along with those who had been injured in the line of duty, and the survivors of those who'd died in the line of duty.

"I think this fund-raiser gets bigger every year," Steve remarked to his ex-partner Drew Barton as they sat together with Drew's wife, Marcie, at one of the tables.

"It's a wonderful thing the Above and Beyond folks do here," Drew agreed. "They've been a great help to us these last few years."

He and Marcie shared an understanding look.

"Hey, partner—" Drew began, changing the topic to avoid thinking about the bad times. "What was that article in *The Daily Sun* all about last week? Since when are you into beating up teenagers in the middle of the street?"

Steve had known he'd hear about the article tonight, and he could only grin wryly at his friend. "It was more a work of fiction than a factual news report."

"That's what all the abusive cops say," Drew countered, chuckling.

Steve finally had to laugh, too. "Lydia Chandler, the reporter who wrote the article, left a message for me at headquarters after the story ran, but I didn't bother to call her back. I didn't see any reason to talk to her again."

"What did the captain do?"

"Let's just put it this way: Donovan wasn't real happy about that headline."

"I can't imagine why," Drew said drolly.

"The kid blew a .8 when Charlie and I got him back to the station. He was drunk and he was driving. I got him off the street. That's all that mattered."

"Good for you."

"You're a good cop, Steve—no matter what the headlines might say," Marcie added to lighten their moods.

Though they were at the Above and Beyond fundraiser, Marcie didn't want to spend the rest of the evening remembering that horrible moment when she'd gotten the call about the accident Drew and Steve had had with the drunk driver.

Marcie noticed that Steve's expression suddenly changed. She glanced in the direction he was looking to see a very pretty young woman standing just inside the main entrance of the ballroom.

"Who's that?"

"That is none other than Lydia Chandler," Steve told them.

"Of 'Police Brutality' fame?" Drew asked, eyeing the shapely, dark-haired young woman, too.

"The same."

"She's brave to show up here after that article. How come you never told me she was this good-looking?"

"Watch it, Buster," Marcie ordered her husband with mock sternness.

"I am watching it," he countered with a grin and a wink at his wife.

"I never noticed," Steve answered him.

"Yeah, right," Drew drawled, still admiring the curvaceous young woman. "Hey, Steve—I hate to tell you this, buddy, but it looks like she's spotted you and she's headed this way."

Steve stifled a groan. The last thing he wanted to do was talk to Lydia Chandler. He hadn't returned her phone call for a reason.

Lydia had planned on attending the fund-raiser with Sandy. At the last minute, though, Sandy had had a family emergency that forced her to stay home. Not wanting to miss the Above and Beyond, Lydia had decided to come by herself.

The research Gary had asked her to do on officers in

the department who'd been killed or injured in the line of duty had been revealing. In the past year alone, one patrolman had been gunned down in cold blood by a drug dealer, and three officers had been seriously injured in separate incidents around the city.

Lydia had also followed the money trail as Gary had directed her to do, and she'd found that 94% of all the funds taken in by the Above and Beyond group went directly to the families of killed or injured officers. There was no graft or corruption anywhere in the organization.

Lydia had been surprised when she'd found a reference to Steve Mason while going through the information. She'd checked it to see what his involvement had been and had found a report that Detective Mason and his partner Drew Barton had been injured when a drunk driver broadsided them while they were on duty. According to the report, Detective Mason had suffered only minor injuries, but Detective Barton had been left partially paralyzed.

The discovery had left Lydia even more convinced that she owed Steve Mason an apology for Gary's headline. She understood far more clearly now the reason he'd acted so quickly to catch the drunk driver earlier that week.

Lydia had hoped the detective would be present tonight, and when she spotted him across the room, she headed his way. She wanted to set things right between them.

"Good evening, Detective Mason," Lydia greeted him as she approached his table.

"Miss Chandler." Steve got to his feet to speak with her.

Lydia had always thought he was a good-looking man, but in a suit and tie, he was downright handsome.

"To what do I owe this honor?" he asked cautiously. Any trust he'd had in her had disappeared the day the article about "Police Brutality" ran in the paper. Still, trust her or not, he had to admit she did look hot in the black cocktail dress she was wearing.

"You didn't return my phone call—" she began.

"I've been busy," he interrupted.

"The reason I called was to apologize for what happened with the coverage of the DUI arrest the other afternoon. I wanted you to know that I'm sorry if the headline caused you any trouble."

Steve was surprised by her candor, and her apology.

Lydia went on, "My editor is big into sensationalism. I knew it was a slow news day when I turned the report in, but I had no idea he would run it on the front page, let alone with that kind of headline. I know you were only doing your job."

"I appreciate your concern."

"It didn't cause trouble for you, then?"

"Nothing came up that I couldn't handle," he told her.

Lydia was relieved. "Good. Again, I apologize. Gary's main goal is selling newspapers—and sometimes he doesn't care how."

"It sounds like your editor's more into fiction than news reporting."

"Off the record, there are times when I agree with you."

"What about you?" Steve asked. "What's your main goal with your reporting?"

Lydia met his gaze straight on as she answered him. "The truth—I've always been about going after the truth."

"Good for you," Marcie put in. She loved women with spunk, and she admired the reporter for seeking Steve out this way and being up front with him. She'd heard there were many in the media who didn't care about anything except getting their names before the public. Obviously, Lydia Chandler wasn't one of them. She invited, "Would you care to join us?"

"I wouldn't want to intrude—" Lydia looked at Steve, unsure if he would be comfortable with her there. She'd caused him enough trouble. She didn't want to spoil the evening for him.

"Nonsense. We can never have too many pretty ladies at our table," Drew said, pulling out the chair between him and Steve for Lydia. "Have a seat. The more, the merrier."

"Thanks." Lydia noticed then that the man who'd offered her the chair was in a wheelchair. She suspected he was probably Detective Mason's ex-partner. She found out her guess was right when he introduced himself and his wife, Marcie.

"It's a pleasure to meet you," Lydia said.

"You, too, Miss Chandler," Marcie replied.

"Call me Lydia, please."

"And we're Drew and Marcie."

They all relaxed a bit now that the introductions were out of the way.

"Detective Mason—" Lydia turned to Steve.

"I think we can be on a first-name basis, too," he told her with a half-smile. "Call me Steve."

"All right—Steve."

He liked the way she said his name, but he had no chance to say anything more to her, for the lights in the ballroom dimmed and the emcee, a local television personality, went to the podium.

The evening's program proved a moving one. The fallen and injured officers were honored, and more than a few tears were shed by those in the audience.

Lydia's appreciation of the officers' sacrifices grew even greater as she listened to the presentation. Their jobs were hard. A lot of the time on duty, they had to deal with the ugly side of humanity, and they could face unexpected danger at any moment when they went on patrol. It was no wonder Steve took his job so seriously. Officers couldn't afford to be lax. One mistake in judgment could cost them their lives.

When the ceremony ended, dinner was served. The four of them made small talk as they enjoyed the delicious fare. As the meal finished up, the music began.

"So what are you going to write about tonight?" Drew asked her. "What angle are you going to use to cover the fund-raiser?"

"I'm not working tonight. I know what good work this group does, and I just wanted to support their cause."

"We appreciate that," Marcie said. "The Above and Beyond group was there for us whenever we needed them these past few years."

"That's good to know. Are you doing all right now?"

"Yes, we are," Drew said firmly.

"I was terrified at first," Marcie admitted, remembering those horrifying days right after the accident. "I didn't know if he was going to make it or not, but things turned out better than I ever dreamed they would. Drew's teaching at the university now. He went back to school and took the courses he needed to become an Associate Professor of Criminal Justice."

"That's wonderful." Lydia was in awe of the man's grit and determination in the face of all the obstacles he'd had to overcome.

"I loved law enforcement too much to give it up completely. This has worked out well for me."

"Yeah, you take off for the academic life and leave me to clean up the streets all alone," Steve put in.

"You're not alone. You've got Charlie to help you. And here he comes now." Drew laughed as he saw Steve's current partner coming to join them. "How hard can your job be when you're working with Charlie?"

"I just heard my name," Charlie said, giving them all suspicious looks. "Why are you talking about me?"

"Drew was complimenting you," Marcie put in.

"I don't believe that for a minute," he laughed.

They were all good friends and at ease with one another.

"Charlie, you know Lydia Chandler from *The Daily Sun*, don't you?" Steve made the introduction.

"I believe we've met in passing. It's nice to see you." He'd been on his way over to see who the woman with Steve was, and now he recognized her. He was surprised that Steve was giving her the time of day, much less sitting down talking to her, but he was sure he'd get the whole story later.

"It's nice to see you, too," Lydia said.

"Is everybody having a good time?" Charlie asked.

"Yes, but we're about ready to call it a night," Drew told them.

"We've got a babysitter tonight, so we have to be home by midnight. It was nice to meet you, Lydia," Marcie said. "Steve, Charlie, I expect to see you both at the barbecue in two weeks. No excuses."

"Yes, ma'am." Steve and Charlie knew better than to give Marcie any trouble.

"Steve, why don't you bring Lydia with you?" Marcie suggested. She'd noticed how the two of them seemed interested in one another, and she'd taken a liking to the other woman.

Steve looked at Lydia and asked, "Would you like to go?"

"I'll have to check my schedule, but it sounds like fun."

"See you then," Marcie bade as she and Drew left.

Charlie moved on to talk with some other people, leaving Steve and Lydia alone at the table.

"So, Steve, what do you do when you're not at work?"

He gave a derisive laugh. "It seems all I do is work."

"Do you have a family?" She'd noticed that he wasn't wearing a wedding ring, but that didn't mean anything. He could be one of those guys who didn't wear a wedding band.

"I'm not married," he answered. "What about you?"

"I'm single, too." Lydia was amazed by how anxious she'd been to hear his answer. "So, what do you do for fun?"

"When I do manage to get some time off, I like to ride my Harley."

Somehow, the news that he had a bike didn't surprise her. "That's awesome."

"You like motorcycles?"

"Oh, yeah."

"I'll take you for a ride sometime."

"You're on."

"So, what about you? What do you do for fun?"

"I like to read a lot."

"We've got to liven you up a little bit." He paused and looked around. His tone was conspiratorial when he asked, "You want to do something wild and crazy?"

"You aren't going to get me arrested, are you?"

"Now, there's a thought." He slanted her a knowing, almost wicked grin before saying, "No, I wasn't going to get you arrested. I was going to ask you to dance."

A slow song had just started.

"Would you like to?" Lydia's heartbeat had quickened at his enticing smile.

"Yes, I would."

They got up, and Lydia walked ahead of him onto the dance floor.

Steve's gaze lingered on her slender, curvaceous form as she walked ahead of him. He found he couldn't look away from the gentle, graceful sway of her hips and the shapely length of her legs. He realized then that if he wasn't careful, Lydia could mean trouble for him. Funny thing was, though, Steve found he liked the thought of being in that kind of trouble.

Lydia reached the edge of the dance floor and stopped to wait for Steve. When he reached her side, he took her in his arms and moved with her out onto the dance floor.

Lydia looked up at him as she followed his lead. Her gaze traced his ruggedly handsome features, the lean line of his jaw and the firm set of his mouth. The scent of his aftershave was heady, and she found herself thrilling to the feel of his strong arms around her. She closed her eyes and imagined herself riding behind him on his Harley. She found the thought decidedly appealing. Lydia realized she couldn't deny it any longer—she was definitely attracted to him. When the song ended, she was sorry to move out of his embrace.

"Thanks," Lydia said.

"My pleasure. You're a good dancer," he complimented her as he escorted her back to the table.

"I was just following your lead, Detective."

"That's what you investigative reporters do, isn't it? Follow leads?"

"That's right."

They were both laughing as they sat down to enjoy more of each other's company.

Gary was feeling quite good about what he'd captured on film that night. He'd moved around the ballroom taking pictures and interviewing people. He'd had no luck getting anyone of authority to speak at length to him, let alone go on record about the highway shootings. Those he'd managed to speak with had been polite but distant when he'd pressed them for details.

After running Lydia's story about police abuse, he'd expected them to seek him out and try to suck up to him and win his favor tonight, but the opposite had happened. It seemed to Gary that anyone of importance had avoided speaking to him. But he didn't care. He already had what he needed.

Gary cast one last glance back across the ballroom to where Lydia was sitting with the detective. He didn't know quite what her game plan was, spending so much time with Detective Mason, but he hoped she was using the man to get some good inside information.

Gary was smiling as he drove back to the office. His article about the police wouldn't run until the Sunday edition, but he had a lot of work to do and he wanted to get started on it tonight.

"Have you heard anything at all new on the sniper?" Lydia asked Steve casually some time later after they'd shared several more dances.

"Nothing. It's real quiet out there, and that worries me. I'm afraid he might be getting ready to strike again."

"'He'? How can you be sure it's a man? Do you know something you haven't told the press yet?"

"No, that's just the profile on this type of killer. It's usually a white male working alone. He's egotistical and likes having the power of life and death over others.

He's into guns and violence, and he's angry with the world and everyone in it."

"That's scary, isn't it?"

"Very. I'm not going to rest until he's caught. I just wish we had something to go on, but he's been so damned good at covering his tracks, there's nothing out there right now. Charlie and I have been all over the crime scenes, and they're clean—real clean. This guy knows exactly what he's doing."

"I hope you catch him before he strikes again."

"So do I. I don't want to see anyone else get hurt."

The disc jockey announced that the next song would be the last of the night.

"Shall we?" Steve invited.

She took his hand and allowed him to lead her out among the other couples. They moved together in perfect rhythm, enjoying each other and the dance.

Lydia found being in Steve's arms a rare pleasure, and she wanted the music to just keep going. But all good things come to an end.

"Good night, folks," the disc jockey announced. "Be careful going home."

Those who'd stayed on until the end began to make their way out of the building to the dimly lighted parking lot.

"I had a good time tonight," Lydia told Steve.

"I'm glad we got to know each other better," Steve said as he accompanied her to her car near the back of the lot.

"I am, too," she said as they stopped beside her Focus.

She unlocked the door, then looked up at him. "This was fun."

"And I didn't get you arrested."

They both laughed.

"I guess we'll have to do this more often," Steve suggested.

"I'd like that."

"So would I," he responded, gazing down at her.

Steve was glad no one else was around, for Lydia looked more beautiful than ever in the moonlight and he couldn't help himself. He took her in his arms and drew her to him. His mouth claimed hers in a gentle, yet sensuous kiss.

A thrill of delight trembled through Lydia at the touch of his lips. She linked her arms around his neck and returned his kiss with abandon. At the sound of voices in the distance coming their way, they broke apart.

They stared at each other for a moment as if seeing one another for the first time.

"I'd better go," she said softly.

"Are you in the phone book?"

"Yes."

"I'll call you."

"I'll be looking forward to it."

"Good night." Steve stepped back.

Lydia got in her car and buckled up.

Steve watched her drive away, then went to find his own car. He headed home, more than satisfied with the evening's turn of events.

# *Chapter Ten*

George sat down at the kitchen table to enjoy a cup of coffee and read the Saturday morning paper. He scanned the headlines, checked out the sports scores and was leafing through the local news section when he saw it.

MYSTERIOUS BENEFACTOR SAVES GRACE

An unknown donor has given new hope to the Saving Grace Animal Shelter. The shelter had been scheduled to close at the end of the month due to falling donations. Bonnie Zimmerman, the director, said that times had been hard in recent months, but not anymore. "My prayers have been answered!" Zimmerman said. "Saving Grace is a no-kill facility, and thanks to the generosity of some wonderful, caring person out there, we will be able to continue our work here with the animals. Thank you. You're a miracle worker! God bless you!"

George had to stop and set the paper aside for a moment; his vision was too blurred by tears to keep reading.

Duchess, believing something was wrong, got up and came to his side. She nudged his arm with her nose and looked up at him questioningly.

"Sweetheart, we did it," George told her with a watery grin as he scratched behind her ears. "The shelter's going to be just fine."

Duchess licked his hand before lying back down, satisfied that her owner was all right.

George managed to finish reading the article then. It was good to know he'd made a difference in the world. He wondered what he could do next to help someone else. He planned to go to five-o'clock Mass. He would seek out Father Richards afterward and talk to him about it.

"I'm ready, Dad," Jim said when he joined his parents in the kitchen.

"You look very nice," his mother told him, admiring the dress pants and long-sleeved white shirt he was wearing. "Are you nervous?"

"A little," he admitted. He'd called the local theater to see if they were hiring the day before and had learned there were openings. The manager had requested to meet him that morning, so he was ready to go to his first-ever job interview.

"You'll do fine," Paul assured him. "Just look the manager straight in the eye and answer his questions. Let him know you're honest and not afraid of hard work."

"I didn't know they were going to expect me to work," Jim complained with a grin.

"Let's get going. You don't want to be late." Paul was taking him to the interview while Belinda stayed home.

"Good luck."

"Thanks, Mom." He gave her a thumbs-up as they drove away.

It was a short trip to the Cinema 10 theater. Paul waited outside in the car while Jim went in. Jim was gone for quite a while, and Paul began to suspect that the lengthy interview meant good news. He was right. Jim was smiling broadly when he came out of the theater.

"I got it!" Jim told his father excitedly as he climbed into the car.

"I'm proud of you, son. When do you start?"

"Mr. Thomas, the manager, said I could start tonight. I told him I had to check with you first."

"That's fine. Why don't you run back in and tell him you can do it. Find out what time he wants you to be here."

Jim did as his father suggested and soon they were on their way home to tell his mother. At five o'clock that evening, he would officially start his job.

"Did your boss say what you were going to do?"

"I'm going to be an usher. I have to wear black pants and a long-sleeved white shirt. They'll give me a vest and a bow tie to wear. That's, like, the uniform. Mr. Thomas said they'd train me to do concessions and box office, too."

"How many hours a week will you be scheduled?"

"While school's on, sixteen hours."

"That'll be just about right. You'll still have plenty of time to get your homework done. Let's get home and tell your mother the good news."

Five-o'clock Mass was crowded as always. George sat in his usual pew near the back. When Mass was over, he made his way out to the church greeting area and stood off to the side, waiting for Father Richards to finish speaking with the other parishioners.

"George, it's good to see you tonight," Father Richards told him, shaking his hand.

"It's good to see you, too. I was wondering—do you have a minute to talk, somewhere more private?" The greeting area was a busy place at Holy Family.

"Sure. We can go over to my office."

"That'd be good."

They left the church and headed to the rectory. Once they were seated in the office with the door closed, George explained what he wanted to do.

"So if you hear of anyone who could use help, let me know."

"That's very kind and generous of you." The priest was in awe of George's plan.

"I've been doing a lot of thinking since we talked last, and I want to do some good while I still can."

"You're sure you want to do this anonymously?"

"I'm sure. I'm not doing this for the glory. I just want to be able to help."

"Let me check into a few things. There's always a need at the food shelter and the St. Vincent de Paul Society. Is there a specific dollar amount you want to give?"

"No."

"All right. I'll give you a call."

"I'll be waiting to hear from you."

Father Richards walked George out to his car and watched him drive away.

He'd always known George was a good man.

George not only practiced his religion.

George lived it.

"I'm a senior at Central, where do you go?" seventeen-year-old Rob Hudson asked Jim as he was teaching him how to get a theater cleaned up quickly before the next crowd of moviegoers was allowed in to be seated.

"I go to North," Jim replied, following his lead going up and down the rows to pick up the discarded popcorn boxes, soda cups and candy wrappers.

"I didn't think I'd seen you around Central. How'd you get that bruise?" Rob had noticed the bruise on Jim's face right away.

"I was in a car accident earlier this week." He didn't offer anything more.

"That must have hurt."

"Yes, it did," Jim told him as he kept working. Not wanting to dwell on the accident anymore, he asked Rob, "Are people always this sloppy?"

"This is nothing," Rob warned him. "Wait until we have a big premiere. It can get real crazy around here. You're in for some treats, cleaning those up."

"Great—something to look forward to."

They finished picking up the big stuff, then got brooms and swept up the rest. Once they'd gotten all the trash bagged and disposed of, they were ready to open the theater doors and let the next group in.

"One screen down and nine more to go," Rob joked when they stepped out into the hall. "You ready to quit yet?"

"Not quite."

Mr. Thomas, a tall, heavyset man with an easy grin, came up to check up on Jim. "How's our newest usher doing, Rob?"

"He can handle a broom with the best of them," Rob said.

The theater manager laughed. "That's definitely an asset in this business. Keep up the good work, you two."

Rob and Jim started down to the next theater, which had just let out.

"Ready for some more excitement?"

"Sure, why not?"

It was several hours later when Jim got his first break. He and Rob went to the employees' room to sit down for a few minutes and have a soda.

"How many hours do you work a week?" Jim asked the upper-classman.

"I usually put in about twenty. I'm trying to save up as

much as I can to help out with college next year, and car insurance is a killer."

"That's for sure." Jim didn't even want to think about what was going to happen to his rates after the accident.

"Do you work again tomorrow?" Rob asked.

"No. Mr. Thomas said I'm scheduled to work Monday and Wednesday nights this coming week."

"I'm in on Wednesday, too. I think you're going to like weeknights better. They're not nearly as busy as the weekends."

"In that case, I'm looking forward to it already."

They finished their sodas and went back to work.

Jim was tired when his mother picked him up at 11:30. He told her how the night had gone.

"Well, let's get home, so you can go to bed and be ready to get up for church in the morning," she said.

"Why do I have to go to church?" he complained. He was used to sleeping late on Sundays.

"Because we're going to Mass in the morning—all of us."

"But I want to sleep—" he argued.

"Your father and I talked about it, and we've decided it's time we started going to church again. We checked the schedule and thought seven-thirty would work out best."

Inwardly Jim groaned at the thought of getting up so early on the weekend.

"Set your alarm," his mother went on. "We need to leave the house no later than seven-fifteen to be on time."

He said nothing more. He knew he had no grounds to argue.

George was having trouble sleeping. It wasn't that anything in particular was hurting; he was just restless. He went to the kitchen for a drink of water. He stood at the sink, drinking his water and staring out the window at the clear, beautiful night outside. He could see the half-moon on the horizon and stars twinkling in the heavens. The weather forecaster had promised a great day tomorrow, and George suddenly knew what he was going to do.

Setting his glass aside, he went into the garage and turned on the lights. The sight of the perfectly maintained red '66 Mustang made him smile—as it always did. George had many wonderful memories tied up with the car. Whenever he took it out for a drive, he always felt like a kid again, and he knew that was what he needed right now.

He needed to feel young and vibrant.

He needed to feel alive.

After all, he wasn't dead—not yet anyway.

As he returned to the house, George made up his mind. First thing in the morning, he was going for a drive. He didn't know where he was going to go, and it didn't matter. Just having some time out on the road would be good for him. He'd have the radio blasting on the oldies station, so he could time-travel—in his mind.

Relaxed and still smiling at the thought of being on

the open road again, George turned out the lights and went back to bed. This time he managed to fall asleep.

Sunday morning couldn't come soon enough.

Steve glanced at his watch and couldn't believe he was still at work. He sat back in his desk chair and stretched wearily. It had been one long day.

"You about ready to call it a night?" Charlie asked from his own desk.

"I guess. There's nothing more we can do here."

They'd spent most of the day following up on the leads that had been called in to the tip line, but to no avail.

"I was hoping that partial on the license plate would help us, but it was useless."

The phone rang on Steve's desk and he grabbed it up right away. If someone was calling at this hour, it had to be important.

"Detective Mason," he answered. He glanced down at the Caller ID on his phone, but the printout read "unavailable."

"You're never going to catch me," a man's voice said.

Steve tensed and immediately sat upright. Any weariness he'd been feeling vanished.

Steve gestured at Charlie, and Charlie knew what he had to do. He started to put a trace on the call.

"Who is this?" Steve sounded aggravated on purpose, hoping to challenge the caller and keep him talking.

"Who do you think it is?" the voice taunted. "Goodbye, Detective."

The phone went dead.

"Damn it!" Steve slammed the receiver down. "Did you get anything on the call?"

"No. There wasn't time. What did they say?"

Steve looked at Charlie, his expression grave. "The caller said, 'You're never going to catch me.' "

"He's wrong," Charlie ground out.

"I know."

The sniper made his way back home from the pay phone, contemplating the chaos that, he had no doubt, was reigning at police headquarters.

He smiled.

It was a wonderful feeling.

He was in complete control.

He could do whatever he wanted to do, whenever he wanted to do it, and they couldn't stop him.

The sense of control and power was intoxicating, for he knew now that Detective Mason had still been at his desk working at this late hour on the weekend. He liked knowing the public servants were hard at work, earning their pay. But it didn't matter how many hours the detectives put in. They would never find him.

He was too smart for them, and he'd prove it to them again next week.

# *Chapter Eleven*

"Mom—I went to church just like you wanted, but I'm not going to that dumb youth group meeting tonight!" Jim protested when they returned home from Mass.

"Yes," Belinda said with determination, "you are."

"Dad—" He turned to his father to plead his case. He didn't want or need to go to the youth group. They were probably a bunch of strange kids he didn't know, and didn't want to know.

"You'll do what your mother says, son. It's time for you to make new friends."

"I don't need any friends."

"Good, then don't make any, but you're still going to the meeting," she told him, effectively ending the discussion. "Plan on it."

Jim turned away, stormed into his room and shut the door. He wasn't sure what his life had become, but his future didn't look very promising right now.

He could go to church.

He could go to school.

He could go to work.

He could go to the youth group.

Period.

The end.

Jim groaned and threw himself on his bed. The sad part of his existence was, he had no one to blame but himself. The one ray of hope he clung to was that once he'd managed to pay back the money he owed his parents, he could start saving to buy himself another car. He'd never have a car as cool as his Camaro again, but the day was going to come when he'd have another set of wheels.

Lydia attended nine-o'clock Mass, then drove home ready to enjoy her day off. The past week had been a long one, and she needed to relax and get some yard work done.

Lydia parked in her driveway and sat in the car for a moment, looking at her house. Her home was her pride and joy. She'd bought the thirty-year-old brick ranch for a good price four years before and had slowly been updating it ever since. Her plan for today, since it looked like the weather forecast of a sunny, warm day had been right, was to plant flowers in the front yard. First, though, she was going to indulge herself and have a leisurely breakfast and read the paper.

Lydia got out of the car and grabbed up her copy of the Sunday newspaper from the middle of the driveway. Once she was inside, she made coffee, poured herself a cup and sat down at the table to enjoy the paper. Granted, there were days when reading *The Daily Sun* was like doing homework, but she knew Gary's article on the Above and Beyond fund-raiser was going to run today, and she was eager to read all about it. She slipped the newspaper out of its plastic covering and unfolded it on the table before her. She stared down at the headline in horror.

KILLER RUNS LOOSE AMONG US
WHILE THE POLICE PARTY THE NIGHT AWAY

Gary's bold headline blazed above a picture of people dancing at the fund-raiser Friday night—and she and Steve were one of the couples. Rage filled Lydia. She understood his "sell papers" mentality and tolerated his need to find the "right angle" for every story, but she couldn't believe Gary would take such a negative angle on something as powerful and uplifting as the Above and Beyond charity.

She quickly read his article and inwardly grimaced at his coldhearted depiction of the events of last night. Gary wrote that it was a raucous party. He focused almost entirely on what the police department didn't know about the sniper and how they couldn't be working on the case if they were drinking and dancing all night. Only one brief line mentioned that the funds raised went to support policemen injured in the line of duty on the families of those killed.

Lydia threw the paper aside in disgust, angrier with

Gary than she'd ever been before. She could not understand what motivated him to print negative things about something as positive as Above and Beyond.

Lydia was tempted to quit—to call Gary and turn in her resignation that morning. She could cut and run. She could move to Arizona and live near her parents, who'd relocated there after her father had retired several years before. She was their only child, and they'd been asking her to move out near them. Right now, living and working in Arizona sounded better than ever.

But even as she considered quitting, the investigative reporter in her began to wonder at Gary's motive for acting as he did. She wanted to know what made him tick. She decided then and there to start looking into his past; she wanted to know what had happened to him to turn him into such a coldhearted, calculating man. If nothing else, checking out his past might give her better insight into how to deal with him.

Her coffee finished, Lydia got up and went to her computer. She did a Google search on Gary and came up with close to 9,000 different listings. She quickly went through them, checking out his past history at various newspapers. She found a short bio that told of his college years in journalism and of how he'd gotten his first job with a major newspaper in Chicago twenty years ago. According to the bio, he'd been named editor-in-chief of a newspaper in Denver and had been working there prior to taking his current position at *The Daily Sun*.

Disappointed that she couldn't find anything more

revealing about his character, Lydia shut down the computer and went to her bedroom to change clothes. She had yard work to do today, and it was time to get at it.

George took his time Sunday morning. He fed Duchess, fixed himself a simple breakfast and looked through the newspaper. He'd noticed the headline about the police fund-raiser, but it sounded so negative, he didn't even bother to read it. He checked out the ads, then put the paper aside. He'd had enough of lazing around indoors.

The sun was shining.

It was warm and beautiful outside.

It was definitely a Mustang day.

Grabbing up his keys and wallet, George went out to open the garage. Duchess looked up at him expectantly.

"Sorry, little girl, you're not going along this time."

He pressed the button to the garage-door opener and waited as the door went up. The bright sunshine poured in, revealing the highly polished red '66 hardtop sitting there, just waiting for him.

George wasted no time. He got in and started it up. The engine roared, and he automatically started smiling as he adjusted the rearview mirror. He decided then and there that doctors should prescribe driving a Mustang to cure whatever ailed you. It was certainly the perfect cure for what ailed him right then. At moments like this, he felt invincible again, and he needed that feeling right now.

He pulled out of the garage and closed the garage door behind him. He drove off down the street, humming along to an oldies tune on the radio.

* * *

Steve was looking forward to the afternoon. It was the perfect day for a bike ride. The frustration of these past few weeks, coupled with the arrogant phone call from the sniper, had left him tense and on edge. He needed to get out on the open road and let the wind blow away his cares.

Steve got his helmet and started to leave the house, then stopped as Lydia slipped into his thoughts. He wondered if she'd be interested in going along with him. Figuring it was worth a try, he got out the phone book and looked up her number. He found her address and phone number easily and gave her a call. When an answering machine come on, he just hung up without leaving a message. Now that he knew where she lived, he figured he could ride by and see if she was around. If not, no loss. Just in case, he grabbed his extra helmet to take along.

Lydia was hard at work planting marigolds in her front flower bed when she heard the roar of a motorcycle coming up the street. There weren't many cycles in the area, and she stopped what she was doing to get a look at the bike. She was impressed by the black and chrome Harley, and she was really surprised when the biker pulled to a stop at the curb right in front of the house.

She smiled in delight when the lean, mean biker took off his helmet and sunglasses and she discovered it was Steve. In his biker boots and riding gear, he looked more like a bad boy than a cop—a very sexy bad boy.

"You want to go for a ride?" Steve asked, giving her an easy grin.

"Oh, yeah," Lydia said eagerly, her heartbeat quickening as she smiled back at him. She took a look down at herself and realized she'd have to clean up a bit before she could get on the bike with him. "I've been working in my garden here, and I'm a little dirty. Can you give me a minute?"

"I guess I can wait a minute," he said easily. "I brought an extra helmet."

"Pretty sure I wouldn't turn you down, were you?"

"I figured if you said no I could always arrest you for something and take you in."

Lydia started laughing. "You'll never have to threaten me to get me on a Harley, but you might have to threaten me to get me off. I'll be right out."

Steve felt more relaxed than he had in days as he waited for her to return.

Lydia went inside and made short order of washing up and changing into clothes suitable for a motorcycle ride.

Steve heard her come out and almost did a double take at the biker babe coming down the porch steps. He'd thought she was hot in the cocktail dress the other night, but in her tight pants, lightweight fake leather jacket and boots, she looked really fine today.

"I heard you were giving free rides," Lydia said, smiling flirtatiously. "I'm ready to go cruisin' if you are."

He held out the spare helmet to her and watched as she strapped it on.

"All set?"

"Let's go."

They got on the bike. Lydia fit snugly against him.

"Hold on tight," Steve advised.

Lydia linked her arms around his waist as Steve pulled away from the curb.

"Where are we going?" she called out to him over the rumble of the engine.

"We're escaping," he called back over his shoulder. "We're going to get out of town."

Steve handled his bike easily in the traffic, but when he got the chance, he turned off the main road and headed away from the city on a quieter route.

"You all right?" Steve asked.

"I'm fine," Lydia answered, enjoying every minute of the ride. She'd never ridden on a motorcycle as special as Steve's Harley. This was one powerful bike. She loved the sense of freedom that came with the wind in her face and the warmth of the sunshine beating down on her as they rode along. It was definitely a glorious day.

Steve knew exactly where he wanted to take Lydia. About half an hour's ride out of town on the River Road was a small country store. They sold soft drinks and sandwiches and had tables set up out back with a view of the river. He knew it would be the perfect place to stop and rest for a while.

They had little chance to talk as they rode along. They simply enjoyed the quiet roads and the lush scenery that surrounded them once they left the city behind.

When at last Steve pulled into the parking lot of the

country store, Lydia had to admit she was glad. Unaccustomed as she was to riding on the back of a Harley, she was getting a bit stiff and needed a break.

"Are you ready for lunch?" Steve asked when he'd turned off the ignition.

"Sounds great."

They left their helmets with the bike and went inside to look around.

River Bend Grocery was an old log cabin that had been fixed up to accommodate modern conveniences like electricity and indoor plumbing. Lydia was enchanted by the rustic feel of the place. She wandered through the aisles, looking at merchandise on display while Steve went to get their food. There were keepsakes and handcrafted items along with children's toys.

Lydia had meant to skip the toys, but then she spotted the kids' plastic version of an old-fashioned Wild West sheriff's badge and she knew she had to buy one for Steve. She made the purchase secretly and hid it in her purse to wait for the right moment to give it to him.

Steve caught up with her once he had their drinks and sandwiches, and they went outside to the picnic area.

"I love this place," Lydia said as they sat down at one of the tables. "How did you find it?"

"Drew had a Harley, too, and we used to go riding together all the time before he got married. We found this place years ago when they first started renovating it."

"They did a nice job fixing it up. I guess they must do a good business, since they're still open."

"They're really crowded on the weekends during the

summer. Some tourist buses actually come out here to let the people have lunch and take in the view."

"How long have you had your Harley?"

"I bought my first bike when I was seventeen, and I've had one ever since."

"You should have moved to California."

"Why?" He couldn't imagine why she'd suddenly brought up California.

Lydia grinned. "Then you could have joined the highway patrol and starred in a sequel to the original *Chips* series."

They both laughed.

"No, my bike is my fun. I don't want to ruin it by turning it into work."

"I have to tell you, I'm very proud of myself."

"Why?"

"I remembered not to smile while we were riding, so I don't have any bugs in my teeth. What about you?"

"I'm good, too," he chuckled, remembering the jokes that used to go around about telling how happy a biker was by counting the bugs in his teeth.

After they'd enjoyed their meal together, Steve suggested, "The trail leads down to the river's edge, if you feel like exploring."

"Sure, let's hike down there."

The gravel path was sometimes steep as it meandered through the woods and down the hillside to a cleared area. They walked to the river's edge to watch the muddy water flowing by.

"It's so peaceful here," Lydia remarked.

They hadn't met anyone on the way down, and they enjoyed the serenity of being alone and away from any vestiges of civilization.

"There are days when I understand why some people turn into hermits," Steve told her.

"You, too?" she agreed, glancing over at him.

"Yes, but not today," he answered.

Their gazes met.

Lydia was suddenly very physically aware of Steve—of his broad shoulders and the powerful width of his chest. Having had her arms around him on the ride out there, she knew how fit he was, and she suddenly felt the need to wrap her arms around him again. Somehow she controlled the impulse, for she didn't want to appear brazen.

Steve, however, had other ideas. The sweet serenity of their isolation encouraged him. He reached out to take her in his arms and then bent down to kiss her.

Lydia surrendered willingly to his embrace. They stood locked in each other's arms, caught up in a moment of pure delight.

His kiss had started out sweetly, but her willing surrender urged him on. He deepened the exchange and brought her fully against him. It was heavenly—and exciting, very exciting.

And then they heard voices coming down the trail.

They broke apart and stood there staring at each other for a moment.

"I think we've got company coming," Steve told her regretfully.

"I thought this was one of those places where the hermits went to live."

"I was hoping." He managed a wry grin.

They turned back toward the trail just as a large family appeared. Several small children ran out into the opening, squealing in delight at the sight of the river so close by.

Steve and Lydia greeted them in passing and started back to the bike. The return trip to town went smoothly. Lydia was even more relaxed and at ease, and Steve loved every minute of having her nestled against him.

"Would you like to come in for a while?" Lydia invited when they pulled into the driveway at her house. She got off the motorcycle and removed the helmet.

"I would, but I've got to get back and check in with headquarters to see if anything new has turned up."

"You think there might be?"

"You never know. I got a strange phone call last night when I was working late. I think it might have been the sniper."

"What did he say?"

"Not much. He was on the line less than fifteen seconds, so there was no tracing the call, and he knew that. He just said, 'You're never going to catch me.' "

"Well, I bet you will," Lydia insisted. "This killer is going to make a mistake, and when he does, you're going to be there, ready and waiting."

"I like the confidence you have in your local police department." He managed a wry grin.

"Hey, some of my favorite people work there. I know what good work they do."

For a moment, their gazes met and held.

Steve wanted to take her in his arms and kiss her again, but they were in the middle of her driveway in broad daylight. He controlled the impulse with an effort. "I guess I'd better be going."

"Oh! Wait! Before I forget—I bought you a present while we were at River Bend."

"A present?"

She took the small package out of her purse and handed it to him.

He opened the bag to find the sheriff's badge. "I haven't seen one of these since I was a kid."

"I thought it suited you."

"Why, thank you, ma'am," he drawled in his best imitation of a Western lawman. He put the badge in a shirt pocket that buttoned down for safekeeping on the ride home.

"You're welcome, and thanks for lunch. Next time, it will be my treat."

"Sounds good. I'll give you a call."

Steve made sure the extra helmet was safely fastened to the back of the bike before heading off.

As Lydia watched him ride away, she was smiling. With the promise of that phone call, she knew he wasn't riding off into the sunset.

# *Chapter Twelve*

Jim sat slumped down in the back seat of his father's car as he pulled into the parking lot behind church near the parochial school.

"Don't look so happy," his mother said, trying to get a smile out of him. "I know we're torturing you, but as parents that's our job."

Her attempt to engage him in banter didn't work. He just stared out the window glumly.

Paul parked and turned off the engine. "Come on, son. We'll walk you in."

"I can go in alone," he told them.

"Not tonight, you can't. It's your first time. We have to make sure you're registered."

The youth group meetings were held in the school cafeteria, so Jim got out of the car and started inside. Other teens were already there, hanging out in the hallway. His parents followed him in.

"Jim! It's so good to see you here," Phyllis Logan

greeted him from the table where she was seated, checking the teens in as they arrived. She volunteered to work with the youth group, and she had a great time doing it. "Are these your parents?"

"Yeah," he answered.

They introduced themselves as Jim looked around for someone he recognized.

"Have you been here before?" she asked.

"No."

"All right, then, go ahead and fill out this form. I hope you'll enjoy yourself."

"Is there anything we need to do?" Belinda asked.

"We'll be done about eight-thirty, if you want to pick him up then."

"We'll be back."

Feeling they'd done the right thing, Paul and Belinda said good-bye to Jim and left him there on his own.

Jim filled out the form Mrs. Logan had given him and turned it back over to her.

"Here's your name tag," Phyllis said, handing him one she'd hand-printed for him. "Now go have some fun. There's kids here from all the schools in the area."

"What do you do here?" He looked toward the cafeteria, where everyone was gathering.

"We have fun. You'll see. Angie!" she called out to a pretty girl who'd just entered the building.

"Yes, Mrs. Logan?"

"This is Jim and he's new tonight. Could you show him around and introduce him to some of your friends?"

"Sure." Angie gave Jim a bright smile. "I'm Angie—welcome to the youth group."

"Hi." He felt a bit tongue-tied, for Angie was the prettiest girl he'd ever seen.

"Where do you go to school?" she asked as she led him off to join the other kids in the cafeteria.

Phyllis was smiling as she watched them go. Angie was Miss Personality. Phyllis knew Jim was in good hands.

"Hey, look! Jim's here!"

Jim heard someone shout, and he was ready to head for the door. He figured it was one of the guys from school, someone who was going to taunt him about the wreck again.

"Hi, Rob! You know Jim?" Angie responded before he could turn tail and run.

"We work together at the show," Rob answered easily, coming over to speak with them and bringing several friends with him.

Jim was surprised to see Rob, and he actually smiled in relief. "I didn't know you'd be here."

"I always show up if I'm not working." He quickly introduced Jim to his pals, then looked back at Angie. "Game night's still on, isn't it?" Rob knew she worked regularly with the group and helped organize the meetings.

"Yes, it is!" she said excitedly. "We'll have a quick meeting first—then it's time to play."

"Play what?" Jim asked, unsure what was going on.

"Games!" she laughed. "We bring them from home. I

brought Chinese Checkers, and I know a couple of the other kids brought Monopoly and Uno. You just sit down at whatever table you want and have fun."

"I brought Aggravation," Rob announced. "I'm the all-time champ!"

"Isn't pride one of the seven deadly sins?" one of the other boys taunted him.

"You're right," Rob said with a sheepish grin. "I'll rephrase that. I play Aggravation a lot and I really like it."

"Which game do you like best?" Angie asked Jim.

"I like Aggravation, too."

"It'll be interesting to see which one of you wins."

They would have kept talking, but Father Richards came into the cafeteria.

"If you'll all have a seat, we'll begin this evening's activities with a prayer," he announced.

When the teenagers had quieted down, he led them in saying the Lord's Prayer and the Hail Mary.

Phyllis took over then to run the business part of the meeting.

Jim respected Mrs. Logan, and he listened attentively to what she had to say. He was slowly coming to realize how wrong he'd been about the group. There were a number of different activities in the works, from game nights to a float trip to a car wash that would help raise money for the poor. When the discussion was over, Father Richards led them in a prayer once more before turning them loose to enjoy themselves.

"I'm taking on all comers at the Aggravation table," Rob announced as he got up. "You up to it, Jim?"

"You bet."

"See you later," Angie said, heading off to play Chinese Checkers with some other girls.

Phyllis went into the kitchen area to start bringing out the snacks for the kids. She found George hard at work there.

"When did you sneak in?" She welcomed him with a warm smile.

"While you were busy talking to Father a few minutes ago."

"Did everything turn out all right at your doctor's visit?" she asked.

"It went fine," George answered, but did not elaborate.

"That's good news. I'm glad you could make it tonight. We've got quite a crowd out there."

"Good. I can't think of a better place for them to hang out and have fun. I drove the Mustang here tonight. You think any of the boys would want to take a look at it?"

"I'm sure they would, and it probably won't be just the boys. When we get done taking the drinks out, why don't you bring the car around and park by the main entrance? That way they can all get a look at it."

"I'll do that," he said as they carried coolers of iced soda out to the refreshment table.

Someone had turned on a boom box, and music was blaring in the cafeteria. George and Phyllis looked around, satisfied that things were running smoothly. It was going to be a fun evening.

* * *

"Anything new come in?" Steve asked Sergeant Riley when he got home and phoned into headquarters.

"We've had quite a few calls today, but they're mostly about crazy boyfriends or ex-husbands with guns," he answered. "There's been no repeated mention of any one person."

"All right. I'll see you in the morning."

Steve was frustrated. He wanted to be following up on leads and tracking down the killer. Steve wanted to stop him before he could strike again—and after that phone call, he had no doubt that he would.

"If you're interested," Phyllis announced to the teens during a break, "George drove his classic Mustang here tonight. He parked it outside in front if you want to take a look at it."

A large number of kids made their way out front to ogle the sports car.

Jim didn't rush outside. There was no point in getting excited about any car. It was going to be a long time before he ever got another one.

"It's a beautiful car," Phyllis said as she came up behind him. She could well imagine how Jim was feeling after the trauma he'd gone through earlier that week. "George has had it all these years, and he's kept it in perfect condition. Come on, I'll introduce you."

George saw Phyllis coming with a boy and made his way over to speak with them.

"Who've you got here?"

"This is Jim. Jim, this is George."

"Good to meet you, son," George told him. "You into Mustangs?"

Jim was staring at the classic car in delight. He'd seen Mustangs on the car shows on TV but had never been around one. "They're awesome."

"Go sit in it," George invited.

"Really?"

"Go on. You're not going to hurt anything," George encouraged him.

Jim opened the door and slid into the bucket seat. His first reaction was to smile.

George saw his expression and told Phyllis, "I feel the same way every time I sit in it."

They stepped away to let the other teens move in for a closer look.

"Think I should let Jim take it for a spin around the parking lot?" he asked Phyllis.

"No—he can't," she said in a quiet voice.

George was puzzled by her answer. "Why not? He looks like a good kid."

She drew him aside to explain. "He is, but he's one of the boys we prayed for the other night. He was the driver—"

She didn't need to say any more. George fully understood. Now he knew why Jim had hung back. "I wondered where that bruise had come from. How's he doing?"

"Well, he's here tonight. This is his first time."

George nodded thoughtfully as he watched Jim. "Good. He's got parents who care about him."

"Very much so."

"All right," George announced, "everybody step back. I'm taking Mrs. Logan for a ride."

"Oh, George—" she laughed.

"Come on. Get in."

Jim climbed out and turned over the driver's seat to George while Phyllis got in on the passenger's side.

The crowd moved back and erupted in cheers when he revved up the engine.

"Go, Mrs. Logan!"

They circled the parking lot.

"I see what you mean, George," Phyllis told him. "It does make you feel young again."

George slanted her a sidelong grin, and in that moment Phyllis had a glimpse of the dashing young man he'd been all those years ago. They pulled to a stop in front of the kids.

"All right, everybody, back inside," George directed once he'd parked the car and he and Phyllis had gotten out.

"I think you should take all of us for a ride," one of the teens said.

"Maybe next week," George joked. "Right now, we've got a car wash to plan."

They filed back inside to finish their games and organize the volunteers who were to work at the fund-raiser.

George was the last one to go back inside. He was still smiling over all the comments the teens had made. He paused to glance back at the Mustang one last time, but as he did, his gaze was drawn past the car to the church.

A great sense of peace filled him at the sight of the steeple silhouetted against the pastel beauty of the evening sky. He gazed at it for a moment longer, then went on inside. It was, indeed, a glorious evening.

As the evening aged, Steve tried to relax, but he was feeling restless. Troubled by the unease that gripped him, he decided to drive back to the crime scenes and take another look around. He needed insight into the killer's motive.

Taking his car, Steve returned to the site of the first shooting. It was in midtown near the hospital district. At this time of night, the area was almost deserted. He got out and looked around, but his search for any insight was in vain. He stood on the overpass and stared down at the cars passing by on the interstate. He noticed that a cross had been placed at the side of the road where the elderly man's car had crashed when he'd lost control after being shot. It was a silent tribute to his loss.

His mood was somber as he tried to imagine how the shooter had planned and carried out his attack without being seen. Even though it had been early morning—a little before seven a.m. when the shots had been fired—at that time of day this was a high traffic area. Someone should have seen or heard something, but despite all the department's best efforts, they'd turned up nothing of any consequence. Whoever the murderer was, he'd had the ability to blend in.

The experts had determined the shot was fired from a point in front of and above the vehicle. The witnesses on the freeway at that time had sworn there were no vehicles or trucks ahead of the victim's car. He had been leading the way on the highway, and he had paid the price for being out in front.

Returning to his car, Steve drove to the location of the second shooting. Looking around, he still found it hard to believe that no one had seen the shooter of the school bus driver. The overpass was open, with unobstructed views in all directions. The hillsides by the exit and entrance ramps were nicely landscaped with shrubs and bushes. If the sniper had used a silencer, no one would have heard anything, but surely if he'd been out in the open, someone would have noticed a person carrying a high-powered rifle, walking along the city streets.

It was almost midnight when Steve made his way to the scene of the last shooting. The residential suburban neighborhood was quiet, but when he parked his car and got out, he noticed that several homeowners turned on their outside lights, then watched him from their windows.

Steve didn't stay long at the site of the young woman's murder. He didn't want to worry anyone, but as he made his way back to his car, a squad car drove up the street and stopped beside him.

"Sir, we've had a report of suspicious activity—" The policeman stopped the minute he recognized Steve. "Detective Mason—it's you."

"Sorry, Officer. I didn't mean to cause any trouble. I was just looking over the crime scene again. I'm glad the residents are keeping an eye out for any suspicious activity."

"Everybody is these days. See you around."

Steve drove home, frustrated and tired.

# *Chapter Thirteen*

*Guide Me, Lord . . .*

"We have breaking news. There's been another reported shooting on the interstate—" the morning news anchor reported.

"Oh no! Not again!" Lydia was in the midst of getting dressed for work when she heard the announcement. She ran into the living room to see what was being reported.

"The shooting took place about ten minutes ago at the Beltline Overpass. No word yet on any casualties. Our camera crew is in transit, and we'll be broadcasting live from the scene as soon as possible."

Lydia threw on the rest of her clothes, grabbed her purse and rushed from the house. She wanted to be on the scene, too.

* * *

Steve had been on his way into headquarters when he'd heard the first call go out. He'd known traffic on the highway would be at a standstill while the investigation was going on, so he'd stayed off the interstate en route to the scene of the shooting. When Steve reached the crime scene, he parked on a side street and ran down to join Ron Allen, the patrolman who was already there. The officer was speaking with another man.

"Ron, what have we got?" Steve asked as he approached the wrecked vehicle.

"The driver's dead," Ron told him.

Steve took a quick look at the victim and knew there was no reason to doubt Ron's determination. The driver had been, as near as Steve could tell, a middle-aged man, and he'd taken a head shot.

"I ran the plates," Ron went on. "The vehicle's registered to one Robert Vogler, and we have a witness—"

"I'm Don Fredricks," the witness spoke up nervously, looking from the policeman to the detective. "I was just driving by and a man stepped right out in front of me on the outer road. He wasn't even looking in my direction—"

The ambulance arrived right then, and so did Charlie. Steve was glad to see that his partner had brought along his digital camera.

"I'll be right back with you, Mr. Fredricks," Steve told the witness. "Stay with Officer Allen."

"All right."

"We've got another one," Steve told Charlie, walking over to talk with him separately.

Charlie took a quick look around and could tell they

had their work cut out for them. Cars were backed up for at least a mile on the highway, and a crowd was forming to see what was going on.

"The only good news is we may have our first witness."

"Who is it?"

"The man over there with Ron."

"Finally—a break."

Steve and Charlie quickly took pictures of the position of the victim in the vehicle, then backed off to allow the EMTs to remove the body from the car. Once the victim had been taken away on a stretcher to be transported to the morgue, Steve and Charlie went back to work. They examined the car inside and out. They wanted to figure out the entry and angle of the bullet, and then find its remains. They finally did. What was left of the bullet was embedded deep in the back seat. They finished photographing the crime scene, taking more pictures of the interior and exterior of the vehicle.

A crowd had gathered to watch what was going on, and people were obviously scared. Extra police officers were called in to help control them and to protect the crime scene.

Steve and Charlie turned their attention back to the witness as the tow truck arrived to take the car away to the impound lot.

"Mr. Fredricks, I'm Detective Mason and this is Detective Tucker. What exactly was it that you saw at the time of the shooting? You said a man walked right out in front of you without looking? Why did you suspect him of being involved?"

"He was dressed in camouflage. And he was carrying a gun. I was driving on the outer road, and all of a sudden he just walked right out in front of me. I had to slam on my brakes to keep from hitting him."

"What did he look like?" Steve asked. He had his notebook out, ready to write down the description.

The witness looked pensive. "He was a white man. He had brown hair, I think."

"Was he short or tall?"

"He wasn't tall."

"Was he wearing glasses?"

"No."

"Were there any distinguishing features you remember about him? Anything that stood out? This is very important, Mr. Fredricks. We want you to be sure of what you're telling us."

"I wish there had been something distinctive about him. I was just so shocked at nearly hitting him and the fact that he was holding a gun that before I could react or do anything, he'd already run off down the side street."

"Did you see what car he was driving?"

"I did see a blue sedan drive off, but it was too far away to get the license plates."

Steve didn't like hearing that the car the witness had seen was blue. "Do you have any idea of the make or model?"

"No. I think it was probably foreign, but I don't know."

"Mr. Fredricks, if you were to see the man again, would you recognize him?"

The witness looked shaken by the question. "I don't know. It all happened so fast—"

"It would be good if you could accompany Officer Allen back to headquarters and sit down with one of the officers with a composite kit, to see if we can come up with a picture that resembles the man you saw today."

"Yes, sir. I can do that."

"Good. Thank you for your cooperation."

Steve and Charlie left him with Ron and made their way back to where Charlie had left his vehicle.

"I'll call in an APB for a white male wearing camouflage driving a blue sedan," Charlie told him.

While Charlie took care of that, Steve climbed up the exit ramp to comb the hillside for clues.

"If the shooter was in camouflage, he could have been lying here in the bushes, just waiting for the right shot," Steve remarked when Charlie came to work with him.

"It makes sense, and it would explain why no one was ever seen firing from the overpasses before."

For the first time since the terror had begun, Steve was starting to feel as if they were actually making progress on the case. They'd found no trace of the shooter, but that didn't mean he hadn't fired the shot from that position.

"What did the chief say?"

"He said he was going to address the media in half an hour and give the description out. He wanted the witness to try to come up with a composite we could circulate. Ron's taking him down to headquarters."

"Good. Now let's get the bullet into the lab and make sure it's a match," Steve said.

They were ready to head back to headquarters when Steve heard someone calling his name. He looked over at the crowd gathered around the crime scene and spotted Lydia.

"Go on back. I'll meet you there," he directed Charlie; then he went over to speak with her. "I wanted to see you again, but not under these circumstances."

"It was the sniper again—"

"Yes, but this time we've got a witness. You might want to get down to headquarters. The chief is going to be issuing a statement within the hour."

"Thanks. Good luck."

"I'm going to need it." He managed a tight smile. "I'll call you."

Lydia hurried back to her car and called in to the office to let Gary know she would be at police headquarters to cover Chief Donovan's address. Gary was terse with her and demanding, as usual, insisting she get back to the office as quickly as possible once the press conference was over.

A short time later, Lydia was at headquarters listening to Captain Donovan's official statement about the events of that morning.

"Earlier today there was another shooting on the interstate. The victim's identity has not yet been released, pending notification of the family. We have a witness who saw a person of interest leaving the scene. The person of interest has been described as a white male with brown hair driving a blue car. He was last seen wearing camouflage and carrying a rifle in the area of the crime. If this person of interest is the sniper, the weapon he was carrying would be a 30-06. Anyone with any additional information is asked to call our tip line immediately. Thank you."

"Captain!" one reporter yelled out as Donovan started to leave the podium.

"Yes?"

"Who's your witness?"

"For security purposes, we are not releasing the person's name."

The reporters understood the precaution, but had hoped to interview the witness.

Another reporter called out, "Why a blue car now, when all this time we've been looking for a green one?"

"A blue car is what today's witness saw leaving the scene of the crime. We'll keep you informed as more information becomes available. Thank you."

Lydia went to the office to write up the story.

"Get in here!" Gary shouted from his desk when he saw Lydia come in. He waited until she was standing in his doorway before asking, "What happened out there today? What have you got? I listened to Donovan on the radio. He said they've got a witness and a 'person of interest' in the case now. What's that all about?"

Lydia quickly related all she'd learned at the crime scene and at police headquarters.

"Who's this witness they say they have?" Gary demanded.

"The police aren't releasing the name."

"But we need to interview the witness! We need to find out what he saw this morning!"

"The police must be concerned about the witness's safety."

"See if you can discover who it is. Dig into it—deep, and get back to me. We've still got time to work this some more."

"I'll do what I can."

"Have they had a composite drawn up yet of their 'person of interest'?"

"They didn't announce that a picture would be forthcoming, but that doesn't mean one won't be released to the media soon. We can only hope."

"The way things have been going, I wouldn't count on it," Gary said sarcastically. "The police have been totally useless trying to catch this guy. It's going to be up to us to find him—that's why I want you on it!"

Lydia didn't even try to argue the point with Gary. Returning to her desk, she went to work.

Steve and Charlie reported in with the results of the tests on the bullet, and it was a match. The sniper had officially claimed his fourth victim—Robert Vogler.

Married and the father of four, Vogler had been a devoted family man. He'd been a successful businessman and was loved by all who'd worked with him. News of his tragic death had left the community even more devastated and on edge, fearful that the killer could and would strike again at any moment.

"Steve—" John Clayton, one of the detectives, called out to him when he returned to headquarters.

"What is it?"

"A call came in for you. The guy's name was O'Malley. He owns a gun shop on the other side of town. He said it was important that he talk to you."

"What about?"

"He didn't say. Here's his number. He said he'd be there working until nine o'clock tonight." John held out a slip of paper to him.

"Thanks." Steve took the number and went to his desk to call the man back. If he owned a gun shop, he might have some reliable information.

"Ammo, Inc., what can I do for you?"

"I need to speak with Mr. O'Malley."

"This is Pat O'Malley."

"This is Detective Mason at police headquarters. I understand you wanted to talk to me?"

"Yes, I do. After I heard what Captain Donovan had to say at the press conference today, I realized I might know this guy you're looking for."

"What do you mean?"

"One of my customers, a guy named Ted Brown, bought a 30-06 not too long ago. He's crazy about that weapon. He's in here buying ammunition all the time, and I don't think I've ever seen him wearing anything but camouflage. He might be your man."

"Do you have his address?"

"Yes, I do."

They spoke a moment longer while Steve took down all the relevant information.

"Charlie! I think we may have something here!" He quickly told his partner what he'd learned.

"Let's run a quick background check on him before we go," Charlie advised.

They did and found out that Brown was currently unemployed. He had been arrested several times for disturbing the peace and currently had an outstanding traffic ticket—a ticket issued to a 1997 Taurus. It didn't say what color the car was, but Steve had a feeling it would turn out to be blue.

They left headquarters and drove straight to Brown's house. It was a small, run-down place on the poorer side of town. When they walked up the path and knocked on the door, a dog started barking wildly inside. They could hear a man shouting at it to shut up. The door suddenly opened in front of them and a thin white man wearing camouflage pants and a green T-shirt stood before them.

"Ted Brown?"

"Yeah, I'm Brown, but what's it to you? Whatever it is you're selling, I don't want any of it!" he declared in hostile tones, eyeing them suspiciously. Men in suits didn't usually walk around in this neighborhood.

"We're not selling anything. We're here because—"

"Because you want me to find Jesus? Get off my porch. I don't want any damned holy rollers hounding me!" Brown stepped back and started to slam the door in their faces.

Steve stepped up and pulled out his badge for Brown to see. "Mr. Brown, I'm Detective Steve Mason and this is Detective Charlie Tucker. We're investigating the sniper killings, and we'd like to ask you a few questions—if you don't mind?"

Brown went still. *They were the law and they wanted to ask him questions about the sniper shootings?* "I don't know nothing about that," he protested quickly.

"If we could speak with you in privacy?" Charlie pressed.

"Sure—come on in," he said, stepping back and holding the door wide to admit them. He knew he wasn't the cleanest-living man, but he wasn't about to give these two detectives trouble, especially not when they thought he was a suspect! "Sit down."

"Thanks, but this won't take long." They remained standing. "We understand you own a 30-06 rifle."

"Yes, I do."

"And where were you this morning about six-thirty a.m.?"

"I was right here, sleeping."

"Do you have anyone who can vouch for that?" Steve asked.

"My wife, but she ain't here right now. Listen," Brown offered, not wanting to act nervous or guilty. "Do you want to see my gun? I've got it right out back."

"If you wouldn't mind?" Steve said.

They followed him to a back bedroom filled with all kinds of hunting gear and a large gun case. They watched while Brown unlocked the gun case and took out a 30-06.

"Here it is," he said, handing it over.

"You only own the one?"

"That's right, and you're welcome to take it with you, if that's what you need to do. Go ahead and run the tests on it. I didn't have nothing to do with any of the shootings, so I ain't got nothing to hide."

Charlie and Steve had hoped they were on to something when Brown was so belligerent, but they realized now that Brown probably wasn't their man.

"Thanks, we'll do that. We'll return the rifle to you in a few days."

"Take your time. I'm glad to help in any way I can."

"We appreciate your cooperation, Mr. Brown."

"Do you want my wife to call you when she gets home from work?"

"That won't be necessary right now. We'll speak with you again after we've run the tests on the weapon."

Even as they said it, though, Steve and Charlie knew he wasn't their man, and the ballistics tests they ran later that afternoon only confirmed that they were right in their assessment.

Gun fanatic that he was, Ted Brown was not the serial sniper.

# *Chapter Fourteen*

"Don't let the bedbugs bite!" Cheryl Hall teased as she tucked her children, four-year-old Kyle and six-year-old Bethany, into bed.

Kyle and Bethany giggled as they snuggled down beneath their blankets.

"Are you ready to say your prayers?"

Together they recited, "Now I lay me down to sleep. I pray the Lord my soul to keep. If I should die before I wake, I pray the Lord my soul to take. This I ask for Jesus's sake. Amen."

"You sleep tight," Cheryl told them as she kissed them both, then turned off the overhead light, leaving the room softly illuminated by the single night-light on the dresser.

" 'Night, Mommy."

"Good night, darlings." She stood in the doorway for a moment, staring at her children, thinking how beautiful they were. They meant everything to her. They made her life worth living.

Cheryl went into the living room of her trailer home and sat down to relax in the recliner chair. Times had been hard this past year. Her husband had deserted her, leaving her cash-strapped with two kids to raise. She'd gotten a divorce and was trying to be hopeful about the future. The way things had been going lately, it seemed everything was finally going to work out okay

Cheryl smiled as she considered how far she'd come. She'd bought the used trailer and relocated to this nice family-oriented mobile home park just three months ago. She'd never owned anything before. Her family had always lived in apartments, and she was glad that Bethany and Kyle now had their own yard to play in. She was taking pride in fixing up her new home, too. It wasn't easy on her salary as a waitress, but she was making ends meet, and that was all that mattered. She was living her life one day at a time, and it was working. At twenty-eight, she had two wonderful kids, and she was happy.

Cheryl settled in for a few hours of watching television, then finally called it a night.

A loud screeching noise erupted through the house and brought Cheryl bolt upright in bed. She glanced at her bedside clock and saw it was two a.m. Her heart was pounding as she tried to figure out what the noise was.

And then she realized there was smoke in the house and Kyle and Bethany were screaming.

"God help me!" she cried, jumping out of bed and

racing down the hall to their room. "Kyle! Bethany! Get out here now!"

Smoke was quickly filling the home, and she could feel the heat of the fire. Her eyes were burning from the fumes and smoke, and she felt dizzy and slightly disoriented.

"Mommy!" Kyle cried. "Mommy, help me!"

"I'm coming!"

She burst into their bedroom to find one wall of the room on fire. Kyle and Beth were huddled together on Beth's bed, too terrified to move.

"Come on! We have to get out of here!" Cheryl shouted, grabbing them up and carrying them from the danger.

The children clung to her, sobbing in fright as she stumbled down the dark, smoke-filled hall. She was growing dizzier by the second, but she knew she couldn't stop. She had to get out of the house. They wouldn't be safe until they were. As she threw open the door and rushed out onto the small porch, she found her next-door neighbors, Irene and Ernie Phillips, were already running over to help.

"We called 911! They're on their way!"

"Thank you! Can you take the kids? I need to go back in and get—"

"You're not going anywhere!" Ernie insisted.

"Ernie's right, Cheryl. It's too dangerous! Wait until the fire department gets here," Irene cautioned.

"But—"

"Don't even think about it. There's nothing's so important that you should risk your life to get it!"

Ernie ran back to his house and unrolled his garden hose. He knew it wasn't much, but it would help a little until the fire department showed up.

Irene, realizing then that Cheryl was clad only in her nightgown, ran back home to get her a coat.

Cheryl stood there in the street watching the house burn with Kyle and Bethany, feeling completely numb and utterly in shock. She hardly noticed when Irene came up to her and slipped the coat around her shoulders.

In the distance, the haunting wail of the sirens echoed through the silent night. The noise grew louder and louder as the fire trucks raced ever closer. When at last the trucks turned into the park, Cheryl's mobile home was almost completely engulfed in flames.

Ernie was still single-handedly trying to battle the blaze, while other residents of the park came out to watch the power of the raging fire in terrified silence.

The firemen took charge of the scene.

"Is everyone out of the house?" one of the firemen shouted out.

"Yes!" Ernie answered.

They directed Ernie to put down his hose and back away, along with the rest of the onlookers. Then they started hosing down the home. The fight was a long one. The firemen did prevent the flames from spreading to the other homes, but when the fire was finally extinguished, there was nothing but smoldering ruins left of Cheryl's trailer.

The captain sought out Ernie once they were certain the fire was out. "Whose home was this?"

"Cheryl Hall's." Ernie pointed her out to him.

The captain went to speak with her. "Mrs. Hall, I'm Captain Davis. Do you have any idea how the fire started?"

"No. I was asleep when the smoke alarm went off. I ran to get Kyle and Bethany, and their bedroom wall was on fire—"

"Did you have any lighted candles?"

"No."

"Did you have any overloaded outlets?"

"No. The night-light was the only thing plugged in in the children's room."

He looked thoughtful. "Have you had any trouble with circuit breakers?"

Cheryl frowned. "One did keep clicking off on me, but I made sure to reset it every time."

"I see. All right." He had an idea of what had started the blaze and would begin the inspection shortly. "We have Red Cross contact information if you're in need of immediate assistance."

"I don't know—" She was dazed.

He was accustomed to dealing with traumatized families. He advised, "You'll need to contact your insurance company, so they can get an adjuster out here to take care of things for you."

Cheryl began to tremble as the reality of what she now faced loomed before her.

*She had lost everything!*

*Everything!*

*She and her children were homeless.*

"I don't have insurance," she said in a voice barely above a whisper.

The captain shook his head sadly.

Irene heard Cheryl's answer and couldn't believe it. She was horrified as she reached out to put a supportive arm around the younger woman's shoulders. "Cheryl—"

"Is there a place where we'll be able to reach you?" the captain asked.

"I don't know." Cheryl was at a complete loss.

"Contact me," Irene spoke up. "If she's not staying here with us, at least I'll know where to find her." She gave him her own name and phone number.

"I'm sorry about your loss, Mrs. Hall," the captain said before returning to the ruined house to begin his search for the cause of the fire.

"Mommy—what are we going to do?" Bethany and Kyle looked up at their mother, terror and insecurity in their eyes.

"I don't know." Cheryl dropped to her knees and took both of her children into her arms. She held them close to her heart, wanting them to feel safe again.

"Cheryl, let's go inside," Irene urged. "You can spend the night with us."

"Thank you."

Cheryl drew the children with her as they followed Irene and Ernie into the safe haven of their home. Once they were inside, Irene gave Cheryl a robe to wear instead of the coat. Then she quickly turned down the double bed in their extra bedroom while Ernie set up a roll-away for Cheryl at the foot of the bed.

Cheryl got Kyle and Bethany to lie down, but it took a while. She could tell they were exhausted, but they were still tense from all that had happened.

"I'll leave the light on and the door open for you. I want to talk to Irene and Ernie for a minute, and then I'll come back and sleep right here with you."

"Mommy," Kyle said in a trembling voice. "I'm scared."

Cheryl went to him and hugged him, giving him a soft kiss on the forehead. "Don't be. Thank God, we're alive. Our guardian angels took care of us tonight, that's for sure. No one was hurt, and that's all that really matters."

"Okay," he whispered.

Cheryl kissed Bethany, too, then went to speak with her neighbors. She found them sitting at the kitchen table, waiting for her.

"How are the kids?" Irene asked, concerned.

"They're scared, but they'll be fine. Thank God, the smoke alarm was working," Cheryl told them as she sat down with them. "If it hadn't been, we'd be dead right now."

Irene reached out and took her hand across the table. "It's a miracle you escaped!"

"I know." She drew a ragged breath. "Smoke alarms are wonderful things."

"What are you going to do?" Ernie asked. "I heard you tell the fire captain that you didn't have any insurance."

"I couldn't afford it. I was just getting to where we were making ends meet, and now—" She stopped, suddenly overwhelmed by what she would be facing in the morning.

"Do you have any family here?"

"No. No one. My parents are dead."

"What about the kids' father? I know you're divorced, but maybe he could help you?" Ernie was trying to find a way to offer her hope.

"No, he lives out-of-state now. I haven't heard from him in over six months."

"Is there anyone you need to call, then?"

"My boss. I'm supposed to work tomorrow, but there's no way—"

"Do you want to call him now?"

"I guess I'd better, so he'll have time to get someone else to cover for me."

"The phone's in the living room by the window," Irene told her.

While Cheryl went to make the call, Irene and Ernie shared a sad look of understanding. They could well imagine the difficulties Cheryl was going to face trying to put her life back together in the days and weeks to come.

"What can we do to help her?" Ernie asked Irene quietly. "The only thing she's got left is her car, and she doesn't even have the keys to that."

"I'll call Father Richards first thing in the morning. Holy Family will help them, and so will St. Vincent de Paul. They're always there for those in need."

"Good idea. We'll get on it right away."

Cheryl came back into the kitchen.

"Did everything go all right?"

"My boss said to take as long as I need."

"Good, at least you won't have that pressure to deal with right now."

"Thank heaven. I was worried he might not understand."

"Well, why don't you try to get some rest? There's a lot you have to deal with tomorrow, and you're going to need your sleep."

"You're right," she answered, then looked at Irene and Ernie with heartfelt emotion. "Thank you. Thank you for everything."

Irene got up from the table and went to give her a big hug. "We'll see you in the morning."

Cheryl went into the bedroom and closed the door. She was relieved to find that Kyle had fallen asleep, but Bethany was still tossing and turning.

"Mommy," she whispered. "I'm still scared."

"I'm here, sweetheart. Nothing's going to hurt you. I promise."

Bethany held out her arms to her mother. Cheryl took off the robe and carefully climbed into bed with the children. She took Bethany in her arms and nestled her close. She could feel the tension ebb from the child as she held her.

Cheryl had been afraid the trauma they'd gone through would torment them all night. She knew she was blessed that Kyle had managed to fall asleep. She pressed a kiss to the top of Bethany's head and thanked God that her children were safe.

Cheryl was exhausted, physically and emotionally,

but tired as she was, sleep still would not come. Memories of the horror just past tormented her. When Bethany finally drifted off, she slipped out of the bed and went to lie down on the roll-away. It was almost dawn before she finally managed to doze off, but what sleep she got was not restful.

Irene was up early, determined to get started helping Cheryl and the children. They were going to need everything from underwear to money to reclaim their lives. It wouldn't be easy getting it all done, but she was going to give it her best try. She took a chance and called Father Richards's office just after seven a.m. She knew he often showed up early, and she was hoping this was one of those days.

"Good morning, this is Father Richards," the priest answered.

"Father, it's Irene Phillips."

"Good morning, Irene. What can I do for you today?" Father Richards liked and respected Irene and Ernie. He knew how involved they were in parish activities and how caring they were in the faith community.

"We need your help. There was a terrible fire here—"

"Are you all right?" he asked quickly, concern in his voice.

"It wasn't our home. It was our neighbor's. She's a good woman—a single mom with two little kids, and she's lost everything. She doesn't have any insurance at all."

Father Richards listened to Irene describe the horror of the fire the night before. "Give the St. Vincent de Paul Society a call, and I'll see what else I can do."

"Thank you, Father." Irene knew he always came through in times of need.

"I'll be in touch."

Father Richards hung up the phone and sat there for a moment, deep in thought about the homeless family. George had said to call him if he heard of anyone in need. He got out his parish phone directory and looked up George's number. If his friend didn't show up for Mass that morning, he'd call him.

"I need to get over there and look around," Cheryl told Irene and Ernie the following morning after they'd eaten breakfast. Kyle and Bethany were watching cartoons, and she was glad. TV would help them escape the reality of their situation for a while. "I know it looks like everything's been destroyed at the house, but I want to try to find what's left of my purse and checkbook and car keys."

"Then let me get you something to wear besides your gown and that robe," Irene said, heading into her own bedroom to go through her clothes. She returned a few minutes later with a T-shirt and a pair of sweatpants. "These should fit you."

"Thanks, Irene. I was wondering how I was going to look digging through the mess over there wearing my nightgown."

"It would have been interesting," Irene said with a grin, trying to lighten her mood. "What size shoes do you wear? I'm a seven. Will that work for you?"

"That's perfect, but don't give me anything good.

They might get ruined when I'm climbing through all the burned stuff."

"I've got just the pair for you—they're the ones I wear when I cut the grass." Irene retrieved them and handed them over to Cheryl.

"The kids can stay here while you do that, if you want."

"That would be best. It might be tricky walking around over there."

"I'll keep them busy for you."

"And I'll come with you," Ernie offered. "You never know what might have survived the fire. We'll dig around and see what we can turn up."

"I called the St. Vincent de Paul Society early this morning and left a message on their answering machine."

"What do they do?"

"They help people. I told them about the fire and left our number. They always get back to those in need within twenty-four hours."

"But I'm not a member of the parish." Cheryl was surprised they would help her.

"It's the Christian thing to do."

Cheryl looked up at Irene, and their gazes met. "Thank you."

Cheryl hurried off to change clothes so she could be ready to find out what was left of her belongings. After going through the charred remains, she would have to find a place to live and get clothes for Bethany and Kyle so they could return to school the next day.

Silently she prayed for the strength to do what needed to be done. The kids needed her to be strong. She needed to protect them. She promised herself she wouldn't let them down.

# *Chapter Fifteen*

Lydia had expected another horrible Gary headline and she wasn't disappointed.

"*Sniper Kills At Will!*" the new edition proclaimed in bold letters. The people were already on edge about their safety, and Gary's inflammatory headlines did nothing to try to calm their fears.

Lydia knew that if she wanted to keep her job, she would have to get used to her editor's ways, but the forthright journalist in her wanted to deal with the facts only, not sensationalism and hype. She felt sorry for Steve and the rest of the police department. They were doing everything in their power to catch this murderer, but he was always one step ahead of them.

The previous afternoon the police had released a composite of the "person of interest," and Gary had placed only a small copy of the picture below the headline.

Lydia sat at her kitchen table, staring down at the picture. Nothing about the man looked familiar. The composite could have been any middle-aged, clean-shaven white man, and she couldn't help wondering just how accurate it was. Though eyewitnesses could sometimes be helpful, often they were inaccurate and could be misleading. She hoped that wasn't the case here. The police needed all the help they could get to catch this cold-blooded killer.

After finishing her breakfast, Lydia headed to the office. She was certain that work would be waiting for her; and if she didn't do it, it wouldn't get done.

Lydia was hard at work at her desk before nine. It was a little past eleven when the office clerk came by and dropped her mail in her in-box. She didn't pay much attention. Gary wasn't in that morning, and she was getting caught up on a lot of paperwork. When she finally turned her attention to the few letters, she didn't see anything that looked important. As she opened them, she found one to be a thank-you note from a gentleman she'd done an article on a few weeks before. Another letter from a subscriber complained about the articles on the sniper. She was tempted to leave it on Gary's desk, but knew there was no point.

And then she opened the last piece of mail to find a computer-generated letter:

*Lydia Chandler—*

*As you are reading this, you already know that I have*

*killed again. I claimed my fourth victim, and no one is any closer to finding me.*

*Do I need to wish you luck?*

*—A Friend*

Lydia stared down at the piece of paper in shock. She looked up, then glanced around the office, trying to figure out what to do. Should she wait for Gary and let the paper get credit for being the first one to be contacted in writing by the sniper? Or should she go straight to the police with it? She knew Steve had gotten an anonymous phone call, but this was different. There might be an actual physical clue here. It didn't take her long to make her decision.

Carefully carrying the note with her, she appeared nonchalant as she made her way to the copier. Lydia made two copies and went back to her desk. Slipping the original and the envelope it had come in in a sandwich bag, she put the bag in her purse and got ready to leave. She told the clerk that if Gary came looking for her, she'd be out for a few hours following up on an old story. It wasn't a lie. The sniper story had been around for a while.

Lydia rushed to her car and drove straight to police headquarters.

"I need to speak with Detective Mason, please," she told the officer at the front desk. "It's important."

"Let me see if he's in. If you'll have a seat, please."

Lydia was nervous as she sat down on the edge of a chair in the waiting area. She hoped against hope that

Steve was in. She wanted to make sure the letter got in the right hands as quickly as possible. Her heart leapt when she saw him coming into the front office.

"Steve—" She stood up.

He immediately came to her.

"Lydia—what is it?" He could tell by her manner that whatever had brought her to headquarters was serious.

"I need to speak with you—in private."

He knew from the tone of her voice that this was no social visit. "Of course. Let's go back here."

He escorted her to a private room and closed the door.

"There's something I have to show you," she began hurriedly, taking the plastic baggy out of her purse and handing it to him. "It came this morning. It's from the sniper."

Steve took it from her carefully and was able to read the taunting message through the bag. "Who's touched the letter that you know of?"

"I did—and our office clerk when he delivered the mail."

"Have you shown it to anyone else?"

"No. No one. This was too important. I made a couple of copies to keep for my records and came straight to you."

"All right, I need to get this down to the lab."

"What more can I do to help you?"

"Right now, nothing," he told her, worrying that since the sniper had picked her to communicate with, she might be in danger. "I do want wiretaps put on your phones at work and at home."

"Wiretaps? Why?"

"In case he tries to make contact with you again. He might call you next time, like he did me that day—you never know. He's interested in you, and I want to make sure you're protected. Be careful."

"Don't worry. I will be," she assured him. "But how should I handle this with my boss? The killer knows I got this letter. He's going to be expecting full coverage of it in the paper."

"Cover it as you would any story."

"I'd better get back to the office, then." Lydia was relieved that she'd come to Steve. "Let me know if you find out anything from the letter."

"I will."

"Will anyone else know about the wiretaps?"

"No. The fewer who know, the better."

"I'll see you later."

"Yes, you will," he promised.

Lydia returned to the office to discover that Gary was at his desk. She knew there could be no avoiding it, so she went to tell him what had happened.

"Gary, I need to speak with you."

He looked up at her in irritation. "This had better be important."

"It is. The sniper contacted me today—"

"What?" He was shocked. "How? Did he call you?"

"No. He sent a letter. Here's a copy of it." She handed one to him.

"Where did you get it? Here or at home?"

"It came here to the office."

"Where's the original?" he demanded, eager to follow up on the story.

"I've already turned it over to the police."

"You did what?" Gary raged. "You went to the cops before you came to me?"

"I gave it to Detective Mason so the lab could check it over for clues. I kept a copy here for us."

"A copy! I want to see the original. Who knows what we could have found out by checking it over! You're an investigative reporter! You're supposed to solve crimes!"

"I'm a reporter! Not a cop!" she countered heatedly.

"And as a reporter, you're supposed to find out the truth about things and *report* them, not give your information to the police department. They're so inept, they're useless."

"Our police department is a fine one," she quickly retorted.

"Yeah, right," he sneered. "That's why they've caught this guy and locked him up."

Lydia had never been so close to resorting to physical violence as she was right then. She wanted to hit Gary—real hard. Somehow she managed to control the desire, but it wasn't easy.

"You can't count on the cops for anything in this case," Gary lectured her coldly.

"You're wrong about that, Gary. We can help, too. We shouldn't withhold important evidence from the police. This letter could save lives. They're going to catch him. I'm sure they will."

"If you believe that, you should turn to fiction writing. Consider yourself lucky that you've still got a job, Lydia," Gary said harshly. "If you hear from the sniper again, I want to know about it first, not last! Now—how are we going to work this?"

"What do you mean?"

"The sniper's contacted you—not a reporter at another paper—*you*! You've got to write back to him. I'll run it on the front page. Get back to me in fifteen minutes. This is big. I've got to make sure it's right."

Gary started working feverishly on the headline for the next edition.

Lydia went back to her desk to think. For some reason, the sniper had chosen to contact her, and she knew it was important to keep that line of communication open. "Sniper Contacts Reporter! Reporter Responds!," she wrote down and then hurried back to Gary with it.

"If he wrote to me once, he may write to me again. I thought we ought to encourage him. If you run this headline, I can write a short response in the article inviting him to stay in touch with me."

Gary had been trying to come up with something more eye-catching, but time was of the essence. "Fine. Let's see what happens. If he doesn't get back to you, we can jerk it up to a higher level in the next edition."

Steve was waiting impatiently for the lab results. He had high hopes that the technicians might find something on the letter that would point to a suspect. When he got the call, though, he learned they had found no DNA. The envelope had most likely been sealed with a sponge. There were multiple fingerprints on the envelope and letter, and the technicians would check those out further, but there had been no match with any prints they had on file. As always, the sniper had proven to be smart and elusive.

George slowly came awake to find Duchess curled up next to him on the bed. He reached down to pet her, and she looked up at him and licked his hand. He glanced over at his radio alarm clock on the nightstand and was shocked when he saw the digital readout on it. It was already afternoon.

George had awakened in severe pain in the predawn hours. He'd tried to tough his way through it, but the agony he'd suffered had proven debilitating. It had already been daylight when he'd given up on being macho and had taken several of the prescription painkillers his doctor had given him. He'd unplugged his bedside phone and had sought escape through sleep. Looking at the clock now, it was obvious the medicine had done its job.

Tentatively George shifted positions in bed. He wanted to test his body before he made any effort to get up. He was relieved to find that the torturous pain he'd endured through the night was gone. He was feeling all right—although these days "all right" was a truly subjective term.

He got up and got cleaned up, believing a hot shower would do him good. And it did. By the time he had dressed and made it to the kitchen to get something to eat, he was feeling like a new man. He made a pot of coffee, grabbed a sweet roll and then noticed the blinking light on his answering machine.

George punched the button and listened attentively to the message.

"George, this is Father Richards. You told me to call you if I heard of anyone in need, and I think there's a family you might be interested in helping. Give me a call when you can, or just come on by the rectory. I should be around most of the day, and I look forward to hearing from you."

George made short order of eating his not-so-nutritious breakfast and then went into his study to call the rectory.

"Father Richards," the priest answered on the second ring.

"Hi, Father. It's George returning your call."

"Thanks for getting back to me. How are you doing?"

For a moment, George thought about telling him the truth, but then decided to keep quiet about his bad night. He was fine now. That was what was important.

"I'm doing real good. What's this you were saying about a family in trouble?"

"Do you know Ernie and Irene Phillips of the parish?"

"I think so."

"Well, they live in the mobile-home community, and in the middle of the night last night, their neighbor's home was destroyed by fire. It turns out the neighbor is a single mom with a young son and daughter, and they had no insurance."

"Are you serious?" He couldn't imagine not having home owner's or at least renter's insurance.

"She was too poor. She couldn't afford the mobile home and the insurance, too. From what I understand, they still have their car, but otherwise, they lost everything."

"Thanks for letting me know, Father."

"If you want any help with anything, just call me."

"I will."

George hung up and looked down at Duchess, who was sitting patiently at his feet. "I think we've got another job to do today."

She barked at him playfully.

George smiled and got out the yellow pages. He needed to find out who sold mobile homes in the area.

# *Chapter Sixteen*

Though Irene and Ernie offered to let Cheryl and the kids stay with them, Cheryl decided it would be better if they stayed at the small motel nearby. The rates were reasonably cheap, and it would give them a little privacy and some time to heal as a family.

It had been a long, exhausting day, but at least Cheryl knew she'd gotten some important things taken care of. She'd dug through the ruins of the trailer, but had found little to salvage. What the fire hadn't burned, the smoke and water damage had completely ruined. The good news was that she'd been able to find what was left of her purse and checkbook, so she didn't have to worry about that anymore, and with Ernie's help, she'd gotten new keys for her car, so she had transportation. That afternoon she'd taken Kyle and Bethany to buy some clothes, so they could go back to school tomorrow. The sooner they resumed their normal routine, the better it would be for all of them.

* * *

"Hey, Father, you want to go for a ride with me?" George invited when he called his friend later that afternoon.

"That sounds like a good time," Father Richards responded. "I'm free for the rest of the day. What have you got in mind?"

"Just be ready in about half an hour. I'll come by and pick you up."

"I'll be waiting for you."

Father Richards was smiling as he hung up the phone. Any time he and George got together, they had a good time.

When George pulled up in front of the rectory in his Mustang, Father Richards came out, smiling.

"What do you say we get something to eat first?" George asked when Father Richards had climbed in beside him.

"Sounds good. To what do I owe the honor of getting a ride in your Mustang?" the priest asked, admiring the vehicle.

"I thought we ought to have some fun tonight."

"Any time you're driving this, you have to be having fun. It makes you feel like a kid again, doesn't it?"

George grinned at him. "It sure does."

They drove to a small local diner called Crown Candy Kitchen.

"You like Crown's?" George asked as he parked.

"Oh, yeah."

They were still smiling as they got out of the Mustang and went inside the small restaurant.

The restaurant owners, the Karandzieff brothers, had taken over the business from their father. They made their own chocolate on site and served wonderful sandwiches, malts, shakes and sundaes. It was a warm and welcoming gathering place for the community, and gather there they did. Luckily, it wasn't too crowded when George and Father Richards went in, and they were seated right away in one of the old-fashioned booths.

Once they'd placed their orders and settled back to enjoy themselves, Father asked, "Did you have time to give some thought to the family I told you about?"

"Yes, and that's where we're going next," George answered. "I called a local mobile-home dealer, and they have several homes in stock that might work. I thought we could ride over there and take a look around after we eat."

Father Richards had known George was willing to help out, but he'd never suspected he would buy the family a new home. The priest was deeply touched by George's generosity and kindness.

"If I take care of the home itself, will they be able to get the clothes and furniture they need?"

"I know Irene already called St. Vincent de Paul for them. I'm sure they'll get some help from them."

"What worries me is that even if they get everything they need to survive day to day, what if she still can't afford insurance? There's no guarantee in life that bad things won't keep happening."

"I know. When people are down and out this way, they need all the helping hands they can get."

"She sounds like a hardworking mom. Maybe she needs a break, like a better job to help make her life more stable."

"We'll have to pray on that for her."

They relaxed for a while and enjoyed their BLTs and malts, then they headed out to the mobile-home dealer to see what they could find. They sat down with the dealer to talk with him before going out to tour the available homes.

"What can I help you with?" Jason Howe, the owner, asked.

Father Richards told him of the family's plight and explained that they were trying to find a way to help them.

"Was there a price range you were considering?"

"Actually, we didn't know enough about this type of housing to estimate. That's why we thought it would be best to talk with you first."

"Well, come out on the lot and I'll show you what we have."

Jason took them through six different models. All were nicely made and roomy. The prices ranged from $19,995 for a two-bedroom, one bath to $35,000 for a four-bedroom, two-bath.

"Whichever one you decide on, I'll give you a fifteen-percent discount to help out."

"We appreciate that," Father Richards said, knowing Howe was probably donating his commission toward the cause.

"What do you think, Father?" George was thoughtful. "Do we buy it, have it delivered and set up for her, and make it a complete surprise, or do we let her pick out the home herself?"

"Though it would be fun to surprise her with a new home already set up and ready to go, I think, overall, letting her make the final decision would be best."

"Fine, we'll do it that way."

"When is a good time for you, Mr. Howe?"

"We're open this evening until nine."

"That should work out. Let me make a quick phone call and find out if she'll be available tonight."

Father Richards went outside to call Irene and make the arrangements.

While he was gone, George looked at the salesman. "Take care of this young lady when she comes in. She's going to need all the help she can get."

"I will," he promised. "Is she a relative or a friend of yours?"

"No. I've never met her."

Jason was impressed by this gentleman's obvious generosity.

Father Richards came back to join them. "A Mr. and Mrs. Phillips will bring Mrs. Hall and her children by this evening."

"I look forward to helping them. This is a wonderful thing you're doing," he told them as they got ready to leave. He'd never known of anyone doing anything like this before.

"We're just doing God's work here on earth," Father Richards said, and with that, they went outside.

Jason walked out with them. Only then did he notice the vintage Mustang parked on the lot.

"That's a nice car you've got there," he called out to George as the older man unlocked the door and slid in behind the steering wheel.

"Thanks!" George responded. He revved up the engine, and both he and Father Richards waved as they drove past him on their way out of the lot.

It was after six o'clock when the phone rang in the motel room and Cheryl quickly answered it.

"Cheryl, it's Irene. How are you this evening?"

"I think we're fine," she answered.

"Would you like to go out and get something to eat? We can go to McDonald's."

"McDonald's?" Cheryl repeated deliberately, and she got the reaction she expected from Kyle and Bethany.

"We're going to McDonald's?" they asked excitedly, their eyes lighting up in anticipation.

"That's right," Cheryl told them. "We'd love to go, Irene. How soon do you want us to be ready?"

"We can pick you up in about fifteen minutes, if that works for you."

"That's perfect," she told her. "And, Irene?"

"Yes?"

"Thanks."

"Our pleasure, dear."

They were ready and waiting when Irene and Ernie picked them up.

The trip to McDonald's was a happy one. The kids relaxed and enjoyed their Happy Meals and then played in the playland, while the adults ate peacefully at a nearby table.

"This was a wonderful idea," Ernie said, smiling as he watched Kyle and Bethany.

"Yes, it was," Irene said, "but we'll have to be going in a minute. We've got another stop to make before we head home."

"I'll get the kids ready to go."

They were soon heading out to the car.

"We can wait in the car for you, if you want, while you run into the store," Cheryl offered. She assumed their next stop would be for groceries. "That way, we won't slow you down."

"There's no need for you to do that," Ernie told her. "You can come in with us."

"Okay, whatever works. You're our chauffeur tonight," Cheryl said, teasing.

It was a short drive to Howe Mobile Home Sales, and Ernie parked out in front of the main office.

Cheryl had no idea why they were there, but figured Irene and Ernie needed something for their home.

"Come on, we'll all go in," Ernie said.

"You're sure?" Cheryl knew what a handful Bethany and Kyle could be.

"I'm sure. We're going to need your help," Irene put in.

"My help? With what?"

Ernie and Irene didn't explain any further.

He just said, "Come on."

They went ahead, leaving Cheryl and the kids to

catch up with them. Ernie held the door and they all filed inside.

"Mr. Howe?"

"Yes, I'm Jason Howe."

"I'm Ernie Phillips and this is my wife, Irene."

"It's nice to meet you. Father Richards said you'd be stopping by." Jason looked past them to the young woman with two small children. "And this is Mrs. Hall, I take it?"

Cheryl was surprised he knew her name. She frowned as she looked from her friends to the salesman.

"Mrs. Hall, it's nice to meet you."

"Hello—" She was cautious as she went forward to join them.

"Feel free to take a look around. We have six models currently available. You can take your time going through them, and if you have any questions, I'll be glad to help."

"I don't understand—" Cheryl was embarrassed to be standing there with the salesman, who obviously thought she could afford to buy something.

"It's all right, Cheryl," Irene said, sensing her tension. "Let's take a look around."

"But—" She looked around in confusion.

"Come on, Kyle. Come on, Bethany. Let's go outside." Ernie distracted the kids to give the women time to tour the mobile homes by themselves.

"Cheryl, now while we've got the chance—let's escape," Irene teased, knowing how precious time away from little ones could be.

The two women went outside and started up the steps into the first home on display.

Cheryl followed Irene inside. She looked around the lovely interior of the new home. It broke her heart to see the beautiful decor and furnishings. It reminded her of all that she'd lost and would probably never have again—not that her house had looked anywhere near this pretty, but it had been hers. It had been her castle, while she'd had it. Cheryl stood there, unable to take another step.

"What do you think of this one?" Irene asked from where she'd already disappeared into the kitchen. When she realized Cheryl wasn't right behind her, she retraced her steps and found her standing there in silence with tears streaming down her cheeks. "Don't cry—"

"I'm sorry, Irene, but I just can't do this." She started to turn away to leave.

"Do what? Pick out a new house?"

Cheryl looked at Irene, her expression tortured. "But I can't afford one. I don't know when I'll ever be able to afford one."

Irene went to her and took her in her arms. She gave her a motherly hug. "Nobody said you had to pay for it."

"Then there's no point in our being here—"

"There most certainly is. You have a guardian angel."

"I don't understand," Cheryl said in an emotion-choked voice.

"I spoke with Father Richards. He said an anonymous donor has offered to buy you a new home."

"But—" Cheryl drew back to stare at her in disbelief.

"Who? Why?" Her tears fell even more freely as she tried to come to grips with what her friend had just told her.

"Someone who believes in living God's Word."

"Oh, my God."

"Exactly."

"How will I ever repay them?"

"This is a gift. The person doesn't want repayment."

Cheryl couldn't fathom such generosity. "This is a miracle!"

Irene gave her another hug, then stepped away. "Now, no more tears—unless they're tears of joy. I'm sure your mysterious guardian angel would want you to enjoy this moment. Let's have fun!"

Cheryl managed a teary smile. "You're right. This is a blessing. How will I ever thank this person?"

"Pray for your mysterious helper. That's the best way."

"I will, believe me."

"Now, what do you think of this kitchen?"

The rest of their time at the dealership was pure excitement for Cheryl. She had loved the older home she'd been fixing up, but the thought that she was going to have a brand-new home left her in awe. Each one of the displays was delightful in its own way.

When she and Irene finished going through all the models, they went looking for Ernie and the children. Ernie, Kyle and Bethany had been making their way through the display homes, too, but at a more leisurely pace.

"Bethany—Kyle—I have some wonderful news for

you," Cheryl told them when she finally tracked them down.

"What, Mom?"

"Well, Irene told me we get to pick out a new home today. Some very kind and generous person has agreed to buy one for us."

"They did?" Bethany gasped, her eyes widening in amazement.

"Who, Mom?" Kyle asked.

"I don't know who it is, and they want it to be that way. They want to surprise us."

Both kids were dancing with excitement.

"So which one do you think we should choose?"

"This one! This one!" both of them squealed.

The home had three bedrooms and a bath and a half. The kitchen and family room were open and airy. It felt right to all of them.

"I like it, too." Cheryl agreed with their choice, but worried about the cost. "How much is it?" she wondered out loud.

"Don't worry about the cost," Ernie advised her. "If this is the one you want, then this is what you'll get."

She started to protest, not wanting to appear greedy and not wanting to risk abusing the kindness of the generous person behind their good fortune.

"That's right. We were told to let Father Richards know which one you picked, and he'll take care of everything from there on."

Cheryl drew a ragged breath as she opened her arms

to her children. They ran to her and embraced her. She knelt down to hold them close and whispered to them. "We have a new home. We have a new home."

Irene and Ernie stood back, gazing at the sight of the mother embracing her children. They would remember the joy on their faces forever.

"Let's make that phone call," Ernie said quietly to Irene.

They left Cheryl and the children there and went to find Mr. Howe to let him know they'd reached a decision. All that remained to be done was to contact Father Richards and to make arrangements with the mobile-home community to see how soon the home could be moved in.

# *Chapter Seventeen*

Lydia read the headline and felt somewhat satisfied with what Gary had done.

SNIPER CONTACTS REPORTER AT *THE DAILY SUN*!
WISHES INVESTIGATIVE REPORTER LUCK
IN TRYING TO FIND HIM
REPORTER RESPONDS
POLICE STILL AT A LOSS

True, Gary had insulted the police department, but that had become the norm for him. Lydia read the article, still wondering why, of all the journalists in town, the sniper had picked her to taunt. The killer had probably thought it would embarrass her, but he was wrong. If anything, contacting her had inspired her. The killer didn't know whom he was dealing with. She was going to do everything she could to help the police catch him.

Lydia set the paper aside and went to get ready for Mass.

* * *

George was relieved when he passed a restful night. He awoke early, which was normal for him. Feeling like himself this morning, he got up and got dressed, ready to go to seven a.m. Mass. There was little traffic as he drove to church, and he made it in plenty of time.

Holy Family was peaceful as he entered. The glowing stained-glass windows, the flickering of the candles at the foot of the statue of Mary, and the reverent silence made it a blessed haven from the outside world. He saw that Lydia was there this morning, too.

George entered a pew and knelt down to pray, thanking God for all the good things in his life and asking for the strength to deal with what he knew lay ahead of him.

"Please stand."

George stood up as Mass began.

Later, when Mass had ended and George and Lydia were leaving together, Father Richards called to him in the greeting area.

"George, I need to talk with you for a moment."

George and Lydia parted company as she went on to work. "How did it go last night?" he asked Father Richards.

The priest smiled at him. "Your generosity has been a blessing for Mrs. Hall and her children."

They went back to his office in the rectory to talk. Father Richards quickly told George what Irene had related about the trip to see the mobile homes.

"The family was completely humbled by your generosity. Irene said it was an amazing moment when Mrs. Hall learned the home would be a gift."

The two men looked at each other with understanding.

"You're a wonderful person, George. I'm blessed to know you."

George managed a gentle smile. "I'm blessed to be able to help them this way. How do you want to handle the financial end of this?"

They worked out the details and then stood up and shook hands.

"I'll keep you posted on how things are going."

"Just let me know the final dollar amount and I'll write a check for you."

"As soon as I get the call, I'll contact you."

"Good—and, you know, I was wondering. Do you think we could get the youth group involved in helping the family in some way? They've got that car wash fund-raiser coming up soon, but maybe we could put together some kind of project where the kids could help them get furniture and the other household items they need."

"I'll talk to Phyllis and see what we can come up with."

"Thanks. If they do something, make sure you let me know. I want to work with them."

"Don't worry," the priest chuckled, "you'll be the first one we call."

Both men were smiling as George left the rectory.

George stepped outside and stood there for a moment, enjoying the glory of the sun shining down on him.

It was a great day.

* * *

The sniper read the morning headline and was satisfied that his ploy had worked. He'd hoped to challenge Lydia Chandler with the note he'd sent her, and it was obvious that she'd taken the bait. Now he'd let her wait for a while. There was no need to write back to her just yet. The media elites might think she was a good reporter, but he knew she wasn't good enough to find him.

The sniper smiled as he considered what he should include in the next message he sent her. Advance knowledge of his next attack would be perfect. That meant the whole town would be on edge, waiting and watching for him to act, and they still wouldn't be able to catch him. He would prove once again just how good he was. He began to plan.

Gary was watching for Lydia when she came in to work. The minute he saw her walk in, he stalked out to confront her.

"The mail should be here in an hour or two. I want to see every piece of mail you get today. I have no intention of finding out you heard from the sniper *after* you've already talked to your cop boyfriend!"

Lydia glared up at him. "I did the right thing, Gary. The sniper is a cold-blooded killer, and the cops need all the help they can get. They're not trying to come up with some big headline to sell newspapers. They're trying to save innocent lives."

"Good for them. In the meantime, I'm your boss. If

you get a suspicious letter today, I want to see it immediately." He turned and went back into his office.

Lydia didn't know why she was surprised by Gary's demand. She should have expected as much from him.

Steve's frustration over the lack of leads in the sniper case was at an all-time high. He considered himself a patient and thorough investigator, but the killer's arrogance was getting to him. The ease and indifference with which this man killed left Steve full of rage. Crimes of passion he could understand, but the cold-blooded assassinations of complete strangers had made the city into a hell on earth.

And it was his job to stop the killings.

Steve got up from his desk and walked over to look out the office window. He stared out at the city's skyline. It was a nice morning, weatherwise. The sky was clear with only a few high, wispy clouds. The city looked clean and fresh.

But Steve knew better.

Somewhere out there a murderer was on the loose—undetected by law enforcement, free to come and go as he pleased, and able to prey at will on the innocent and helpless.

Steve lifted his gaze, and in the distance, he could see the silhouette of the steeple of Holy Family Church. Cynically he wondered where God was when all these terrible things were happening.

He had been raised Catholic. His parents had been

good and faithful parishioners, and he'd kept at it, too, for a while once he'd moved out on his own and become independent. But after the horror of the wreck with Drew and the continual ugliness he saw every day in his job, his faith and his belief in God had been tested. Sometimes he found himself wondering if God really existed.

And today was definitely one of those days.

Steve turned away from the window and went looking for Charlie. If nothing else, they could go back to the gun shops and gun clubs today and see if anyone had heard or seen anything new that might give them a lead on the shooter. He would also keep checking in with the detective assigned to watch Lydia. Since the sniper had chosen her for his contact, he might get in touch with her again. They had to be ready for whatever came next.

"Here she comes now," announced Frank Morris, the owner of the Good Eats Diner, when Cheryl came through the door that morning. "It's about time you showed up."

"I'm sorry. I—" She stopped, fearful her boss truly was angry with her for missing several days.

Before she could say more, Frank and all the customers went to give her hugs.

"I was teasing. We've been worrying about you."

"Yes, we have," the customers echoed.

"How are you? How are the kids?" Frank asked.

"It was terrible. If it hadn't been for the smoke alarm, we'd all be dead."

"But the kids are all right?"

"Yes. They're at school. I managed to get them some clothes so they could start back."

"Well, we were all here hoping you'd come in this morning," said Carl, one of the regular customers. "We took up a collection for you. We heard you didn't have any insurance, so we sure hope it helps."

He presented her with an envelope.

Cheryl looked down at the cash-stuffed envelope in her hand, then lifted her gaze to the loving people who surrounded her.

"Thank you," she said in an emotion-choked voice. "Thank you all so much!"

She gave each of them another hug, crying as she did so. When everyone had finally calmed down, she carefully stowed the money in her purse and got ready to go to work.

"How are things going?" Frank asked. They all knew that her life was going to be real rough for a while.

"That first day, I didn't know what I was going to do. We lost everything—and I do mean everything. It was scary. I was trying to stay calm for Bethany and Kyle, but there were moments when I almost lost it. I still don't think everything has really sunk in with me, but the most amazing thing happened."

"What?"

"Someone at Holy Family Church is buying me a new trailer."

Everyone in the diner was shocked.

"You're kidding!"

"I know," Cheryl said humbly. "I reacted the same way when my friend Irene told me."

"Who is it? Anybody we know?"

"The person who's doing it wants to remain anonymous. This is like a gift from God."

"I go to Holy Family," Carl spoke up. "But I haven't heard a word about this."

"Whoever my secret guardian angel is, I love them very much, just like I love all of you."

It was a lovefest at the diner that day. Frank had put a jar in a prominent place on the counter asking for donations for Cheryl's family, and as the day passed, all the regular customers pitched in. The generosity and caring she'd experienced over these last days touched her to the depths of her soul.

When she got off work later that afternoon, Cheryl knew what she wanted to do. She was scheduled to pick up Kyle and Bethany at Irene's, but she called and asked if it was okay if she was a few minutes late. Irene and the kids were in the middle of a big game of Sorry, so her friend told her to take her time.

Cheryl wasn't sure exactly what she was doing, but she drove to Holy Family and parked out front. She'd been in Catholic churches for weddings and funerals, but she'd never been in one simply to pray. Her religious background had been one of church-hopping. Her parents had never settled on any particular Protestant church. They'd only gone occasionally, usual at Christmas and Easter, and the rest of the year they'd slept late on Sunday mornings.

Cheryl lingered in her car for a moment, gathering her nerve, then bravely got out and walked up the steps. She'd heard Irene and Ernie say Holy Family was open to everyone, and she guessed she was going to find out if that was true right now.

She went inside and crossed the greeting area to enter the church itself. The door closed quietly behind her, and she was overcome by a sense of peace and holiness. There were a few other people sitting reverently in the pews, deep in prayer.

Slipping into a pew near the back, Cheryl sat there gazing up at the altar. In the silence of her heart, she offered up thanks and praise for the generosity that had been shown her these past few days. She prayed for blessings on all those who'd helped her, especially her secret guardian angel. She was still in awe of the magnitude of the gift.

Cheryl remained there praying for a while longer, then got up to go. She didn't want to impose on Irene's good nature too long. As she left the church and started across the greeting area again, a priest came out of one of the side rooms.

"Good afternoon," he greeted her with a kind smile.

"Hi," she answered a bit nervously, not quite sure how to bring up the subject on her mind. "Are you Father Richards?"

"Yes," he answered.

"I'm Cheryl Hall."

She didn't have to say any more. Father Richards recognized her name right away.

"It's a pleasure to meet you," he said, coming over to her.

"You, too." She smiled at him. "I came by—I wanted to thank you—"

"Irene Phillips has been keeping me informed on how things are going."

"I can't tell you how much your help means to us." She paused, for she was about to be overwhelmed by emotion. She met his gaze as she added, "Tell whoever was kind enough to help us that it's been a miracle. We were homeless—destitute—but because of this person's generosity, my children and I are going to have a home again."

Father Richards was touched by the depth and sincerity of her emotion.

"Please," Cheryl went on. "Tell them thanks for us, and if there's ever any way I can repay them for their kindness, let me know."

"Just keep this person in your prayers," Father advised.

"Oh, I will. You can be sure of that. I've already been thanking God for this blessing."

They shook hands, and then Cheryl left to pick up the kids. Her heart was full of love as she drove to Irene's house. She didn't know how she was going to do it, but for the rest of her life, she was going to try to take care of others in need the way she'd been helped. The kindness and generosity she'd experienced were wonderful things.

Cheryl made it to Irene and Ernie's to find her friends eagerly awaiting her.

"Mr. Howe called. He wants you to call him back. He's got the information about the home for you."

"May I use your phone?"

"Of course!"

She called the owner of the mobile home dealership.

"Mr. Howe? This is Cheryl Hall."

"It's good to hear from you. Thanks for returning my call. I wanted to let you know that everything has been taken care of. I've spoken with the manager of your community, and we're all set to move you in on Friday."

"That soon?" She was surprised and delighted.

"That's right. Your manager said he had a different site within the community that would work for this particular home, if that's okay with you."

"That's fine. I'm just so surprised that everything's been taken care of so quickly."

"We're glad to do it. You've had a rough time, and getting back in your own home will help."

"Thank you, Mr. Howe."

"One last thing—I wanted to let you know that the taxes and insurance have been paid up front for an entire year. You'll have no financial obligations to worry about while you get back on your feet."

Cheryl hung up the phone, speechless. She'd been worrying about insurance. She'd known she had to have it and she'd been frantically trying to figure out how to pay for it. Now even that worry had been taken from her.

"What is it?" Ernie and Irene were puzzled by her stunned expression.

She looked over at them. "The taxes and insurance have been paid on my new home."

"Oh, Cheryl! That's wonderful!" Irene exclaimed.

"And they'll be moving it in on Friday!" She looked at her son and daughter. "We get our new home on Friday!"

"Yeah!" Bethany and Kyle were overjoyed and started jumping up and down.

Just for pure silliness, Cheryl and Irene joined them. Ernie only looked on smiling.

# *Chapter Eighteen*

Steve and Charlie returned to headquarters empty-handed late that afternoon. It had been a long, frustrating day, but they were getting used to that.

"I think any personality profile done on me would read 'Handles frustration well,'" Charlie said as they started up to the office.

"You have to be able to handle it if you're going to work this job," Steve agreed.

They checked in to make sure nothing of significance had happened while they were out, and, as they'd suspected, nothing had. None of the leads from the tip line had panned out, and there had been no further contact from the killer.

Charlie called it a day first. Restless and feeling uneasy, Steve stayed on at his desk. A few more tips had been called in to the hot line in the last few hours, so Steve took the time to go over those. He found nothing of any significance, though, and finally decided to quit around seven p.m.

Steve decided to give Lydia a call before leaving the office just to make sure she was all right. He called her at home first and got her answering machine. He left a message, then tried her cell phone. When there was no answer there, he grew concerned. He placed a call to Don Parkins, the officer doing Lydia's surveillance.

"Don, it's Steve. I was trying to call Lydia Chandler, but I can't get hold of her. Is everything all right?"

"She's in church right now. That's probably why she's got her cell phone turned off."

"Okay. Thanks. Stay on it."

"I will," he assured Steve.

Steve hung up, wondering what Lydia was doing at church on a weeknight.

"I beat you here tonight!" Lydia teased George when he arrived at the prayer-group meeting at church a little late.

"Good, then I won't have to be sitting around here worrying about you," George countered good-naturedly. "I saw that article in this morning's paper. Did the sniper really contact you?"

"We were just talking about that before you got here, George," Mary added.

"Yes, the sniper sent a letter addressed to me at work," Lydia told him.

"That is so frightening," Phyllis put in. "Aren't you worried that he knows who you are?"

"It's scary, all right, but the police are keeping me under surveillance, so I'm not too worried."

"I'm glad they decided to do that. I want you protected," George said.

"We all do," the others chimed in.

Mary called the group to order, and they began the program for that night. When they'd finished the material on the Ten Commandments, they closed the evening with prayers. George prayed for the family that had lost their home to the fire, and that Lydia would be kept safe from harm. Lydia prayed for the sniper to be caught so there would be an end to the terror gripping the city, and Phyllis prayed for all the students she knew who were going through difficult times in their lives.

"Phyllis, did Father Richards speak with you about getting the youth group involved in helping the family who lost their home in the fire?" George asked her as they were getting ready to leave.

"Yes, he did, and I thought it would be a great thing for them to do."

"I do, too." He quickly recounted all the trauma the mother and children had been through and their dire financial situation. "From what I understand, they are going to be in a new home soon—"

"I know," Mary interrupted. "My friend Irene told me someone from the parish was kind enough to donate a new mobile home for them."

"That's wonderful! Who was it?" Lydia asked.

"That's the strange part. Whoever donated the home is keeping their identity secret."

"That's weird," Lydia said. "Why would anyone keep it a secret when they were doing something nice for someone?"

"Probably because they don't want any glory from it, they only want to help out," Phyllis added. "Like that donor who bought the building for the Saving Grace Animal Shelter."

"I hadn't heard about that. When did that happen?" Mary asked.

Phyllis related what she knew about the gift to the shelter. "Lydia, it just occurred to me—that would make a great investigative report for you. You could check into these stories and find out who's behind all these good deeds. It would be so nice to have a headline that dealt with a Good Samaritan instead of the sniper for a change."

"But, like you said, what if this Good Samaritan doesn't want their identity revealed?" George asked. "We know how good Lydia is at tracking down leads and finding the facts in a case, but if this person's cover is blown, it might ruin the whole thing. They are doing good works, you know."

"George is right about that," Lydia agreed, "but I agree with Phyllis, too. It would be wonderful to have some other news on the front page besides the sniper. Some good news."

"But anyway, back to what I was thinking," George went on. "The last I heard, none of the family's furniture, clothes or household items survived the fire. They've got nothing left."

"We can get the kids on this right away. Has the family been in contact with St. Vincent de Paul?" Phyllis asked.

"I believe so."

"Maybe we can organize the project through them."

"Give me a call and let me know whatever it is you'd like me to do," George said.

"I'll do that," Phyllis promised.

As she left the church, Lydia couldn't stop thinking about the generosity of the mysterious philanthropist. She tried to imagine who would be making such big donations and not tooting their own horn. In this day and age, that kind of charity was very rare. When corporations or CEOs gave money away, they always wanted media coverage to make sure everyone saw them signing the checks.

But not this person.

Whoever this was, they truly were doing things the way God wanted them done—for the benefit of those in need, not for one's own profit and glory.

Lydia knew she would enjoy writing an article about such a wonderful person, but with Gary running the paper, she doubted she would be allowed to—at least not until the sniper was caught and locked up behind bars. Only when it was a slow news day did an article of merit like one about a Good Samaritan stand a chance of getting in *The Daily Sun*.

As she thought about slow news days, she found herself wondering what had happened to the teenager who'd wrecked his car. She hoped the boy who'd been injured was doing all right, and that the driver had learned his lesson.

"You're right," Jim told Rob as they worked together that evening at the theater. "I do like working weeknights best."

"It's definitely a lot more laid-back than the weekends."

The low attendance at weeknight showings left little to be cleaned up.

"That was fun at the youth group the other night," Jim said.

"Yeah, we usually have a good time. Isn't George cool?"

"He's the old man with the Mustang, right?"

"That's him. He's been coming to the meetings for as long as I've been going. I've heard him talk about his Mustang before, but that was the first time he ever showed up with it."

"You don't see many Mustangs like that anymore. They're pretty rare."

"That's why I was surprised he brought it up there to show us. You into cars?" Rob asked.

"I had a Camaro."

"Had?"

"Remember when I told you I was in an accident last week?"

"Yeah."

"Well, the accident was my fault. I was driving and I totaled my Camaro."

"Man, that's terrible," Rob said sympathetically. "Thank God, you were all right."

"I know, but I loved that car probably as much as George loves his Mustang."

"You'll just have to save up your money and get another one when you can."

"That's my plan."

"Once school's out for the summer, you can ask the boss for extra hours."

"I'll do that. The faster I get some money put away, the better."

"Speaking of money, it's time to get ready to earn our keep. Cinema Five is just about to let out."

The two ushers, armed with their brooms, headed toward the theater.

Lydia's phone was ringing as she came in the door at home.

"Well?" Gary demanded when she answered. He saw no reason to bother with saying hello.

"Nothing," she answered. "There's been no attempted contact at all."

"Damn! All right, you've got ten minutes. You can fax it to me, e-mail me or read it to me, I don't care, but I want another communication from you to the sniper. It's going to be front-page news, so make it good."

"Ten minutes?"

"That's right. Get on it—*now*." He hung up.

Lydia sat silently for a moment, trying to decide the best way to get a reaction out of the sniper. She'd tried coaxing him with her first response, but nothing had happened. Whatever she did now, it had to be something that would provoke him.

Without wasting another moment, she picked up the phone and called Steve at the office, hoping he was still there.

"Detective Mason," he answered in his professional manner.

"I'm glad you're still there."

"What's up?" He could tell she was concerned about something.

"Since the sniper made no effort to contact me today, my editor wants to run another letter from me to the sniper tomorrow to try to draw him out."

"All right, what are you thinking?"

"That's what I wanted to run past you. This maniac seems to enjoy seeing himself in the news, so I thought it might be time to jerk his chain—to print something that would get a quick reaction out of him."

"Like what?"

"I think I need to belittle him in some way. Say something like 'You're real brave and fearless. That's why you go around hiding and shooting unarmed, defenseless people, and then write me at the newspaper to brag about it.' "

"It could be dangerous," Steve cautioned.

"It already is, but it's worth it if it will help you catch him before anyone else gets hurt."

"We'll have to be very careful how we handle this."

"I have 'Sheriff' Mason watching over me," she said, trying to lighten their conversation. "You can't get much safer than that in this town."

"Yes, ma'am. I do my best." Steve played along just to keep their mood from getting too dark. "Call your editor and get that note to him. This could work."

"Thanks."

They hung up, and Lydia called Gary back at the office.

"What have you got?" Gary demanded impatiently.

"This should draw him out," she declared, ready to start reading her note, but Gary didn't give her a chance.

"*Him?*" Gary rudely interrupted. "Why are you so sure this sniper is a man? For all we know, this could be some pissed-off, menopausal woman with a gun!"

"The one eyewitness said it was a man," she argued.

"And we all know how reliable eyewitnesses are," he disparaged. "Have you talked to your detective boyfriend lately? Has he told you something I don't know? Has he given you a heads-up on anything that hasn't been officially released to the public yet?"

"No, and for your information, Steve Mason is not my boyfriend," she denied.

"Oh, really? It sure looked like he was, at the fund-raiser the other night, dancing all cheek-to-cheek," Gary taunted.

"We danced, Gary. That's what you do when they play music at those kinds of social occasions."

"Right," he said dismissively. "Let me hear this note."

"'An Open Letter to the Sniper: You are real brave and fearless, aren't you? That's why you go around shooting unarmed, defenseless people from hiding places, and then send me an unsigned letter bragging about it. You're nothing but a gutless coward. You must be too scared to contact me again. Sincerely, Lydia Chandler.'"

Gary was quiet for a minute, then told her, "E-mail your letter to me right away. I've saved room for it. It'll run tomorrow morning."

Lydia hung up and went to get online. She said a silent prayer that the ploy would work.

# *Chapter Nineteen*

*Lord, Give Me Hope . . .*

*THE DAILY SUN*'S OWN AWARD-WINNING
INVESTIGATIVE REPORTER
LYDIA CHANDLER CALLS SNIPER A COWARD!

Lydia expected a bold headline from Gary as she sat down at the kitchen table with her paper a little before seven the next morning, and he didn't disappoint her.

She read over the letter she'd sent him and was glad to see he hadn't changed the content. Now it was just a matter of waiting. The next move was up to the sniper. She had no idea what the killer might try to do, but she had to be ready.

It was so early and Lydia was so on edge that she actually jumped when the phone rang.

*Could it be the sniper already?*

The only way she stayed calm as she answered the

phone was knowing the line was tapped. She was profoundly relieved when she found the caller was Steve.

"Good morning," she told him.

"Yes, it is. It looks like your boss took care of things, so all we can do now is wait and see what happens. If you need anything today, just call. If I'm not at the office, they'll know where to find me."

"I will."

"I was wondering—would you like to go out to dinner tonight?"

"That is a wonderful idea. I get the feeling it's going to be a real long day at work, so it would be nice to have something to look forward to."

"Plan on it, then, and I'll give you a call later on this afternoon, once I know when I'll be able to get away."

They spoke for a moment longer, then hung up.

Lydia was delighted at the prospect of seeing Steve socially that evening. She only wished they could hop on his bike and take off again as they had over the weekend. For that little while, they'd been able to pretend that the harsh, ugly world they lived in didn't exist. It had been heavenly while it lasted. She hoped they could find a way to block out the real world again that evening. She was certain they both needed a little peace in their lives.

The sniper read the newspaper and chuckled to himself at the reporter's pitiful ploy. He'd instinctively known Lydia Chandler would rise to his challenge when he'd sent her that first note, and she'd reacted just as he'd expected her to by printing not just one letter back to him, but two.

He was aware that she had recently won a media award for best investigative reporting, and that was why he'd singled her out. He was certain she was confident of her abilities as a journalist and possibly even a bit arrogant following her win. He had no doubt that Lydia Chandler thought she could outsmart him. She probably assumed that by insulting him and getting his ego involved, she could taunt him into responding to her, but he wasn't falling for that.

He was in control of the situation.

He always had been.

And he always would be.

Of course, he knew it couldn't hurt to play along. He would turn things around and let the reporter think she could entice him into revealing his identity, while all the while he'd be toying with her for his own enjoyment.

Smiling broadly at the thought, he went to his computer and began to type out his response.

Phyllis Logan saw Jim in the hall at school and sought him out.

"I know you're new to the youth group, but I wondered if you're busy this Friday after school?"

"No, I don't have to work at the show until Saturday night," Jim answered. "What do you need me to do?"

She quickly explained what she'd heard about the

homeless family. "If you could check with Rob and find out if any of the other kids are available, I'll see what I can come up with to help the family."

"Is it okay if I let you know tomorrow?"

"Sure, that will be fine. I'll talk to you then."

Phyllis had already called the local food shelter to get the family a supply of food. She was working with St. Vincent de Paul to find some furniture and other household goods. She hoped by the time the weekend was over, the family would be happily settled in their new home.

George had meant to get up and go to early Mass that morning, but he hadn't been able to. He'd awakened just before dawn, once again in terrible pain, and when he'd tried to get up, he had experienced a devastating sense of weakness. He'd rested for a while, then dragged himself from bed to get his pain medication. He'd lain back down, praying the medicine would take effect quickly.

George was discovering that he did not handle being sick very well. He was used to being in complete control of himself, brain and body, and now that was changing rapidly. It was like he'd thought before—the warranty really was up on his body parts, and there were no mechanics around who could give him a tune-up.

Still, once the painkillers kicked in, George could pretend he was fine again. He got up and got moving. When he retrieved his morning paper from his driveway and read the headline about Lydia, he grew worried. This was a very dangerous thing she was involved in, and he prayed it would turn out all right and that she would be protected from all harm.

The evening couldn't come quickly enough for Lydia. Steve had called in the mid-afternoon to tell her he'd be by to pick her up around seven o'clock, so she was ready and waiting for him. It had been a disappointing day. There had been no response whatsoever from the sniper. No one had tried to contact her or to call in anything new to the tip line. The lack of immediate response troubled her, but she realized the sniper was playing a very frightening game and would not necessarily respond normally to insults and challenges. She would have to bide her time and wait to see what the next day's mail delivery brought.

Lydia heard a car in her driveway and went to look out the front window. At the sight of Steve, so tall and handsome, getting out of his car, her heartbeat quickened. She hurried to welcome him. He was coming up the front walk as she stepped out onto the porch.

"You're right on time," she complimented him.

"I got lucky—nobody called after we talked. Are you ready?"

"Let me get my purse."

He followed her inside and waited in the foyer while she went to get her purse.

"So you didn't hear anything more, either?" he asked.

"No. It was quiet all day, and even though he initially thought it was a good idea, Gary started complaining that he had wasted good front-page space on my letter. Knowing Gary, he's probably afraid that since I insulted the sniper, he won't contact us at *The Daily Sun* anymore."

"Your editor always complains about something, doesn't he? Ignore him. The last time the sniper contacted you it was by snail mail. If he contacts you again, he'll probably do it the same way. We'll have to wait and see what tomorrow's mail delivery brings."

"Let's don't even think about tomorrow," Lydia said. "I want us to enjoy ourselves tonight."

"So do I," Steve agreed as she stopped before him. He gazed down at her, seeing her beauty and her innocence, and he couldn't help himself. He took her in his arms and drew her to him.

Lydia was mesmerized by his tenderness and surrendered to his embrace. She welcomed his kiss and responded warmly to him. When at last they broke apart, Steve smiled down at her.

"I think we'd better go get some dinner."

"I think you're right," she agreed, but, in truth, she wanted nothing more than to go back into his arms and stay there. She felt safe in Steve's arms—and excited.

They went out to his car, after she'd locked up the house, and drove to a nearby Italian restaurant. Steve was aware that one of the plainclothes officers from the department was keeping tabs on them, so he took an appetizer out to the officer, to help him pass the time while they were inside. They enjoyed a delicious dinner and deliberately didn't speak of the sniper.

"What made you decide to go into police work?" Lydia asked.

"My father was a cop. He liked seeing the bad guys locked up, and so do I," Steve admitted.

"Your work is definitely a calling," she told him.

"I don't know about that—"

"Of course it is. You've been blessed with a special talent for your work. Not everyone can do what you do," she complimented him.

"I don't look at it as a blessing," he denied.

"You should. Think of all the people you're helping by catching criminals and keeping them off the streets so they can't hurt anyone. It's no wonder St. Michael is the patron saint of policemen. You're strong and moral men."

"You have to be strong to deal with what we have to deal with every day."

"Well, I've been praying for God's help in catching this killer."

He gave her a jaded look as he said, "If I were you, I wouldn't count on God a whole lot."

She was surprised by his response. "Why do you say that?"

"If there is a God, why—"

Before he could finish his remark, their conversation was interrupted.

"Lydia? I can't believe it!"

She recognized the man's voice immediately and looked his way. "Brian?"

A tall, handsome, blond-haired man came up to the

table and gave Lydia a warm hug the moment she got to her feet.

"It's so good to see you," Brian Thompson said when he set her away from him. "It's pure luck that you're here tonight. I've been thinking about you since I got into town."

"Let me introduce you to Steve," Lydia began. "Brian Thompson, this is Detective Steve Mason. Steve, this is Brian, an old friend of mine."

Steve stood up and shook hands with the other man. "Would you like to join us?"

"Thanks, but I'm here on business tonight."

"What are you doing back in town?" she asked.

She and Brian had dated seriously two years before, but when his company offered him a promotion that meant a transfer out of state, he'd taken it with no thought to their relationship at all.

"We've got corporate meetings here all this week," he explained. "I know you're still with *The Daily Sun*. I saw the headline about you this morning." He looked at Steve, wondering if the detective was with her socially or for her protection. "Good luck catching this nut," he said to Steve.

"Thanks. We're working on it," Steve answered.

"Brian—" one of his business associates called him.

Brian realized he had to go. "It was wonderful to see you, Lydia. If I can get away, I'll give you a call and maybe we can get together while I'm here."

He hurried off to catch up with his business associates.

Lydia and Steve sat back down at their table. They

were quiet for a moment. Steve was wondering just who Brian was. He'd embraced Lydia so easily that it was obvious they were close.

"So, who's Brian? An old friend?"

"I guess you could call him that," she answered. "We dated for a while, but he took a transfer out of town and things were never the same."

Steve looked her in the eye and smiled slowly as he said, "I'm glad."

Caught up in his mesmerizing regard, Lydia realized the truth of her feelings, too. "So am I."

At her age, Lydia was mature enough to realize that she hadn't known Steve long enough to be serious about him, but even as she tried to be logical about her feelings for him, there was no denying them. She was attracted to Steve as she'd never been attracted to another man.

"So, tell me more about you," Steve encouraged as they settled back in at their table. "Did you always want to be a reporter?"

Her eyes lit up at his question. "Oh, yeah. I like getting the truth out there. It's important for the public to know what's really going on."

"You don't kiss and tell, do you?" he asked with a grin.

"That could prove to be a very interesting investigation, depending on who you were kissing," she said teasingly. "But can you imagine the headline Gary would come up with for that article?"

"I don't even want to go there." Steve started laughing at the thought.

"Neither do I," she laughed, too.

They finished their dinner, enjoying every moment, and then returned to her house.

"Can you come in for a while?" Lydia invited.

"No, I'd better go," he said regretfully as he remained standing in her foyer. "With an officer on duty watching the house, I don't want to put your reputation at risk."

"You're a very special man, Steve Mason," she said, touched by his concern. It was a rare quality in men these days. "I know you have to leave, but—" She paused.

Intrigued, he asked, "But what?"

"If I'm going to write that article we were talking about, I need to begin my investigation—"

"What article?"

"You know—the one where I 'kiss and tell,'" she said with a slow, inviting smile.

"I'd be pleased to help you with your research," he volunteered, closing the distance between them.

"I will need your assistance—"

Steve took her in his arms and claimed her lips in a passionate kiss. Lydia met him fully in that exchange. She clung to him, reveling in being held so close to him, and she gave herself over to the pleasure of his embrace.

When they finally ended the kiss and moved apart, Lydia looked up at him, deliberately keeping her expression serious.

"I'm sure I'll need to do more research in the future—if I'm going to do the 'kiss and tell' article justice."

"All you have to do is call me. I'll be glad to help you in any way I can with your investigation."

"I'll remember that."

They were both smiling as he left her.

# *Chapter Twenty*

Gary was again watching for Lydia when she came into the office.

"Remember what I told you about the mail," he carped. "Nothing gets out of this office that I don't take a look at first."

"Right." She went to her desk, not wanting to get into an argument with him. It was going to be a tense enough day as it was, waiting to see if the sniper would respond. The pressure Gary put on her only made things worse.

Jim got to school early and went looking for Mrs. Logan before classes began.

"I talked to Rob and Angie last night. They said they could help out after school today, and they were going to call a few other friends. I told them I'd let them know where you wanted us to meet."

"Thank you, Jim. I really appreciate your help. When

you talk to them this afternoon, tell them to meet us at church around four-thirty."

"We'll be there," he promised.

Phyllis called George at home during her lunch hour to let him know of their plans, and he told her he'd be there, too.

Gary and Lydia were both watching anxiously for the mail delivery, just as they had the day before. The minute the mailman arrived, they hurried to the front of the office to meet him.

"I can't believe how popular I am around here," the mailman quipped.

Gary ignored him and took the stack from him. He cut off the clerk who was standing there, waiting to distribute the mail in the office.

The mailman had a feeling nobody wanted to make small talk that day, so he quickly left.

"Let's see what we've got here," Gary said, sorting through the bundle.

The clerk knew better than to challenge the boss. He backed away, letting him do whatever he wanted with the mail.

Lydia didn't trust Gary. She stood right beside him, watching carefully as he quickly went through the big stack, letter by letter.

And then he found it—a plain envelope with a computer-generated label on the front, addressed to Lydia.

"I think we've got it," Gary said with almost savage

delight as he held the envelope by the upper corner for her to see. "What do you think?"

"It is the same," she confirmed.

"All right!"

"Be careful!" Lydia ordered, not wanting the letter to be contaminated by him. "Let's put it in a plastic bag and get it over to police headquarters."

"You might as well slow down, Lydia. This letter isn't going anywhere until I'm finished with it," he snarled at her. "This is breaking news, and we're covering it!"

Other reporters in the office suddenly realized what was going on and gathered around to watch.

"That letter is mine, Gary!" Lydia said hotly. "Give it to me."

"If you want your job, you'll shut up right now," Gary sneered at her.

"No," she challenged, refusing to be intimidated by him. "If you want *your* job, you'll hand over *my* letter right now! It's a federal offense to tamper with someone else's mail. That letter is addressed to me. It's mine!"

Gary did not immediately back down. He stood there giving her a look that could kill.

"Do I have to call Detective Mason and tell him you're interfering with the investigation?" When he didn't react immediately, she ordered, "Sandy, call police headquarters and get Steve on the line—"

Sandy reached for a phone and began to dial.

Gary swore loudly and held out the letter to Lydia.

"Never mind, Sandy," Lydia said.

Her friend hung up and looked on in fascination to

see how this confrontation would play out between Lydia and the boss.

Lydia took the letter from him and laid it on a nearby desk. Very carefully, she slit the envelope open with a letter opener and then shook the envelope. A small sheet of paper fell onto the desktop and she read:

*Dear Lydia Chandler,*
*Thanks for all the publicity. You say I'm a gutless coward. I say I'm a very good shot. I'll stay in touch, for there's more to come.*

*—A Friend*

"He's going to kill again, and he's bragging about it," Lydia said, sickened by his perversion.

"He's one ballsy son of a bitch, I'll say that for him," Gary remarked.

Lydia ignored Gary's crude comment as she carefully picked up the note and made a copy for her file. She placed the original, along with the envelope, in a plastic bag to safely transport it.

"I'm going to police headquarters to turn this in. I don't know when I'll be back."

She drove quickly to headquarters and went straight to the front desk.

"Is Detective Mason here? It's important I speak with him right away."

"Let me see if I can find him for you," the officer at the desk told her.

A few moments later, Steve came hurrying down to meet her.

"Lydia? What have you got?"

"Another letter." She held the plastic bag out to him.

Steve took it from her and read the message through the bag. *"I'll stay in touch, for there's more to come—"*

"We've got to get this to the captain right now. Come with me."

Steve led the way through the maze of corridors to Captain Donovan's office. He didn't pause, but walked in unannounced with Lydia by his side.

"It's from the sniper. He says there's more to come," Steve told his boss grimly as he held the bag out to him.

Donovan took it and read the cold-blooded message. He looked up at them. "We're going to beef up patrols starting now, and I'll talk to the state to see if we can get more helicopters down here to help us out."

"Good. I'll take the letter down to the lab for tests, but I've got a feeling it's going to turn out like the last one."

"The sniper's shrewd, that's for sure, but we're going to catch him," Captain Donovan said with fierce determination.

"If there's anything you'd like me to do—anything I can help you with, let me know," Lydia offered.

"Steve's got you under surveillance, right?"

"Yes."

"And your phones are tapped?"

"Yes."

"Then all I want you to do is be careful and keep an

eye open for anything out of the ordinary. This sniper's made no attempt to call Steve again, so you're our one and only contact with him right now."

"I will."

Captain Donovan looked down at the note in the bag again. "All right, get this down to the lab, Steve. Who knows? Maybe we'll get lucky this time—but I'm not counting on it."

Steve and Lydia left the captain's office.

"I'll call you and let you know what the results are," Steve promised.

"Thanks."

"Are you interested in going to the barbecue at Drew and Marcie's Sunday?" Steve asked.

"I'd like that. I know she mentioned it at the fund-raiser."

"Good, I'll pick you up."

"On the bike?" The thought of sitting behind him on the motorcycle with her arms wrapped around him thrilled her—even if it was only for the short ride to Marcie's house. Just being that close to Steve would be wonderful.

"You got it," he said.

Steve gazed down at her, thinking that he couldn't wait to be with her again, away from work. The fact that she liked riding the bike with him excited him. She wasn't like other women he'd dated. She didn't care about helmet hair. She honestly enjoyed the adventure of the ride. If they hadn't been standing there right in the middle of headquarters, he would have kissed her. Somehow, he didn't think that would be considered professional behavior while on the job, but it was an intriguing thought.

"I'm looking forward to it."

"So am I."

Lydia left him, and Steve was forced to go back to work. Some days were rougher than others.

Cheryl stood with Irene and Ernie, watching in excitement as Jason and his crew from the mobile-home dealership finished setting up her new home. They'd been awestruck by the way the crew had been able to maneuver the trailer onto the lot.

"This is so amazing," Cheryl said with tears in her eyes. "Only a few days ago, I was crying in sorrow, and now I'm crying for joy."

Irene impulsively hugged her. "I can't wait to see the kids' faces."

"They are going to be so thrilled," Cheryl agreed.

Jason Howe came over to them then and held out two sets of keys to Cheryl. "These are for you."

"Thank you," she said in an emotion-choked voice.

"You're welcome," Jason said, feeling good about what his crew had just accomplished. "If you want to go in now, I can show you around."

They followed him up the steps of the small porch and went inside.

Cheryl looked around in breathless wonder. The display she'd gone through had been furnished. This one, empty as it was, looked huge. She couldn't believe how spacious it was. "It's beautiful."

"You picked out a quality product. This manufacturer makes good homes," Jason assured her. He walked her though the home and gave her the instruction booklets that came with it. "The stove, microwave and refrigerator all come with it. If you have trouble with anything, anything at all, just give me a call. You're under warranty."

Cheryl had had no idea all the appliances would be provided, too. She was stunned.

She and Jason shook hands, and then Jason and his crew left.

"This is perfect for you," Irene remarked.

"It's such a blessing." Cheryl looked to the two friends who had stood with her through all her troubles. "And all because someone from Holy Family wanted to help me. Do you have any idea who it was?"

"None. Father Richards refuses to say. Your Good Samaritan wants it that way."

"I've never known anyone so generous before."

"This is a rare person, for sure."

"Irene? Ernie?"

They could tell by the tone of her voice that whatever she was about to say was serious. They both looked at her.

"I was wondering—would you mind if I started going to church with you? I don't know a lot about Catholicism, but I can learn. I've watched you living your faith, and now this—it makes me want to be a part of something so wonderful and loving."

"Oh, Cheryl," Irene said emotionally. "You are welcome to go to Mass with us any time. And, by the way, here." She reached in her pocket and took out a small crucifix. "I got this as a housewarming present for you."

Cheryl took the crucifix from her, holding it, cherishing it.

"I had Father bless it."

"I'll make sure to hang it somewhere prominent so I never forget."

"That will be wonderful. How much time do we have until the kids show up?"

"About an hour."

"Why don't we go get my cleaning supplies and my vacuum, and give the house a quick once-over? Ernie even said he'd help us."

"You're going to help me clean house, too?" Cheryl smiled at her friends. "You really are saints!"

They were all laughing in delight as they hurried to get the cleaning supplies.

It was almost three-thirty when Cheryl had to stop cleaning and go pick up Bethany and Kyle. On days when she worked, she had the school bus drop Bethany off at Kyle's preschool. That way she could pick them both up at the same time when she got off. She headed there now, excited about bringing them back to their new home.

Bethany and Kyle knew this was the day that they

were moving out of the motel. They could hardly wait for their mother to come for them, and when she finally walked into the preschool, they went running up to her.

"I take it you're both ready to go home?" Cheryl asked, her eyes aglow with the joy that filled her as she looked lovingly down at her son and daughter.

"Yes!" they shouted.

Cheryl checked them out with the supervising teacher and they went out to the car, ready to celebrate.

"We don't have any furniture yet, but we've got a home, and that's all that matters."

"We can sleep on the floor," Bethany said bravely. "We'll just pretend we're camping."

"That sounds good to me!" Cheryl agreed.

She heard both children gasp when she pulled up in front of their new home.

"We're here!" Kyle shouted.

"Yes, we are. We're home!" Cheryl said excitedly.

They got out of the car and raced up the steps. The two children were almost jumping up and down with excitement as they waited for her to unlock the door and let them in. When Cheryl finally got the door open, Kyle and Bethany ran gleefully inside and raced through the home, squealing in delight as they checked out every room.

At any other time, Cheryl would have scolded them for acting so wild and crazy, but she had to admit, she felt like jumping for joy herself.

It was just a short time later when the doorbell rang.

Cheryl went to answer it, expecting it to be Irene and Ernie.

Irene and Ernie were there, but with them were a bunch of teenagers, a middle-aged woman and an older man.

"Cheryl, this is my friend Phyllis Logan and this is George Taylor. They work with the youth group at church, and they've brought you some 'housewarming presents.' "

Cheryl was shocked as she looked from the lady named Phyllis to the man named George. "You have?"

"We sure have," George spoke up, smiling. He could see the surprise in the young woman's face, and it tickled him to know she was so appreciative. "Shall we start unloading? We've got a truck full of furniture out here. Where would you like us to put everything?"

"I don't know—" Cheryl was speechless. "Just come on in. We'll figure something out."

"All right, kids, you heard the lady," George directed the teenagers. "Let's get all the boxes and furniture inside."

The teens all went to work under George's supervision. Jim and Rob worked together to carry the mattresses, box springs and bed frames inside. The other kids carried in a kitchen table and chairs and a small sofa. All the furniture was used, having been donated to charities in town, but it was in good shape. After the furniture was in, the kids began to carry in bags of linens and kitchen items. It took them the better part of an hour to get everything inside the home and set up.

"Who are these kids?" Cheryl asked George as she

watched them working so diligently to make her life better.

"They're part of our youth group."

"They're wonderful."

"I'll let them know you think so," he promised. George had been studying the young mother, and he was impressed with her. She was humble and loving, caring and determined, and he knew the secret helping hand he'd given her and her children would make a monumental difference in their lives. He offered up a silent prayer, thanking God for giving him the means to help them and asking that the family would live safely and happily in their new home.

When they'd finished unloading everything and were about ready to leave, Ernie stopped them.

"You aren't going anywhere," he directed. "I called in an order for pizza and soda. It's going to be here any minute, so let's all relax and enjoy ourselves."

Irene and Ernie brought some outdoor folding chairs down from their house, and, when the food arrived, the housewarming party began. They said grace over the food and then dug in. Kyle and Bethany went to sit with the teenagers, and the teens doted on them.

"What's your name?" Kyle asked one of the teenage boys as he looked up at him adoringly.

"I'm Jim, and your name's Kyle, right?"

"Yeah. Where'd you get all the stuff you brought us?"

"There are different charities that offer things for people in need."

"That's nice," Kyle said seriously.

"Yes—you're right. It is." And as he answered the boy, Jim realized just how much their efforts had been appreciated that day. The time they'd volunteered to help out had truly made a difference in this family's life. A sense of goodwill and peace that Jim had never experienced before filled him.

"You kids about ready to head home?" George called out, rallying his troops.

The teens quickly gathered together. They thanked Ernie for the pizza and then got in their cars to leave.

Kyle, Bethany and Cheryl stood with Irene and Ernie, waving good-bye to Phyllis, George and all the teens as they drove off.

That night, when everything had calmed down and Cheryl was home alone with her children, she gathered them to her and together they said a prayer of thanks for all the blessings they'd received.

God truly had been watching over them.

# Chapter Twenty-one

George was taking it easy on Saturday. He'd gotten a good night's rest and had slept quite late for him. It was after nine when he awoke, and he was surprised to find he actually felt halfway decent. He celebrated by keeping to his normal routine—he made coffee and read the paper.

The headline "SNIPER THREAT HANGS OVER THE CITY" was predictable for *The Daily Sun*. It certainly wasn't breaking news. He turned the page, uninterested in Lydia's editor's rantings.

George was thoroughly enjoying his relaxing morning when the phone rang.

"George, this is Father Richards. How are you doing today?"

"As a matter of fact, Father, I'm doing fine this morning."

"That's good to hear—real good. Listen, I've got a letter here that was just dropped off for you."

"A letter?"

"It's from Mrs. Hall. Do you want me to mail it to you or do you want to pick it up?"

"I tell you what, I'm planning on going to five-o'clock Mass, so I'll get it from you then."

"I'll see you at five."

It was a madhouse at the movie theater that afternoon. Two new movies premiered, and the crowds were big. Jim started work at three o'clock, and it was nonstop action. When Rob showed up to work the five-to-close shift, Jim was glad to see him. They had a few minutes to talk before the next movie let out.

"How are you holding up?" Rob asked, grinning.

"Last weekend was nothing compared to this."

"You should have been working here the weekend the new *Star Wars* movie opened."

"I can imagine."

"So, what did you think about last night?" Rob had noticed that Jim was very quiet on the way home the night before.

Jim was a little uneasy being completely honest, but then he realized if he couldn't talk to Rob, he couldn't talk to anybody. He looked up at his friend. "It was awesome."

Rob smiled at him. "I know. I felt the same way, and, man, the guy who helped them, secretly buying that trailer for them—that's amazing. First off, to have that much money to give away, and second, to actually do it."

"Think they'll ever find out who he was?"

"I doubt it."

"Well, would you look at who's here," Mike Williams called out to Sam Orrico and the rest of their friends as they headed to the screen where the movie they'd come to see was playing.

"It's old front-page-news himself!" Sam taunted.

The other guys laughed loudly when they spotted Jim.

Jim groaned inwardly at the sight of the "in crowd" from school. He'd been avoiding them as much as possible at school, but there could be no avoiding them now.

"Who are these guys?" Rob asked him quietly, standing at his side as the group approached.

"I know them from school."

Rob could tell these guys had it in for Jim, so he stayed right beside him.

"Jimmy, you look real good in your usher outfit. Nice bow tie, don't you think, ladies?" Mike asked their dates, obviously enjoying himself at Jim's expense.

Jim tensed as they all laughed derisively at him.

"It must take a real man to wear an outfit that cool," Sam said sarcastically, "and carry a broom around."

"It does," Rob put in before Jim could say anything. "You should try it sometime."

Mike paid no attention to the other usher with Jim. "Hey, Jimmy, when the movie's over, you want to race? I could meet you out back and—oh, wait a minute. That's right—you don't have a fast car anymore, do you? In fact, you don't have any kind of car anymore, do you?"

Jim tried to ignore their taunts and jibes.

"You're right, Mike. He can't even drive," Sam threw in, enjoying the bullying.

Jim held himself sternly under control. He told himself he was at work and these guys weren't worth it.

Mike went on, "Yeah, his daddy probably picks him up after work—"

Jim told himself he had a job to do.

"Or his mommy," Sam put in, not about to give up.

At that remark, even their dates laughed.

"Jimmy, is your mommy's car fast? We could meet you after the movie and race you. What do you think?"

Jim was ready to explode. He had paid the price for his own stupidity. He was dealing with the results of the bad choices he'd made. He would always regret what he'd done, but he couldn't change what had happened. Still, he didn't have to put up with any more of this hateful ridicule.

"His mommy's got to be a better driver than he is."

Jim's hands were clenched into fists at his sides as he fought to control his temper, but the last remark snapped his self-control. He started to erupt, taking a threatening step forward, ready to shut them up.

Rob anticipated Jim's reaction and put a firm hand on his arm to stop him.

"Let it go," he told him.

Mike, Sam and the rest of their crowd moved off, still laughing over how clever they'd been.

Jim stood stiffly unmoving, his rage and humiliation eating at him.

"It's not worth it," Rob advised. "You'd lose your job if you went after them—even though they do deserve it."

Jim finally let his rage go, and he managed to look over at his new friend. "Thanks."

Rob grinned at him. "You're welcome. Come on. The movie's letting out. Let's go to work. And you know . . ."

"What?"

"No matter what those guys say, there are some girls who really do think we look good in these bow ties and vests."

Rob was glad when he finally managed to get a laugh out of Jim. They headed in to clean up the theater.

Five-o'clock Mass was crowded as always. George was there in his usual pew, enjoying the sense of peace and love that surrounded him. When it came time to offer each other a sign of peace, he did so happily, shaking hands and smiling at those around him. He was delighted when he caught sight of Irene and Ernie sitting across the aisle a few pews ahead of him. With them was the Hall family. The fact that the young mother and her two children were attending Mass touched him deeply. Later, when he went up for Communion, he nodded to them as he passed by their pew, and they smiled back joyfully at him.

"The Mass is ended, go in peace," Father Richards pronounced. He reverently left the altar and waited in the greeting area to speak with the parishioners as they made their way out to the parking lot.

George found Irene and Ernie there speaking with Father Richards along with Cheryl and the children.

"It's good to see you," George told them.

"You, too," Cheryl responded. "Thanks for all your help the other night. It was wonderful. The kids were great."

"They're a good bunch," George agreed.

"Cheryl's interested in joining the church," Irene told him. "We were just checking with Father to find out when the next session of the Rite of Christian Initiation of Adults begins, and then we'll have to see about getting the kids into the Parish School of Religion classes."

George was impressed that Cheryl was interested in learning about becoming Catholic. "That's wonderful. There's a good bunch who run the RCIA program. I think you'll enjoy it," he told Cheryl.

When they'd gotten their information and moved on to leave the church, Father Richards looked over at George and smiled.

"There's just no telling how far a good deed will go, is there, George? Come on back in the sacristy. I've got the letter there for you."

Father Richards led the way into the room where he prepared for Mass and got the envelope out for George.

"Thanks, Father."

"Thank you, George." They were alone, so he went on. "What you're doing is truly amazing. Holy Family is blessed to have you in the parish."

"I feel blessed to be here. You know that." George was

humbled by his praise. "Let me know if you hear of anything else."

"I will, and if you need me, just give me a call."

They shook hands, and George left church. After he'd settled in his sedan, he opened the letter.

*To Whom It May Concern,*

*My name is Cheryl Hall. I'm the mother of two wonderful children, Kyle, 4, and Bethany, 6. I had to write this letter to thank you for the incredible kindness and love you've shown my family. The fire that claimed our home was heartbreaking, but at the darkest moment of our existence, you came into our lives like a Guardian Angel, saving us and helping us. Through your loving kindness, we have come to appreciate even more fully the unconditional love God has for each and every one of us. You have shown the world the power of faith in action. You are a very special person.*

*Kyle, Bethany and I want you to know that you will always be in our prayers and you will always be loved. Thank you for our miracle.*

*Should you ever need us for anything, you only have to ask.*

*Yours in Christ,*
*Cheryl, Bethany and Kyle Hall*

The honest emotion in the letter touched George deeply. Tears burned in his eyes as he folded the letter and put it back in the envelope. He stowed it safely in his console, then started up the engine.

As he got ready to drive, George looked up and saw that the sun was just beginning to set. The sky was bathed in a multitude of vibrant pastels, and the high-flying clouds glowed softly with an inner light. He loved sunrises and sunsets. He often thought they were a sneak preview of what the glory of heaven would be like.

George drove home filled with a great sense of inner peace.

Cheryl Hall and her children were safe and happy in their new home tonight.

Life was good.

Jim and Rob sat together in the employee lounge later that evening. Jim had just confided in Rob the truth of all that had happened the night he wrecked his car.

"Man, that's terrible," Rob sympathized. "Bet you'll never do anything like that again, will you?"

"No, I learned my lesson. I still can't believe I was that stupid. I don't know why I cared about impressing them. They weren't my friends."

"That's for sure."

"And I don't think I'll ever drink again—not even after I turn twenty-one."

"Yeah, I know what you mean. My dad drinks a lot. It can get ugly around our house sometimes. It isn't worth it."

"You're right about that. We can have fun without it, right?"

"Sure, like working here," Rob said, smiling. "Look at

the great time we're having tonight. Not everybody has cool jobs like we do."

"Speaking of which, we'd better get back out there. I've still got an hour to go before I get off."

"Lucky. I'll be here until at least one or two a.m."

"I guess Mr. Thompson likes me best, since he gave me better hours," Jim teased laughing.

"We were lucky we didn't have to work last night, too, as busy as the weekend is. I'm glad I had the night off, so I could help Mrs. Logan and George take all that stuff over to that family."

"Me, too. I felt sorry for those little kids. Think how awful that must have been for them—losing all their toys."

"They're going to be fine now, thanks to whoever bought the new home for them."

"Hey, do you think the guy who's got all that money to give away might feel sorry for me and buy me a new car?" Jim fantasized.

"Ah—no," Rob answered, quickly ending his fantasy. "I think you're probably going to be on your own when it comes to getting another car."

"Too bad. I guess that means I really do have to get back to work, huh?"

"You got it."

They left the lounge to take care of business.

Lydia couldn't believe how excited she was about seeing Steve the next day. She'd gone through her wardrobe three times, trying to find just the right outfit to wear. She kept telling herself it was just a barbecue—that they would probably be sitting outside all day, visiting and having fun—but it felt more special than that since she was going to be with Steve.

She was definitely attracted to him. There was no doubt Steve was sexy. He was by far the most attractive man she'd ever dated, and the most interesting.

As a detective, he'd seen a lot of the ugliness in the world—like the accident with Drew and all the other things he'd had to deal with over the years. She realized that might account for the negative remarks she'd heard him make about God. He seemed to doubt that God even existed.

Lydia was puzzled by that kind of reaction, for she always clung to God all the more when bad things happened. God knew she needed His help and strength, and she was always grateful for His guidance. Somehow, she decided, she was going to have to show Steve that God was right there, active in his life, whether he recognized Him or not. It might take some work, but ultimately it would be worth it. She wanted Steve to know just how blessed he really was.

As Lydia went to bed, she offered up a quick, quiet prayer that she would be granted the wisdom she needed to guide Steve, and she thanked God for bringing him into her life.

# *Chapter Twenty-two*

"What a glorious day it's turned out to be!" Marcie said as she and Lydia sat out on the patio in the backyard. "Last night the weatherman said it might rain, but we got lucky."

"Yes, we did."

"So, how long have you really known Steve?"

"Socially or professionally?"

"Well, I know at the fund-raiser you started off calling him Detective Mason, so I figured you weren't too close then." Marcie was curious. Since Steve, Charlie and Drew were inside watching the end of a baseball game, she knew they had a few minutes of "chick time" to talk.

"Workwise, I've known him for a year or so, but socially, we only started seeing each other since the fund-raiser."

"Steve doesn't date a lot, so I'm glad to hear that."

"He doesn't? Why not?" Lydia was surprised by the news.

"I guess it's because he's too dedicated to his job—or

maybe he just hadn't met Miss Right—until you came along."

She smiled. "I like your second guess better."

"Ah—so there is something going on here," Marcie laughed with delight.

"There definitely is on my part," Lydia confided.

"His, too," Marcie assured her. "I saw the way he was looking at you earlier when you didn't know it."

Lydia was thrilled. "So how long have you and Drew been friends with Steve?"

"Steve and Drew were partners for two years before the accident, so about seven years now. That's why I know you're special. I've always told Steve he could bring a date whenever he came over to see us, but until today, he never has."

"I'm glad he did. It's nice getting to know you better. Last weekend we went for a ride on the Harley and ended up out in the country. That was a great escape for both of us."

"Escaping is good every now and then."

"Especially with all the terror over the sniper. That's all my editor cares about at work—getting the scoop on the sniper investigation."

"I understand that the public wants to know what is going on, but sometimes I think the TV, radio and press go too far with their coverage."

"Do you think the public really wants the constant, unending coverage, or do they put up with it because they have no choice?" Lydia asked.

"I don't know."

"There is other news out there. Have you heard about the secret Good Samaritan in town?"

"No." Marcie was intrigued. "What Good Samaritan?"

"We have no idea who it is, but we know somebody over the course of the last couple weeks has given money to rescue the Saving Grace Animal Shelter. In fact, the person actually bought the building the shelter was located in and gave Saving Grace the title. Then this week a family lost its home in a terrible fire."

"Oh no!"

"Yes. And someone bought a brand-new mobile home for them. Again, anonymously."

"Are you sure it's the same person?"

"We don't know. There haven't been any public statements made. I'd love to look into it and do a series of articles about our Good Samaritan, but there's no trail to follow. The gift to the animal shelter was handled through an attorney, and the family who lost everything in the fire got their gift through the pastor at my church, Holy Family."

"So you go to Holy Family? We're at St. Joseph's."

"What about Steve?" Lydia asked.

"What about him?"

"Do you know what religion he is?"

"He's Catholic. After the accident, he went to Mass with me several times to pray for Drew's recovery."

"I was wondering. The few times God's come up in our conversations, he's sounded kind of negative" Lydia said.

"See if you can get him to go to church with you one Sunday. That'd be a good way to tell where he stands."

"I'll work on that. Thanks, Marcie."

"I can see the headline in *The Daily Sun* now: 'Steve Goes Back to Mass.'"

"I wonder what headline my boss would come up with for a story like that. He'd probably go with something like 'The Sky Is Falling.'"

They both laughed.

"But since it would be a good story with a good ending, he probably wouldn't let you cover it," Marcie said.

"You're right. He doesn't care."

"He sounds like a real fun guy to work for," Marcie said facetiously.

"Fun would never be in any character description of Gary," Lydia said. "He likes to keep everybody on edge—and not because it will help you do a better job."

"I'm glad I don't work for him."

"What do you do?"

"I'm a nurse. I work at the hospital in the ER."

"That's exciting work."

"We appreciate quiet days, that's for sure."

"What's for sure?" Drew asked as he, Charlie and Steve came outside to join the women.

"That quiet days are good in the ER. I was just telling Lydia about work. Is the game over?" Marcie asked.

"We won."

"Good, now how about lighting the grill? Lydia and I are getting hungry."

"Your wish is our command," Drew told them.

"If only that were true." Marcie grinned at Lydia and said, "I think they're probably hungry, too."

"I think you're right," Lydia agreed.

Drew started up the gas grill while Steve went back inside to get the meat. Charlie sat down with the ladies to take it easy.

"I'll let those two real domestic guys take care of the cooking," Charlie said. "I'll bat cleanup."

"So you're the manly man of the bunch, are you, Charlie?" Marcie teased.

"You said it, babe!"

"You're just a glorified maid, Charlie. It takes a real man to cook these steaks," Steve said as he came out with the platter.

Charlie looked between his two friends. "So which one of you is the real man?"

"We both are," Drew told him. "We're going to take turns."

"Yeah, yeah, I still say batting cleanup is the best spot in the lineup."

Marcie and Lydia got the side dishes ready, and it wasn't long before dinner was on the table.

They enjoyed the delicious steaks, and Charlie actually did clean up afterwards.

"I'm going to have to invite him over every night," Marcie mused. "I could get used to living like this—my own private cook and my own private maid."

"That's right, woman," Drew said, grinning at her. "You're living the good life."

"I already knew that," she agreed, going to kiss him. She was grateful for every minute they had together.

It was after dark when they finally called it a night.

Charlie left first, then Drew and Marcie watched as Steve and Lydia rode off on the bike.

"I think they make a great couple, don't you?" Marcie asked.

"Steve may just have met his match with Lydia. She's one sharp woman."

"I hope it works out for them. I like her a lot."

"She could turn out to be the best thing that ever happened to him."

"I was thinking the same thing."

They shared a smile and went inside.

Lydia enjoyed the ride home. The powerful roar of the Harley and the cool wind in her face thrilled her. She closed her eyes for a moment as she held tightly to Steve, cherishing their closeness.

"Here we are," he said as he pulled into her driveway and parked.

"Thank you, that was so much fun." Lydia climbed off the back of the bike and took off her helmet.

"Marcie and Drew are very special people."

"They are," she agreed. "Do you want to come in for a while?"

"For a few minutes."

He left their helmets with the cycle and followed her to the door. He was aware of the unmarked car parked just down the street and he was glad to know surveillance was on the job.

Lydia unlocked the door, and they went inside. When she shut the door behind them, the moment Steve had been waiting for was finally upon him. He took her in his arms.

"I've been wanting to do this all day," he murmured just before he kissed her.

Lydia didn't have the chance to respond verbally, but her reaction to his kiss told him all he wanted to know.

He deepened the embrace, bringing her tightly against him, loving the feel of her soft curves crushed to him. She had been a temptation while riding on the back of the bike with him, but in his arms, she was a pure delight.

Lydia lifted her arms and linked them around Steve's neck to draw him even closer to her. Being in his embrace was heavenly. She loved the feel of his hard-muscled body against her. When his lips left hers to seek the sweetness of her throat, she arched against him as excitement coursed through her.

Steve wanted more. He wanted to pick her up in his arms and carry her off to her bedroom. He didn't want this moment to end, but he knew it had to. He sought her lips once more in a deeply passionate exchange. Then he ended the kiss and moved a little away from her, putting some distance between them. He was a man who prided himself on being in control, but Lydia was proving to be his biggest temptation ever. She was definitely testing his limits.

"Steve—?" Lydia looked up at him questioningly. She'd been completely caught up in his kiss, and it troubled her that he'd broken it off. "Is there something wrong?"

He gave her a slow, seductive, knowing grin that set her heart racing even faster.

"Oh, no, Lydia. There's nothing wrong. The trouble is, everything is too right," he admitted.

"I don't understand."

Steve lifted one hand to caress her cheek. "You are one beautiful woman, Lydia Chandler."

She looked up at him, her eyes aglow with the depth of what she was feeling for him. "Thank you."

"Just the truth, ma'am," he said, bending to kiss her very gently.

"The truth is, Steve Mason, I think I'm falling in love with you," she whispered when he drew back.

Steve smiled down at her, deeply touched by her confession. "I know. I feel the same way, and it's all happening so fast—"

"It's kind of scary, isn't it?"

"Very—but it's good scary."

He gathered her close again and kissed her once more, deeply, passionately.

"Definitely 'good scary,'" Lydia agreed when they'd ended the embrace and finally moved apart. "Would you like something to drink?"

"I would, but I'd better go since we've got company out there watching your house. It's going to be nice once we catch the sniper. Then we can be alone."

"That's another reason why we have to solve this case fast," Lydia agreed.

They shared one last sweet kiss.

"Lock up," he ordered as he left her.

And she did.

George realized as he sat watching television that evening that he had definitely overdone it that day. He'd gotten up feeling relatively good and had spent the day outside doing yard work. The grass had needed mowing, and there had been weeds in the flower beds that had to come out. He'd always loved working in the yard, but judging from the way he was hurting tonight, it looked as if those days were coming to an end.

"What do you think, little girl?" he asked Duchess as she lay quietly beside him. "Think it's time I found us a yard man?"

She looked up at him adoringly and wagged her tail in approval.

"That's what I thought," George chuckled. "Maybe I can get one of the boys from the youth group to do it. There might be a kid there who needs some extra pocket money. I'll give Rob a call first and see if he's interested."

He was friends with Rob's parents through the prayer group, and George knew Rob would be a good choice. But if Rob didn't want the job, he was sure the teen would know another boy who might be interested. If not, the fund-raiser car wash was scheduled for the following Saturday. All the teens would be around that day, and he would probably be able to find someone then.

"One thing we have to make sure of, though," George

said to Duchess. "Whoever we hire had better like dogs, right?"

Duchess woofed her answer and wagged her tail again for emphasis.

"Right." He smiled and reached down to pet her.

# *Chapter Twenty-three*

*Save Me, Oh Lord . . .*

Jayne Crawford got up and eagerly got dressed for her early-morning run with her dog, Grizzly. The weather was beautiful. The sky was clear. The temperature was hovering around 70. It was the perfect morning to get out and get her blood moving before she had to go to work.

Grizzly was ready and waiting for her, standing by the front door. The big shepherd mix always kept her going when they jogged on the trail through the park. Jayne hooked up his retractable leash and opened the door, ready to head out on their adventurous run. With any luck, they would get a full three miles in this morning.

Woodland Park was centrally located, just a few blocks from her house. It was a big park, adjacent to the main freeway that led downtown. Jayne liked running on the trail there in the mornings because it wasn't very crowded.

They ran on the sidewalk to the park's entrance and the beginning of the trail, and then set out at their usual steady, ground-eating pace. Grizzly loved being outdoors. Being cooped up inside all day while his mistress was at work didn't sit well with him. So he took full advantage of this time outside, darting here and there as he kept pace with his mistress.

It was on one of these forays that Grizzly saw something moving in the brush down the hillside near the highway. He charged toward it, intent on rooting out whatever animal was hiding there.

Jayne had been keeping a steady pace, listening to music on her iPod, when Grizzly jerked savagely against the leash, snarling and barking. Caught completely off-guard, she lost her hold on the dog. She quickly took off her headset and gave chase, calling out to him. Jayne feared at the rate he was charging, he might end up on the highway, and she certainly didn't want him anywhere near the traffic, light though it was right now.

Grizzly had no doubt about what he was after. He started to attack just as the gun was fired. The shock of the gunshot startled him, but only for an instant. He attacked with even more ferocity. Barking wildly and biting, Grizzly tore at the arm of the man lying hidden in the brush.

Retaliation was fast and cruel.

The sniper had just been taking aim and getting off his shot when the fierce dog attacked. He swore loudly at the unexpected assault and bashed the dog's head as hard as he could with the butt of his rifle. He'd knocked the dog off him, but not before the beast had chomped down on his forearm, biting him severely and tearing his camouflage jacket.

Jayne had been running after Grizzly at full speed when suddenly a loud noise rent the air. She stopped in her tracks and stood there unmoving, unsure of what was happening and of what she'd just heard.

Had it been a gunshot?

Or had a car backfired?

And then Jayne glanced toward the highway and realized a car on the interstate had gone out of control and crashed into the center divider. Traffic was coming to a screeching halt behind the wreck, and smoke was starting to rise from the engine of the damaged vehicle.

At that instant a man—a white male dressed in camouflage and carrying a rifle—jumped to his feet from the brush where Grizzly had disappeared some distance ahead of her.

"You!" Jayne shrieked in terror at the sight of the gunman.

The shooter turned and fled the scene.

"Wait! Stop!" Jayne yelled, still confused by all that had happened.

The man didn't pause or look back. He ran like a man possessed, charging headlong toward a clump of trees and disappearing into the overgrowth.

Jayne stared after him for a moment, then ran down to the brush to find Grizzly. She found her beloved dog lying unmoving in the tangle of bushes. He was bleeding from a severe wound to his head. She dropped to her knees beside him and got out her cell phone.

"911."

"The sniper! He just shot someone on the highway! Here by Woodland Park!"

"Where are you?"

"I saw him! I saw him running away!"

"Ma'am, where are you?"

Jayne quickly gave the operator her exact location.

"Stay where you are. I'll send an officer to assist you momentarily."

Jayne stayed with Grizzly, waiting anxiously for the cops to show up. She was terrified that the madman would return, but though she kept watch, she saw no sign of him. She heard a helicopter close in on the area and hover overhead, and then finally several police cars arrived on the scene.

She waved frantically at them, and an officer ran to her side.

"I'm the one who called in. I saw him. He hurt my dog." Jayne was frantic.

"I'm Officer Warren." The officer took a quick look at Grizzly and saw how serious the wound to his head was. "I don't know if anything can be done for your dog. We can put in a call to your veterinarian, if you want."

"Yes—yes, please! We have to save him!"

He got the veterinarian's name and number from her and radioed headquarters to let them make the call. As he was finishing up, Steve arrived on the scene.

"I'm Detective Mason," he told Jayne as he joined them. "I understand you saw the shooter?"

"Yes! Yes, I did! I'm Jayne Crawford. We were out for a run and then—then Grizzly went crazy—"

"Grizzly?"

"My dog."

Then Steve saw the injured animal.

"Grizzly knew something was wrong. He got away from me and ran down here and attacked whoever was hiding in these bushes. I saw the man get up and run away."

"What did he look like?"

"He was a white male—wearing camouflage."

"Would you be able to identify this person again if you saw him?"

Jayne looked stunned for a moment as she tried to envision the man who'd so brutally injured Grizzly. "I only got a quick glimpse of him, but I think so."

"How tall was he?"

She frowned. "Not very. I think he was shorter than normal."

"And in which direction did he run?"

"Over there—through those trees." She pointed the way.

Steve knew they needed the Canine Unit on the scene right away. He told Officer Warren to get on it while he finished speaking with the witness.

"What happened on the highway? Was someone shot?" Jayne asked worriedly.

"A bullet hit the car," Steve explained, "but the

driver was not shot. He's got just a few bumps and bruises from hitting the guardrail."

"Thank God," Jayne said, amazed that the driver had survived the horrible attack.

"What have we got?" Charlie asked as he came running up.

"The shot was fired from here. The witness's dog went after the shooter."

Steve knelt down to get a closer look at the injured dog. As he examined the animal, he suddenly realized what he'd found.

"Charlie! Take a look at this!"

Charlie knelt beside him, and together they carefully shifted the unconscious dog to the side. There, crushed in the grass, was a ripped piece of bloodstained camouflage cloth.

Steve and Charlie looked at each other as hope surged within them.

"Let's just hope that's not the dog's blood on the cloth," Steve remarked.

"I don't think it is." Charlie studied the position of the cloth and where the dog had been lying.

They quickly took the necessary precautions to cordon off the area and then very carefully got the piece of cloth ready to be taken to the crime lab in an evidence bag.

When Dr. McDonough, the vet, arrived on the scene, Grizzly was carefully placed in the back of his vehicle, so he could transport the animal to Harvest Plaza Animal Hospital for emergency treatment.

"I want to go with Grizzly," Jayne insisted.

"As our only witness, we need you to stay here with us for now. We'll be glad to drive you to the vet's office once we've finished our investigation."

Officer Warren had directed the Canine Unit into the area where the sniper had fled. They were able to track him for a distance, but it was obvious that he'd parked his car nearby and had driven off. He'd left nothing behind in the brush as he'd run.

Once they were certain the search team wouldn't be bringing anyone in for her to identify, Charlie took notes of Jayne's contact information and then drove her to the vet's office. Steve remained behind to inspect more of the crime scene and take the necessary photos.

Steve caught sight of Lydia in the crowd of onlookers and media, and he went to speak with her.

"He struck again," he told her.

"But no one's dead this time," she said with great relief.

"It's a miracle, that's for sure, and we have some blood to check for DNA."

"How did that happen?"

He quickly explained how the dog had attacked the sniper while he'd been hiding.

"So a dog named Grizzly saved the day," Lydia said with heartfelt sympathy for the dog's owner. "Will you let me know what you hear about him?"

"I will. Let's hope the blood on the cloth turns up something. I've got to get back to headquarters. I'm sure the captain will have a news conference sometime later today."

"Maybe I'll see you then."

They parted company.

Lydia remained at the scene of the wreck, interviewing those she could find who'd witnessed what had happened. It was almost ten a.m. before she made it into the office. She had a great idea for a headline and couldn't wait to run it past Gary.

"What did you find out?" Sandy asked Lydia, anxious to know what the sniper had done this time.

Lydia told her all that had happened. "I can't wait to tell Gary the angle I've got for tomorrow's headline. Where is he? I need to talk to him right away."

"He called in sick this morning with the stomach flu. He said if he was feeling better he might come in later this afternoon, but from the way he sounded when I talked to him, I doubt he'll make it. He probably just said that to keep us on edge, worrying that he might show up."

"Who'd he put in charge?"

"He said you were—lucky girl," Sandy said sarcastically.

"Yeah, then if anything's wrong, I take the hit."

"It can't be wrong. If you're in charge, things can only get better around here."

"Thanks for the vote of confidence."

"You're welcome. Now, let me hear your idea for tomorrow's headline and lead story."

"I don't want to glorify this guy the way Gary does. How's this? '*Sniper Misses! Police Are Closing In! Arrest Expected Soon!*' "

"Perfect. It'll scare him and put him on edge."

"That's what I want. I want him running scared. I want him to make a big mistake so the cops can get him off the street."

"Are you going to ask Gary about it?"

Lydia gave her friend a knowing look. "Only if I have to. He's sick, you know, so I don't want to bother him."

"I understand. Go, girl!"

"If you hear when Captain Donovan is going to have the press conference, let me know right away."

"I will."

The sniper was filled with rage as he doctored his injured left arm. The filthy mutt! He hoped he'd killed it. It deserved to die for what it had done! It had caused him to miss his shot!

And he never missed!

Fury ate at him.

He stared down at the wound on his arm. It was deep and ugly. He'd always heard German shepherds could be fierce, and now he knew it was the truth. He should have shot the damned dog and its owner, too!

He flexed his arm, testing its strength, and he was relieved to find he could still use it. That was good news. The dog attack wasn't going to stop him.

Nothing was going to stop him.

Wrapping up his injured arm, he went in to watch television. He wanted to see what the media were saying about the shooting. He liked knowing he was in the news—even if the results of his shooting hadn't been what he'd hoped this time.

* * *

It was early afternoon when Captain Donovan came to the podium.

"I'll read a statement and then I'll take your questions," he informed those at the press conference. It didn't surprise him that the place was jammed. Reporters from all the media were anxiously awaiting his announcements.

"At six-fifteen this morning, another shooting occurred on the interstate. We are fortunate that the shot missed the driver, but the car was damaged, and consequently crashed into the center guardrail. We had a witness who saw the sniper fleeing the scene. The witness owned a dog that attacked the sniper. The dog did tear off part of his camouflage jacket sleeve, and it was bloodstained. The lab is working on that now. Know that we are doing everything in our power to track down this killer and bring him to justice." Captain Donovan paused to draw a breath before he took on the endless barrage of questions he knew was about to come. "Now for your questions—"

Everyone started yelling at him at once, and he held up his hands to try to regain control.

"Please—it will be much more effective for all of us if we do this in an orderly fashion. Now—Ken Rockwell, *The Evening News*—what's your question?"

"Captain Donovan, you said there was another witness. What description do we have to go on now? Did this witness see anything different from the first one?"

"Today's witness claims the shooter is a white man of less than average height, wearing camouflage."

"And you say he was bitten on the arm?" another reporter called out.

"We have determined that from the evidence at the crime scene—yes."

"So the public should be looking for a short, white guy with an injured arm?"

"That's right, and our tip hot line is still open," the captain announced, giving out the number once again.

"Captain Donovan—" Lydia called out.

"Yes, Lydia?"

"Was a vehicle seen leaving the crime scene?"

"No. The shooter ran off on foot into some trees and brush in Woodland Park. By the time we arrived, he was gone."

"So, is this 'Classic Little Man Syndrome' we're dealing with here? Have we got some little guy who's out there shooting at people, trying to get even with everybody who picked on him all his life?" the first reporter asked.

"It could appear that way, but at this point in time we can't definitely say that is the sniper's motive."

Another reporter asked, "This 'syndrome,' Captain—how can shooting and killing complete strangers make you feel like a big man or make you feel like you're getting even with bullies from your past?"

"If that does prove to be the motive, you can ask the sniper when we bring him in. That will be all for today. We'll follow up as soon as there is more information."

* * *

Lydia called Steve the minute she got back to the office. She felt lucky to catch him at his desk.

"I've got a quick question for you," she said. "Tell me about this 'Little Man Syndrome.' "

"I heard that somebody brought it up at the press conference," he began. "What it amounts to is that a certain type of man becomes very insecure because of his small stature. While growing up, the individual suffers taunting and teasing from other kids, and as an adult, that individual wants to get even. He wants to let the world know he's bigger and badder and better than everyone else. He wants to show the world how good he really is."

"Why don't people like that just become CEOs? That would show everybody how smart they are."

"But they're not smart. That's the problem. And that's why they choose violent ways to act out their frustration and fury."

"Would it be appropriate for me to mention the syndrome in the article I run tomorrow?"

"Go for it. We may be way off base here, or we could be right on. Give it a try. The worst that can happen is nothing."

"My editor's out sick for the day, and he put me in charge. I thought I'd put the 'Little Man' thing in my headline. If anything would set him off, that would."

"That sounds good. Just be careful."

"I will."

"I'll talk to you soon."

"I'll be waiting for your call."

# *Chapter Twenty-four*

The phone rang and Lydia quickly answered it.

"Lydia—what's going on down there?" Gary demanded. "What have you heard from police headquarters?"

"I take it you're feeling better?" she asked.

"No, as a matter of fact, I'm not, but that's neither here nor there. Answer my question," he snapped at her.

"The press conference was held several hours ago—"

"I know that," Gary sneered. "I watched it on television. What have you heard since then? Have any announcements been made about blood types? Has the witness remembered anything else? Have any other witnesses come forward?"

"No. There haven't been any new developments at all."

"All right—so what did you come up with for tomorrow's headline?"

"*Sniper Misses! Police Are Closing In! Arrest Expected Soon! Suspect Could Have 'Little Man Syndrome.'* "

"You're going with that?" He was incredulous. "Nobody cares about some stupid syndrome! They want to know what the killer's going to do next."

"The syndrome theory may explain the sniper's motive and could be key to the investigation," she argued hotly. "Why else would this guy be shooting complete strangers?"

"That's the best you could come up with? It's pitiful! Maybe I should have put a sports guy in charge instead of you. Or better yet, one of the college interns!" he raged on. "What about the dog that attacked the sniper? Is it still alive or did he kill it? What about the car crash? What happened with the driver? How badly was he hurt? Come on, woman! Get with the real story! You're an investigative reporter. Find out all this stuff! That's why I pay you your salary."

He hung up on her abruptly, leaving Lydia staring at the phone, shaking her head in absolute disgust.

"I take it that was Gary?" Sandy asked from Lydia's office doorway.

"You could tell?"

"Oh, yeah. Your happy expression gave you away. What's he after?"

"Probably a headline like *Sniper Kills Dog Bare-handed After Fending Off Savage Attack!*"

"That would really win him some friends at the Saving Grace Animal Shelter."

"When has Gary ever worried about winning friends?"

"So, what are you going to do?"

Lydia was angry with Gary over his insults, but knew

she had to look past that. She was in charge today, and it was her job to do the best she could for *The Daily Sun*.

Lydia was thoughtful for a moment and then got a sudden twinkle in her eye.

"What are you thinking?" Sandy asked. She'd seen that look on her friend's face before and knew it usually meant trouble.

Lydia's thoughts were racing as she realized this was the perfect opportunity to cover the story she'd been wanting to do for days. The Good Samaritan in town was doing wonderful, generous deeds, and he was doing them anonymously. It was time to get the word out about all his good deeds. If the sniper had "Little Man Syndrome," relegating him to page two might get a reaction out of him.

"You know," Lydia said, grinning broadly as she came up with the perfect headline for the next edition, "maybe, since I am the one in charge, I should do what I want to do—what I think is best."

"And exactly what are you thinking?" Sandy could tell by Lydia's expression that she had a devious plan in mind, and she was with her friend all the way.

"Gary will get his sniper story—"

"All right." Sandy waited for what was to follow.

"But it's not running on page one."

"It's not?" Sandy was startled.

"That's right. I'm going to put the sniper story on page two on purpose. It might really annoy the killer to be ignored that way. If he is one of these 'Little Man Syndrome' people, he'll be in a rage being relegated to the second page. And besides, I firmly believe it's time we covered the Good Samaritan story in depth."

"You're brilliant," Sandy agreed in delight. "What do you want me to do?"

"Dig out everything we've got on the family that lost their home in the fire, and then be ready to leave here in five minutes."

"You don't want much from me, do you?" her friend laughed.

"You're a professional. You can handle the pressure," Lydia said with a smile.

"I'll make sure your faith in me is warranted."

"Good. We haven't got a lot of time. I want to get out to the Saving Grace Shelter so we can take some pictures, and then see what we can do about speaking with the family who were given a new home."

"I'm on it." Sandy hurried from the office.

Five minutes later they left the building, on their way out to Lydia's car.

"The animal shelter is open until six," Sandy informed her. "Here's what I found about the family. The mother works at the Good Eats Diner, and she's probably there right now. We can stop by and interview her first, if you want. It's on the way to the shelter, and then we can head on out there afterward."

"Sounds good. You know, you should look into becoming a reporter. You'd be real good at it!"

"I'll think about that career choice."

They were laughing as they drove to the Good Eats Diner and went in.

"Hi! How can we help you?" a young woman welcomed them.

"We're looking for Cheryl Hall," Lydia said.

The woman's expression turned cautious as she eyed the two women. "I'm Cheryl Hall. What can I do for you?"

"It's great to meet you," Lydia went on. She introduced herself and Sandy, and told Cheryl why they were there. "I want to do a front-page article on our mysterious Good Samaritan, and I wanted to hear your story."

"It's quiet right now," Cheryl said, glad there weren't many customers. "Let me tell my boss that I need a few minutes off. Go sit at a table. I'll be right back."

She disappeared in back for a moment, then came to sit with them as another waitress came out to wait on the few customers in the diner.

Twenty minutes later, Lydia and Sandy were sitting there still going over Cheryl's heartwarming story.

"Whoever this person is, they're a godsend. I don't know how my kids and I would have survived without the help we got."

"Have you heard anything more from your Good Samaritan?"

"No. Not a word. It was all handled through Holy Family, but Father Richards was sworn to secrecy. He wouldn't reveal anything to me. I sent a thank-you note to the person through Father, but there's been no response to my note."

"This is so awesome," Sandy said, trying to imagine the type of person who could be so completely generous without any ulterior, selfish motive.

"Yes, it is," Cheryl agreed. "I thank God for my guardian angel every day, and so do my son and daughter. In fact, this gift has affected me so deeply, it's brought me to church. I'm going to begin taking instructions at Holy Family."

"That's wonderful," Lydia said. "I attend Holy Family, too, so I'll see you there."

"I'll look forward to it."

"Mrs. Hall, we were wondering if it would be possible for us to come by your house a little later this afternoon and get a picture of you and your kids to run with the article?" Lydia asked.

"We'd be honored," Cheryl told her. "What time would you like to come by? I get off work at five."

"How's five forty-five?"

"That'll be great. We'll see you then." Cheryl gave them her address and directions to the house, and then went back to work.

Lydia and Sandy left. They had to visit the shelter before they met Cheryl at her home.

Saving Grace Animal Shelter was open for business. When Lydia and Sandy went inside, they were immediately impressed by how clean and neat the facility was.

"Can I help you?" a pretty young woman at the main desk called out to them as they stood just inside the front door looking around.

Lydia and Sandy made short order of introducing themselves and explaining why they were there.

"It's great to meet you," the young woman said. "I'm Leann. I volunteer here. Let me go get Bonnie Zimmerman for you. She's the owner. She's the one you want to talk to."

They waited patiently, looking around at the dog and cat toys for sale, and soon Bonnie came out to greet them.

"It's a pleasure to meet you. Leann tells me you want to do an article about the shelter in *The Daily Sun?*" Bonnie was excited about the possibility of some more publicity.

"Yes. We're following up on your mysterious benefactor and wanted to let the public know how things were going now that you own the building."

"That is so wonderful! Let me give you a tour first; then you'll have an idea of what we do here. Since we were helped out so generously, things have really taken a turn for the better. Adoptions are up, and cash donations are coming in far more regularly."

"So the gift has turned out to be one of those that keeps on giving," Lydia remarked.

"You're right. We've been very blessed by this stranger's generosity. I've never learned who it was, but I've always felt since that remarkable day that I have a guardian angel."

She showed them around the building, stopping to let them pet the animals and give them treats.

"I wish I were home more," Lydia said regretfully as she petted a cute three-legged dog. "I'd love to have a dog."

"I see you and Trinity get along real well," Bonnie said with a smile.

"Trinity is his name?" Sandy was intrigued.

"That's right. He was dropped off right at the time

when I thought I was going to have to close the shelter down. The man who left him never told me his name. Shortly after that, the godsend of a gift came to us, and I decided Trinity was the perfect name for him."

"It is," they agreed.

Lydia and Sandy stayed on a little longer, admiring the work the shelter did before leaving for their meeting with the Hall family.

They made it on time to the Hall family's home and took several pictures of the mother and two children in their new environment.

Lydia and Sandy got back to the office in plenty of time to get the article finished and the headline set for the front-page coverage.

"You know, Sandy, I think I need to change the headline I ran past Gary earlier today. I know I told him I'd be leading the article with '*Sniper Misses! Police Are Closing In! Arrest Expected Soon! Suspect Could Have 'Little Man Syndrome!*' But now I think '*Dog Wins! Sniper Loses!*' is much more effective for the lead, since the article is going on page two."

"That works for me."

"Good. Now, for our real lead story . . ."

Lydia sat down at her computer and went to work. It felt wonderful to be writing about something uplifting and heartwarming for a change. She knew there would be a price to pay for running the article, but she didn't care. Gary had left her in charge, so she was going to do it her way.

When the paper went to press, the headline for the

front page read, "SECRET GOOD SAMARITAN HAS THE POWER TO CHANGE LIVES! ANONYMOUS DONOR SAVES ANIMAL SHELTER AND HOMELESS FAMILY!"

The article on the sniper ran as she'd planned on page two. She made a point of mentioning "Little Man Syndrome" and hoped by downplaying the coverage, she might get another rise out of the murderer.

Lydia didn't know what to expect the next day, but she was ready for whatever might happen. If she read the public right, she believed readers wanted some relief from sniper stories. She knew she would soon find out.

Rob was glad when he discovered that Jim was working Monday night with him. "I was hoping you'd be here."

"How come?"

"My mom got a call. You know George, the old man who owns the cool Mustang?"

"Yeah."

"Well, he's looking to hire somebody from the youth group to start doing his yard work. You want the gig?"

"Why don't you take it?"

"Between working here and being on the cross-country team, I don't have time. Mom said George asked whether you'd do it if I couldn't."

"He did?" Jim was surprised that the elderly man remembered him at all.

"Yeah. Do you want to call him, or do you want me to have my mom do it?"

"Why don't you have your mom call? I'm sure my parents are going to want to talk to him before I go over."

"That's a good idea. I'll tell Mom tonight to give your folks a call."

"Thanks." Jim truly was grateful. He needed to make all the money he could so he could pay his parents back.

Steve and Charlie spent most of the day checking in with stores that sold army surplus. They passed out descriptions of the sniper and asked everyone to be on the lookout for a short white male with an injured arm. They also went house to house in the neighborhood of the shooting, interviewing the home owners and asking if they'd noticed any strange cars in the area that morning. All their hard work turned up nothing, but they were used to that.

The good news was that they knew the killer's blood type now. The sniper was A+. Now all they had to do was catch him.

"You know, I'm feeling real good about this," Charlie remarked.

"You are?" Steve was surprised by his partner's optimism.

"Sure. All we have to do is arrest every short white male who's A+ and run DNA tests on them. Then we'll have our killer."

"That's brilliant," Steve agreed, knowing Charlie was joking. "In a city this size, that's going to be, what?—100,000 to 150,000 men?"

"Well, if we had them all locked up, the shootings would stop. And besides that, once we sort through them, we'll find the guy with the dog bite and we'll have him nailed."

"You tell Captain Donovan your plan. I'll back you all the way."

"Hmmm, there'd probably be a problem coming up with the jail space."

"Not to mention the lawsuits we'd be facing."

"Maybe it wasn't such a good idea after all."

"You think?"

They both laughed, trying to ease the tension that always came when they kept hitting dead ends.

"It's going to be interesting to see what Lydia does with the paper tomorrow morning." Steve went on to tell Charlie about his earlier conversation with her about bringing "Little Man Syndrome" into her article.

"The sniper isn't going to like that."

"Exactly. That's why her idea is perfect. Let's just hope we're ready for him when he erupts."

"We will be. I want this guy off the streets."

"So do I."

George went to bed early that night, still exhausted from all his hard work that morning. As he was resting in bed, flipping channels, he heard a news report on one of the local stations and stopped to listen.

"St. Francis de Sales Parish is reporting that the roof on their more-than-a-century-old church desperately needs to be replaced, and they have very little money to work with. It's in a poor area of the city, and rumors are circulating that the church may be forced to close if the funds cannot be raised in a timely manner."

George lay there, not believing what he was hearing. He'd grown up in that neighborhood. He'd gone to the church and attended the parish school. St. Francis couldn't close! It was a beautiful old church. They didn't make them like that anymore.

Determination filled him, and he knew what he was going to do the next day. It was time to go back to his old stomping grounds and take a look around.

It seemed that God had once again revealed to him where he was needed.

# *Chapter Twenty-five*

*Lord, Give Me Strength . . .*

Lydia got up and went to Mass in the morning. She knew she was going to need all the strength she could get to make it through the day.

Lydia was certain Gary's first reaction when he saw the paper was going to be anger, but if she got the response she hoped from the sniper, she figured he'd get over it. Maybe then he'd learn to trust her reporter's instincts a little more. Arrogant as he was, she sincerely doubted Gary would change, but it was worth a try.

She got to church early and knelt down in the pew to pray. She prayed for the wisdom to know what to do and the fortitude to carry through and do it. She also prayed that the sniper would be caught and peace would come to their community again.

As she was praying, she noticed someone slip into the

pew across the aisle from her. She glanced over and smiled when she saw it was George.

They nodded to each other and both turned their thoughts back to their reason for being there—God.

George knelt down and offered up his prayers, too. As the hours of the long, pain-filled night had passed, he'd come to believe that the end might be sooner than he'd thought. Dr. Murray had said he had up to six months—but now he realized that "up to" were the key words in that sentence. He'd thought he'd just overworked himself yesterday, but now he was realizing he was more than just sore and tired. He'd come to Mass to pray for guidance on how to handle things, and then he was going to go home and take another pain pill. He didn't like relying on them, but if that was what it took to get him through the day, then that was what he would do.

Barely controlled fear ate at him as he offered up his prayers. He'd hoped to just drop dead one day and be done with it. He was looking forward to going to heaven and being with God, but he was suddenly concerned that he might linger in pain for a long time—weeks, maybe a month or two, and the thought of being helpless and miserable and hopeless terrified him.

He'd always been strong.

He'd always been the one who'd helped others.

He'd never needed help.

*Pride is one of the seven deadly sins.*

The thought slipped into his mind, and he couldn't help grinning at the revelation.

George didn't know if it was the Holy Spirit talking

to him or his guardian angel, but he'd heard the voice in his head many times in his life and knew the wisdom and insight it always offered.

"Blessed are the meek," George prayed silently, appreciating the heads-up that God had just given him. "And please give me the strength to be meek," he added, smiling to himself again.

He would try to accept whatever came his way graciously and do whatever was necessary to deal with it.

Father Richards began Mass then, and George turned his full attention to the altar.

When Mass had ended, George and Lydia left church together, making small talk. They saw Father Richards talking with parishioners in the greeting area and went to say hello.

"Lydia, I can't tell you how delighted I am with your lead story today," the priest told her, smiling at both of them.

"What's your lead story?" George asked.

"We covered the Good Samaritan today," she answered.

"The Good Samaritan?" He was puzzled.

"You know, the secret philanthropist who's been helping out those in need around town," Lydia said. "Nobody knows who it is—except, of course, Father here, and he's not talking."

"That's right. My word is my honor. I promised not to reveal the Good Samaritan's identity."

"Surely there's some way Lydia can get it out of you," George teased. "She's one fabulous investigative reporter."

"Yes, she is, but I think it should be up to the Good

Samaritan to reveal him or herself. What was done in the paper this morning was excellent. You'll have to get a copy and take a look, George."

"I've got it at home, I just didn't stop to look at the paper this morning."

"Let me know what you think, George. I felt so good putting something uplifting on the front page today," Lydia told him.

"You decided? Where was your editor?"

"He called in sick, so I got to make the decisions yesterday."

"Well, I'm glad you did," Father said. "The world needs more good news. Keep it up."

"I'll try."

They all moved off, ready to get on with the day.

"See you at prayer Wednesday night," George told her as they went outside.

"I'll be there," Lydia promised, looking forward to it.

When George got home, he unwrapped his newspaper and sat down to read Lydia's article. The headline touched him deeply.

"Secret Good Samaritan Has the Power to Change Lives! Anonymous Donor Saves Animal Shelter and Homeless Family!"

His heart swelled with emotion as he read the interviews with Bonnie Zimmerman and Cheryl Hall. It was good to know he'd truly made a difference.

Now he just hoped Lydia didn't suffer any consequences for doing something different with the front page. He hoped, too, that if she got good feedback on the article, her editor would loosen up and let her do more articles of this nature.

The sniper was outraged as he stared down at the front page of *The Daily Sun*. The headline was about some idiot Good Samaritan who was giving his money away, and the byline was Lydia Chandler's!

Where was *he*?

Where was the headline about his shooting and the dog he'd killed with his bare hands?

Where was the news about *him*?

The sniper was shaking as he threw down the newspaper. As soon as his arm was healed, he'd show them. The authorities thought he'd been dangerous in the past, but they hadn't seen anything yet. He'd be on the front page again. There was no doubt about it.

Lydia was just entering the office when Rose, the switchboard operator, called out to her.

"You're not going to believe it!"

"Believe what?" Lydia wondered.

"The number of phone calls I've gotten this morning, thanking us for running the Good Samaritan story on the front page. Everyone was saying how sick they were of hearing about the horrible sniper."

"Did you keep track of the number of calls?"

"Yes, I did. So far, and it's still early, I've had sixteen people call in. If they're taking the time out of their busy mornings to call me, I wonder how many e-mails we're getting?"

"I'll check it out and let you know. Thanks!"

Lydia was flying high as she went into her office. Her instincts had been right! They hadn't had this kind of positive reaction to an article in ages. She couldn't wait to let Sandy know when she came in.

Sitting down at her desk, Lydia booted up the e-mail service and printed out all the letters that had been sent to the paper complimenting them on the coverage of the anonymous donor.

*"Nice lead story . . ."*

*"Thank you for the uplifting coverage . . ."*

*"It was great to have a morning headline that didn't leave me hysterical . . ."*

Lydia was going to show them all to Gary when he showed up—whenever that would be. She didn't know if he'd recovered enough from the flu to come in today or not.

She had no more than formulated the thought when she heard him shouting in the outer office and realized what she was about to face.

"Where the hell is she?" Gary yelled as he came charging through the main office area, a man in a rage. He stopped when he caught sight of her seated at her desk. He stood there glaring at her through the glass partition.

Lydia met his hate-filled regard straight on.

"Get into my office now, Chandler!" he exploded, storming off to his office.

Serenely Lydia gathered up the e-mails and followed him.

All those who were already at work looked on in sympathy. They could only imagine what she was going to face this morning.

Gary was standing by the door, waiting for her to enter. Once she was in, he slammed the door behind her and stalked over to stand behind his desk. He glared at her.

"What did you think you were doing!" he demanded waving the front page at her.

"You put me in charge. I ran with the story I thought best for the front page." She met his regard coolly and without flinching.

"You cleared the sniper headline with me. I wanted the sniper story there on page one! It should have been our lead story. That's what you told me you were running!"

"I had a change of heart. I thought this would make a better lead story, and the feedback is coming in already," Lydia told him.

"What are you talking about?" he seethed.

"There have already been sixteen phone calls saying how much readers liked the article this morning, and at least twenty-five e-mails already—and it's only eight-thirty!"

"You probably sent them yourself," he raged hatefully.

"I did not," she denied. "I didn't have to. I know what the public wants, and I gave it to them."

"That's only forty-one people out of a hundred thousand. Who knows how many sales we lost because of your idiocy!"

"Watch it," she snapped back at him.

"Listen to me, Lydia. If we don't stay on the sniper

story, it will never get solved. The cops aren't capable of solving it. They're totally useless! They can't figure it out."

"Why do you hate the police department so much?" Lydia challenged.

"Why do you *love* them so much?" he shot back. "Oh, wait, I know. You've got the hots for that detective, Steve Mason!"

"Gary—" There was an even harder edge to her voice as she somehow controlled her temper.

"The police aren't doing their job. They've proven it over and over again. How many dead bodies have to litter the streets before they catch this sniper? Good old Detective Mason doesn't have a clue! I'm beginning to think the cops couldn't find the shooter if he was delivered by UPS to police headquarters in a labeled box!"

"You are way out of line."

"Am I?" he went on, irate. "Am I? We—the taxpayers—pay the cops' salaries! They're supposed to protect us and keep us safe, and they're not doing it! I do my job." He paused and looked at Lydia with a cold-eyed glare. Then he suddenly smiled, an icy smile. "Too bad you didn't do yours!"

"What are you talking about?"

"You're fired, Lydia. Get your things and get out of the office—my office. *Now!*"

Lydia couldn't help herself. Gary was so over the top with his rage that she started laughing, which only made him more furious.

"Did you hear me?" he snarled, leaning over his desk in a threatening manner.

"Oh, yeah. I heard you," she answered, still trying to stop laughing.

"What are you laughing about? What's so funny?"

She looked straight at him as she replied, "You are! I'm laughing at you!"

"What!" He almost came at her physically.

"You sounded just like Donald Trump on his TV show—'You're fired,'" she imitated.

"Get out of here now!"

Gary stormed around his desk toward her and grabbed her by the arm to physically shove her out the door.

But Lydia wasn't about to let him manhandle her. She swung out at him. "Don't touch me!"

She landed several solid blows, hitting him in the arm as hard as she could to break free of his painful grip. She was shocked when he actually seemed to wince in pain from her attack, for she knew that, compared to a man, she wasn't very strong.

"Get out!" Gary ordered. He shoved her toward the door.

"No problem."

Lydia left his office.

"Lydia?" Sandy said, terrified at having witnessed their argument. "Are you all right?"

Sandy had come in with several other reporters, and they were standing around in shock.

"I'm fine. Just fine," Lydia replied. She stopped at her

desk only long enough to grab her few personal possessions.

She started to leave, then turned to look straight at Gary, who was still standing there watching her from his office doorway.

"I don't need you, Gary. I can get a job anywhere in this town in the blink of an eye. I'm an award-winning journalist. What are you?"

He was seething as he watched her go. When she'd left, he realized all the other newspaper employees were standing around staring at him.

"What are you looking at? Get back to work or I'll fire you, too!"

They quickly got busy, not wanting to face his wrath that day.

# Chapter Twenty-six

Lydia was deep in thought as she drove home. She'd expected repercussions from Gary, but she hadn't anticipated he would react so violently. She shook her head in confusion. She'd always known he was a bully, but to manhandle her that way at the office was positively bizarre.

And then there was the way Gary had flinched when she'd struck back at him. She couldn't believe he was that much of a wuss.

Lydia frowned.

He'd called in sick yesterday—

And today his arm had been sore—

Lydia was shocked by a possibility that, until this moment, had never occurred to her.

She found herself holding her breath as she thought of it.

*There was no way it was possible.*

*No way—*

*Or was there?*

Lydia actually found herself trembling as she reached home and went inside. She knew what she had to do. Not too long ago she'd checked on Gary's background. Now she was going to dig even deeper. She had to know more about this man. She had to find out if her instincts were right.

*If Gary was the sniper, it would explain a lot.*

First, though, she wanted to talk to Steve and tell him what had happened at work. She called his office, but he was out, so she left him a message to call her.

Lydia went online and e-mailed Sandy, asking her to either fax or e-mail her a copy of Gary's resumé right away. Then she went back to the website where she'd gotten the info on Gary the first time she'd checked on him. She made notes about the newspapers in Chicago and Denver that he'd worked for.

When the e-mail from Sandy came with his resumé, Lydia found additional references to a newspaper in Phoenix, another in Anaheim and several others in various cities. The information about the Phoenix paper excited Lydia, for Heather, one of her friends from college, worked there now. She called Heather at her office. When she got her voice mail, she left a message, telling her she was working on an important story and needed her help right away. She let her know what information she was looking for and asked her to call back ASAP.

Lydia checked out each of the other newspapers' websites to get contact information. When possible, she jotted down phone numbers, wanting to call rather than e-mail. She e-mailed the other papers, telling them Gary had applied for a job at her company and asking them about his work record as a reference.

Once she was off-line, Lydia started making calls. She began with Chicago. Human Resources confirmed he'd worked there for a short time right out of college, but they knew nothing more than that, since it had been so long ago. Her next contact was the paper in Anaheim. The person she spoke with remembered Gary clearly.

"He was a character, all right," Will Martin, the editor of the paper, told her. "He applied at the Police Academy first and was admitted, but couldn't make the grade, so he came to us. We hired him on and he worked his way up to an assistant editor before he moved on. That was quite a few years ago. How's he doing now?"

"He's here as editor of *The Daily Sun*."

"Well, tell him I said 'hi.' "

"I will."

*Police Academy—*

*Gary had gotten into a Police Academy and failed—*

The evidence was coming together in a frightening way, but Lydia knew she had to wait for more answers. She couldn't jump to a conclusion yet. True, it might take a while to hear back from everyone, but that didn't matter. What mattered was learning the truth about Gary and his past.

The phone rang a short time later, and Lydia was delighted to find it was Steve.

"What are you doing at home? Are you sick?" he asked, worried about her.

"No. I'm not sick. Gary fired me!" she told him.

"He what?" Steve was shocked by the news.

"He fired me first thing this morning. He was in a real rage."

"I can't believe it."

"Neither can I, but it happened, so don't try to call me at the office anymore. I won't be there."

"All right. I'm glad you let me know. Listen, Charlie and I are in the middle of some work here, so I've got to go. I'll give you a call later this afternoon. How's that?"

"Talk to you then."

Lydia didn't even consider mentioning her suspicions about Gary to Steve just yet. She was conducting her investigation, and until she had something more concrete to go on than her gut instinct, she wasn't going to the cops.

With nothing more to do but wait, Lydia let herself relax for a little while.

By mid-afternoon, she'd heard back from another one of the papers. She was told that Gary had never worked there in any kind of editorial capacity. He'd been there merely as a part-time beat reporter—a far cry from what he'd claimed on his resumé. Just as Lydia had thought on more than one occasion, Gary was proving to be quite a fiction writer—and this time where his resumé was concerned.

It was late afternoon when Steve called back.

"How about going out to dinner tonight?" Steve invited, thinking that after the day she'd had, she might want to get away for a while.

"Thanks, but I think I'm just going to stay home tonight. I'm still a little upset over what happened today, and I've got some things I have to work out." She hadn't heard from any of the other sources yet, and she didn't want to risk missing their calls.

"Oh—okay." Steve was surprised she'd turned him down. But when he thought about it, he realized she probably needed time alone to lick her wounds and get over the trauma of losing her job. It had to be hard on her, being let go that way. "I'll talk to you tomorrow."

Lydia regretted not being able to spend time with Steve, but right then her investigation was more important. She had to get to the bottom of this—and fast.

"Thanks for driving me over, Dad," Jim told his father as he pulled into the driveway at George's house.

"I wanted to know where you were going to be, and I want to meet Mr. Taylor before you start working for him."

"Do you have to?" Jim asked, a little embarrassed that his father had to check on him so closely. "He's with the youth group. He's the guy I told you about who's got the old Mustang."

"I know, and that's great, but you're my son, and I need to know you're safe."

Jim just grunted and got out of the car. He started up the walk toward the front door, leaving his father to follow him.

Duchess barked when the doorbell rang, and George mustered enough energy to get out of his recliner chair and answer the door. He went out on the porch to speak with his visitors, shutting Duchess inside.

"Well, hi, Jim. Glad you could make it today," he welcomed him. "And who do we have here?" He knew it had to be the boy's father coming up the walk.

"George, this is my dad, Paul Hunt. Dad, this is George."

"It's nice to meet you, George."

The two men shook hands.

"I appreciate your bringing Jim over. I've been a little under the weather lately and can't seem to get all my yard work done. I'm glad Jim's interested in taking on the job."

"He's a hard worker. If you need anything else, just let us know," Paul told him.

"Thanks. Do you want to take a look around the yard with us?"

"No, I've got some errands to run. How long do you think it will take him to finish? I'll stop back by and pick him up."

"About an hour, maybe an hour and a half," George answered.

"I'll see you then." Paul looked at Jim. "Work hard, son."

"I will, Dad."

George and Jim walked around to the backyard. George showed him where the mower and other yard tools were in the shed and turned him loose.

"If you need any help with anything, just come in the back door and get me."

"Are you sure you want me to walk right in that way?"

"It'll be fine. You like dogs, don't you? Duchess won't

give you a minute's peace. She'll try to lick you to death," he chuckled, knowing how affectionate she was.

"That's cool."

"Get to work," George told him, smiling.

Jim did just that. He found he liked being his own boss. He knew what he had to do. He knew how long he had to get it done. Yard work wasn't easy, but Jim could definitely see the difference when he finished, and he was pleased.

"George?" he called out as he let himself in the house.

Duchess barked and ran to greet him. Jim stopped to pet her.

"Are you all finished?" George asked as he got up from where he'd been reading in the living room.

"Yes, sir." Jim was just coming out of the kitchen with Duchess by his side.

"How about a cool drink? I've got some soda."

"Thanks."

George got him a can of soda from the refrigerator and gave it to him. "I'm going to take a look around and see if there's anything you missed. Since this is your first time, I want to make sure."

Jim followed him outside, and he noticed how slowly the older man was moving. He wondered why. At the youth group meeting, George had been lively and seemed to enjoy himself. Now it looked as if he was in a lot of pain.

"Are you okay?" Jim asked.

George managed a smile for him. "Some days I'm older than others." He gave a short laugh.

Jim smiled, guessing he meant he was just a little stiff and sore that day.

George took a quick look around and was completely satisfied with Jim's work. "I'm impressed. You did a good job."

"Thanks."

"Shall we go sit on the front porch and wait for your dad to come back?"

"Sure."

"I'll let Duchess out so she can sit with us."

They settled on the cushioned wicker chairs to relax and talk for a while.

"So tell me, Jim. I know you're new to the youth group. Why did you decide to join up?"

Jim looked a little embarrassed as he answered, "My parents made me."

"I'm glad they did, but you don't sound very happy about it. The kids in the youth group are a fun bunch. You made some new friends there, didn't you?"

"Yeah. They were nice, and I work with Rob, so at least I knew him to start with."

"That was good."

"I would never have had to join, though, if I hadn't gotten into trouble," Jim admitted, deciding to open up to George so he'd know the whole truth about him.

"What happened?" George had heard a little of the story from Phyllis, but he wanted to hear Jim's version. He seemed like a real good kid at heart. George liked him.

Jim took a deep breath and told him the whole story,

including the fact that his parents were making him repay them. "I was stupid."

"No, you're not a stupid boy, you just made a stupid choice that day. Now you're paying for it, that's all."

"I guess."

"Did you learn your lesson?"

"Yes, but some of the guys were up at the show last weekend, and they tried to pick a fight with me while I was working."

"What did you do? How'd you handle it?"

"Thanks to Rob's being there with me, I didn't do anything. I just took it. I tried to ignore them."

"Good for you. You did learn."

"I don't know why I cared about hanging around with those guys. I don't know why I thought I needed to impress them."

"Trust me, that kind of stuff is normal for teenagers. My son went through some hard times in high school, too."

"You have a son? Where is he?" Jim asked, surprised by the news.

George managed a sad smile. "My boy, Alex, died when he was in his late twenties. He had a heart condition."

Jim looked up at him and said, "I'm sorry."

"So am I. Alex was a good boy, and he had to deal with a lot in his short life, so I know he's happier where he is right now."

Jim frowned.

"In heaven."

"Oh."

George realized their conversation was too serious. He wanted to enjoy Jim's presence. "Want to go take a look at the Mustang?"

Jim's eyes lit up. "You bet!"

When Paul returned to pick up his son a short time later, he found Jim and George in the garage toying with the Mustang.

"Jim told me you had one of these. It's really a beauty," Paul said as he admired the car.

"It's my pride and joy. I take it up to the youth group meetings every now and then to let the kids have a look at it."

"And I bet they go crazy."

"They do," George affirmed.

"We'd better get going. It's a school night," Paul said.

"Jim did a good job on the yard, so I'd like him to show up every week."

"That's great." Paul was glad Jim had done a good job.

"Here's your money, Jim. Give me a call over the weekend when you know your work schedule at the show, and we'll figure out what day you can come over next week."

"I will, and thanks, George." Jim was surprised when George gave him twenty-five dollars.

"No, thank *you*. It's good to have someone I can trust. I'll see you next week."

George watched until Jim and his dad had driven away; then he went back inside. He sat down heavily. He was surprised he'd managed to move around as much as he had with Jim and his dad, but it had been fun.

He was paying the price now, though, as exhaustion claimed him. He closed his eyes wearily, too tired to move and barely able to think.

*The end was coming much faster than he'd thought—*

*He had to get his affairs in order—*

He had spoken with his attorney that morning and had arranged for a sizable donation to be sent to St. Francis de Sales church for the roof fund. He was glad he'd taken care of that, but now he realized, there were still a few other things he needed to attend to—

Duchess nuzzled his hand, sensing something wasn't right.

"It's okay, sweetheart." He petted her, enjoying the peace that came from her nearness and devotion. "It's okay."

George closed his eyes to rest and try to regain some strength. When he felt a little stronger, he would call the attorney back and make arrangements for two of the most important parts of his life—Duchess and the Mustang.

# *Chapter Twenty-seven*

*Lord, Hear Our Prayer . . .*

Lydia passed a restless night. By five a.m. she was wide awake, so she got up and dressed to attend early Mass. She knew she would need help today if she was going to break this case wide open.

When Lydia reached Holy Family, she was surprised to find that George wasn't there. He was a regular, so that was unusual for him. She hoped nothing was wrong. She hoped he was just sleeping late that morning. After Mass, she hurried home to take up her vigil, waiting for Heather's return call. It was after ten a.m. when her friend finally called.

"Lydia? It's Heather. How are you?"

"I'm fine," Lydia said, not wanting to go into what had happened yesterday at the office. "What about you?"

"Things are going great out here. I love it."

They spoke of social things for a few minutes, rehashing some of their college adventures, and then got down to business.

"I checked into this Gary Newman for you, and, believe me, if you're working with him—watch out."

"What are you talking about?"

"I talked to some of the reporters who worked with him here, and according to them, Newman was a real freak."

"What do you mean?"

"They said he was vile to work with. He had nearly violent mood swings. The guys said he was on them constantly and would push them to make things up if they didn't have what they needed for a story."

That news didn't surprise Lydia. "What else?"

"According to the women who remember him, he sexually harassed one female reporter to the point that she taped some of his phone calls to her and hired a lawyer to go after him. Everybody said she kept referring to Gary Newman as 'that little weasel'! Newman quit the paper and left town once she'd gotten the lawyer."

"What a low-life," Lydia sympathized.

"Exactly."

"Is she around so I could talk to her?"

"She quit the paper and left the state."

"Who could blame her?"

"Yeah, everybody here said Newman seemed angry all the time, like he was filled with a deep, driving rage, but nobody could figure out why, and, to tell you the truth, nobody really cared. They were just glad he was gone. Does that help you any?"

"Yes. It does. I appreciate it. I've got another question for you."

"All right."

"Could you check and see if anyone in the office remembers what kind of car Gary was driving when he worked there?"

"Hang on a sec while I ask around." Heather put the phone down and went out to ask some of the other reporters. It didn't take her long. "Consensus has it that he drove a dark green Taurus. Does that help?"

"Oh, yeah." Lydia couldn't believe it—a dark green sedan! "I owe you big time, girlfriend."

"I'll hold you to that! Good luck, and let me know what happens with your investigation."

"Don't worry. I will—and one last thing. What was the name of the woman Gary harrassed there at the paper?"

"They said her name was Barb Landon."

Lydia was shocked. The sniper's third victim had been named Barbara Landon.

*It fit.*

*It all fit—the rejection by the Police Academy—the rejection by a woman.*

"Thanks, Heather."

Lydia knew she had to verify one more thing before she could notify Steve. She called Sandy.

"*Daily Sun*. How can I help you?"

"Sandy, it's Lydia. Listen, did Gary come into the office today?"

"Oh, yeah," she answered miserably. "He's here. I should have been so lucky that he'd stay home sick again."

"Thanks. That's all I needed to know."

"What's up?"

"I'll get back to you."

Lydia hung up the phone. She was an investigative reporter, and that was exactly what she was going to do right now—investigate. Now that she was certain Gary was at work, she could head over to his house and take a look around. She especially wanted to take a look in his garage. She knew he drove a blue car to work these days, but if there was a green sedan parked in his garage—

Lydia knew it was time to fill Steve in on what she'd turned up on Gary. She called Steve at headquarters and got his voice mail.

"Steve, this is Lydia. I think I'm on to something important. I have a suspicion that Gary Newman, the editor at *The Daily Sun*, might be the sniper. I've been doing some checking and I've found a lot of strange, erratic behavior in his past and a connection to one of the victims, not to mention a lot of lies. Gary's at work this morning, so I'm going over to his house right now to take a look around. If there's a green sedan parked in his garage, we may have our man. He's not tall, he's white, he keeps his hair short, and his arm was sore yesterday. I'll let you know what I find out." She left Steve Gary's street address and got ready to leave.

Sandy had been busy at her desk, but she got up to go check on a reference and noticed that Gary wasn't in his office.

"Where's Gary?" she asked one of the other reporters.

"He said he wasn't feeling good again. He said he was going home to rest for a while and then he'd be back."

"Great," Sandy muttered.

Sandy remembered Lydia asking about Gary's whereabouts, and decided she should give her friend a heads-up that he had left the office. She called Lydia at home and left her a message. She had a lot to do, so she didn't give it any further thought and went back to work.

Lydia was grimly determined as she drove to Gary's house. She was aware of the surveillance cop following her at a respectable distance and was reassured. If anything did go wrong, he'd be close by to help out.

Lydia parked on the street in front of the house, for she didn't want to do anything that might look suspicious. She wanted any neighbors who might be watching to think she was stopping by for a visit. She locked her purse and cell phone in the car so she wouldn't have to worry about them while she was snooping around.

Going up to the front porch, Lydia rang the doorbell and waited. She knew no one would answer, so it was a perfectly safe ploy. She looked around and noticed the drapes were tightly drawn; there would be no getting a look inside. She waited a moment longer, as if hoping someone might come to the door, then walked around to the back of the house to check out the detached garage. This was the moment she'd been waiting for. She just hoped she could get a look inside.

The garage was an older building with only one window high up on the side. It was going to be tricky getting a look inside, but the good news was, the window was hung with only a half-curtain.

Lydia was ready for the challenge. She looked around and saw a filthy old trash can up against the house. She pulled it over and situated it beneath the window, then climbed on top of it. It was a precarious perch, but she managed to balance herself as she peered in the garage.

There wasn't a lot of light inside, but there was no mistaking the dark green color of the sedan locked up there.

Steve had called in to headquarters to check his messages. The first message intrigued him and he returned it immediately.

"Marrett and Downing, Attorneys at Law," the receptionist said.

"This is Detective Steve Mason. I'm returning Mr. Downing's call."

"One moment, please."

"This is Sean Downing."

"Mr. Downing, this is Detective Mason."

"Thanks for getting back to me so quickly. I don't know if this is of any interest to you in your investigation of the sniper shootings in your area, but I just realized when I heard the victim's names that one of them had been a client of mine a few years ago. Ms. Barbara Landon had been sexually harrassed by a man named Gary Newman at the newspaper where she worked here in town. He was quite obsessed with her. She quit her job and left the state to get away from him."

"His name was Newman?" Steve repeated, shocked by the revelation.

"That's right. I don't know his whereabouts now, but it might be worth looking into."

"Thanks, Mr. Downing. I'll be in touch."

Steve hung up. *They had it! Gary Newman was connected to one of the victims!*

He quickly listened to his next voice mail. It was from Lydia, telling him of her suspicion about Gary, and he immediately knew what he had to do. He called Lydia at home, and, as he'd expected, he got her machine. Next, he tried her cell phone, but she didn't answer. Troubled, he called the officer who had her under surveillance.

"This is Officer Jacobs."

"This is Steve Mason. I've been trying to get hold of Lydia Chandler, and she's not answering her phone. Do you know where she is?"

"Yes, she's at a house on Sycamore."

"What's she doing?"

"Well, she went up to the front door and when nobody answered, she went around back."

"Can you see her right now?"

"No, but there's no one else around. It's a quiet neighborhood."

"Don't trust it. Don't let her out of your sight! The man who lives there might be the sniper. I'll be there in five minutes." Steve broke off the communication and concentrated on his driving. He had a bad feeling about this.

* * *

Lydia was excited and scared as she climbed down off the trash can.

Gary was their man—

Gary really was the sniper—

No wonder he wanted all those front-page stories about the sniper!

No wonder he always wanted to make the sniper look smart and the cops look stupid!

Wanting to get in touch with Steve right away, Lydia started around to the front. She wanted to let him know he would need a search warrant to get into the garage and inspect the vehicle. She thanked God that Gary was still at work. That way they could get this done before he had any idea that they were on to him. There was no telling what kind of trouble might erupt if Gary got wind that the police were closing in on him.

Lydia was hurrying around the corner of the house when, to her shock and horror, Gary pulled into the driveway in the blue sedan she'd always believed was his only car.

Gary saw Lydia at the same instant, and his expression turned thunderous. He stopped right in front of her and put his car in park. He had no idea what she was doing at his house, but he intended to find out. He turned off the engine, then very carefully reached out and got his handgun out of his console. He put it in his pocket and got out of the car.

Lydia had been standing frozen in place as she watched him park and get out of the car to confront her. Panic threatened to overwhelm her. Her instincts were telling her to run and find a hiding place, but she knew it was too late. Gary had seen her, so she had to deal with him.

Lydia realized she was about to find out just how good an actress she was. She desperately hoped she was Academy Award material. Deciding to play out her role as a pitiful ex-employee who desperately wanted her job back, she took the initiative and walked toward the car, her expression serious.

"What the hell are you doing here?" he demanded.

"Looking for you," she said. "Since you stayed home sick yesterday, I thought you'd be home again today."

"You're lucky I decided to take part of the day off." He looked at her suspiciously. "What do you want?"

Lydia dropped her gaze from his and drew a ragged breath, before looking up again. "I want to apologize."

"You? Apologize?" He was surprised. She was usually annoyingly certain of herself.

"That's right. I was out of line yesterday. You are the boss, and I shouldn't have blown up at you the way I did. I've learned a lot from you during the time we've worked together." Silently she admitted to herself that that wasn't really a lie.

"Yeah, you learned how to annoy me." He was watching her suspiciously, trying to figure out if she was lying or being honest. Something just didn't ring true about what she was feeding him.

"Let's just say we both kept each other on our toes," she offered. "But anyway, I wanted to let you know I was sorry for what happened. I didn't want to part ways like that."

She started to move on down the driveway past him, knowing she should get away. The officer who had her under surveillance must be close by, and she wanted to move into the street, where she could see him and be seen.

Gary was studying her carefully, almost believing her, until he noticed how she glanced down the street.

"Lydia, what were you doing in my backyard?"

"Looking for you. When you didn't answer the door, I thought you might be out back." She sensed his growing disbelief and got ready to take off. "I'll see you later, Gary. I've got to go now."

She started past him, but he was ready for her move. He grabbed her by the arm and held her in a viselike grip.

"You're not going anywhere, my little investigative reporter—"

"What are you doing? Let me go." She tried to pull free, but he had too good a hold on her.

"I'm not a mushroom, Lydia," Gary sneered, smiling a cold, deadly smile at her. "You can't feed me bullshit and keep me in the dark."

"What are you talking about?"

"Come on. You wanted to visit with me. Fine, we'll visit—inside."

He started up the driveway, almost dragging her along.

"No!" Lydia started to fight him. She deliberately turned and hit him as hard as she could in his wounded arm.

"You bitch!" He slapped her and kept moving up the driveway, wanting to get out of sight.

"Hold it right there!" Officer Jacobs shouted as he appeared at the end of the driveway.

"What is it, Officer?" Gary asked, looking over at the cop.

"You're under arrest," Officer Jacobs stated, watching him cautiously.

"For what?"

"Personal assault. Release Ms. Chandler *now!*"

"She's my girlfriend," he lied. "We're just having a little fight—"

"You heard me, sir. Release Ms. Chandler and step away from her now."

Gary didn't hesitate to act. He reached into his pocket for his handgun and turned on the officer.

# *Chapter Twenty-eight*

Lydia was struggling to break free from Gary. She was desperately hoping he would follow the officer's orders.

"Gary! You heard the officer. Let me go."

"Never," he snarled.

It was then that she saw the gun in his hand, and her desperation turned to pure terror.

"Look out!" she shouted to alert the officer.

She threw herself at Gary with all her might, hoping to jar him and make him miss.

The officer started to dive for cover, but Gary managed to get his shot off in time. Gary watched in satisfaction as the officer collapsed and lay unmoving in the driveway.

Lydia screamed in horror and tried to resist as Gary dragged her toward the house. Gary knew some of his neighbors would have heard the shot and would be calling the cops, so he had to get her inside.

Steve had suspected there might be trouble and deliberately approached Gary Newman's house from the side street. He'd just gotten out of the car when he'd heard the gunshot. He'd immediately radioed for backup and rushed through the yard, gun in hand, to check out the situation. He didn't know who'd fired the shot. He hoped it had been Officer Jacobs, but even so, he found himself silently praying that Lydia was all right.

Staying close to the shrubs, Steve moved quickly and furtively around the back of the house. He came upon Gary trying to force Lydia inside.

"Hold it right there, Newman!"

At the sound of Steve's commanding order from behind them, relief flooded through Lydia.

Steve was there!

Everything would be all right!

Gary recognized Steve's voice instantly and was shocked that her cop boyfriend had shown up. He swore loudly and spun around, holding his gun on Lydia as he faced Steve.

"So, Lydia, it looks like your cop boyfriend has finally shown up to save you," he taunted. He enjoyed knowing that she was trembling as he held her pinned against him. He knew he was all-powerful now. He'd already killed one cop. He had a gun on Lydia, and soon he'd have her boyfriend begging for her life. He smiled. Life really was good some days.

"Release her now," Steve directed in a cold, authoritative voice without taking his gaze off Gary. He'd dealt with his kind before and knew this was a deadly situation.

"In your dreams," Gary sneered as he backed ever

closer to the house. "I've got her, and there's not a damned thing you can do about it."

"That's where you're wrong, Newman. I've already called for backup. We know you're the sniper. We know about your connection to one of the victims. We know you flunked out of the Police Academy. We know you're a total loser, and right now, you're going to lose again," Steve taunted him. If he could get a reaction out of him, he might be able to get the drop on him. He couldn't let any harm come to Lydia.

"That's what you think!" Gary hissed, growing red in the face at Steve's insults. "I've got my gun and I've got your woman. There's no way I can lose."

"You want to bet?" Steve said, taking a step closer.

Gary backed slowly toward the house.

Lydia was filled with terror as Gary pressed the gun ever more tightly to her side. She lifted her gaze to Steve's and saw the look of steely determination in his eyes. They shared a look of understanding, and she realized what she had to do. Gary's hold on her was fierce, but she knew his arm still had to be sore from the dog attack. That would be his weak spot, and hitting him there would be her only hope of breaking free before he managed to drag her inside the house. If she didn't try to escape right now, she doubted she would survive the coming showdown.

Lydia knew it was up to her to take action. She looked straight at Steve as Gary continued to back toward the house and gave him a quick nod.

With all the force she could muster, Lydia jammed

her elbow into Gary's injured forearm and pushed herself away from him.

Gary had been so intent on keeping an eye on Steve as he backed toward the house that he was caught off guard by the painful jab. For an instant, her attack stunned him, and in that instant, she fiercely tried to tear herself from his tight grip.

Gary struggled to keep a hold on her, but in the fighting, his gun went off.

Steve didn't hesitate. He fired at Gary.

The bullet slammed into Gary's shoulder. His gun flew from his grip, and he collapsed, bleeding heavily on the ground.

Steve ran forward and grabbed up Gary's weapon. He checked to make sure Gary wasn't going anywhere, then started to rush to Lydia's side. She'd fallen to the ground when Gary's gun had gone off, and he feared she'd been wounded. His concern for her safety vanished, though, when she started to move and get up on her own.

"Lydia—you're all right?" Relief filled him. He holstered his gun and quickly helped her up.

"Don't worry about me! I'm all right. Gary shot Officer Jacobs out front!"

Steve cast one last quick look at the moaning and groaning Gary.

"Do you know how to use a gun?" he asked.

"I think so."

Steve handed her Gary's weapon. "Keep an eye on him."

He ran around front to the end of the driveway where Officer Jacobs lay, bleeding. Steve turned the wounded policeman over and applied pressure to his wound to stop the bleeding. As he was tending to him, a patrol car pulled up, along with an ambulance.

"Here, take over!" Steve ordered, turning Jacobs's care over to the paramedics. Then he directed the other officers. "The shooter is around back."

They ran with Steve back to where Lydia was standing guard over Gary. Steve carefully took the gun from her and handed it over to the patrolmen.

"He's the sniper," he informed them.

"Good work, Detective Mason," the officers complimented him.

Gary was groaning as they took him into custody. An EMT came up to treat him so he could be transported.

Neighbors came out of their houses to watch the police in action.

Gary was enough aware of his surroundings to look at Lydia with unbridled hatred as the EMT worked on him. "I'm not done with you yet, you bitch!"

Lydia didn't cower before him. She knew even more now what a pitiful excuse for a man he was.

"Yes, you are," she told him, looking him straight in the eye.

"Get him out of here," Steve ordered.

He stood by Lydia's side, watching as they carted Gary away. One of the other patrolmen came to speak with them.

"How's Jacobs?" Steve asked, worried.

"He lost some blood, but his wound isn't life-threatening. He should be all right."

"Thank God," Lydia breathed, beginning to tremble again as her momentary rush of courage gave way to the realization of what she'd just been through.

Steve slipped a supportive arm around her. "Are you sure you're all right? Do you want to go to the hospital, too?"

"No—no, I'm fine." She leaned against him, appreciating his strength supporting her. She looked up at him. "Thank you," she said in a breathless, emotional voice. "You saved me."

At that moment, Steve didn't care that he was on duty. He didn't care that there were fellow officers around. All he cared about was that she was unhurt. He held her close and bent down to kiss her right there in front of everybody.

"You're my hero, you know," she told him, still clinging to him when they ended the kiss.

"I'm just thankful I got here in time," he said, then managed a half-grin as he got ready to scold her. "But I have to ask, why did you come to his house all by yourself? Why didn't you wait until I could come with you?"

"I was on a roll with the investigation. I left you a message before I came here. I didn't think Gary would show up. I called the paper, and my friend said he was there at work, so I thought it would be safe to take a look around."

"I guess you found out different, didn't you?"

"Yes, Detective," she told him, suitably chastened.

"Don't let this happen again," Steve said.

"Yes, Detective, but we don't have to worry about that. You've got him. You arrested the sniper!"

"Yes," he said with satisfaction, quickly explaining to her how he'd received the phone call from the lawyer informing him of the connection between the female victim and Gary and how he'd been on his way to investigate Gary further when he'd gotten her call. "We did."

Charlie showed up on the scene then, and Steve realized he had to get back to work. The media people would be showing up at any moment, and he had to be ready to handle the onslaught.

Lydia called Sandy at the newspaper to tell her what had happened.

"You can't be serious." Sandy was in shock. "I knew he was a sleazeball, but I had no idea—"

"That was the problem, no one else did either. But now *The Daily Sun* doesn't have an editor. You'd better call the owners."

"I will, and you might as well get in here and start working on tomorrow morning's lead story."

"Are you saying I've got my old job back?" Lydia asked, smiling.

"As far as I'm concerned, you never left. Hurry up! We've got deadlines to meet!"

Lydia sought out Steve where he was working on the crime scene investigation and told him she was going back to work at the newspaper.

"I want to see you tonight," he told her.

"I know. Now that the sniper's been caught, we can really be alone," Lydia said, giving him an inviting smile.

"I'll be over at seven."

"I'll be waiting for you."

Roberta DuBray, the secretary at St. Francis de Sales Church, was sorting through the morning's mail when she found an envelope addressed to their pastor, Father Whited, from an attorney. Knowing it had to be important, she hurried to give it to him right away.

"What's this?" Father Whited looked up at her, puzzled.

"I don't know. That's why I thought you'd better take a look at it right away."

Unsure what to expect, the pastor opened the envelope and took out the contents. He was startled to find a formal, legal letter informing him that an anonymous donor was contributing to the fund for the needed repairs to the church. A cashier's check for $20,000 was enclosed.

Father Whited looked up at Roberta, his expression one of complete and utter amazement. "I think a miracle just happened."

"What?"

"Look at this." He held out the check for her to see.

"Oh, my God!"

"Exactly."

"Who did it?"

"It may be the same Good Samaritan who saved the animal shelter and helped that family after the fire. The lawyer says the donor wants to remain anonymous," he informed her.

"Prayers really do get answered," Roberta said, in awe of the blessing they'd just received at the parish. Everyone had been so worried that they wouldn't be able to raise the money, and now a complete stranger had come to their aid.

"Yes," Father Whited said with certainty. "They do."

# *Chapter Twenty-nine*

*Peace Be With You . . .*

The prayer group was ready to begin, but there was still no sign of George.

"Did anybody hear from George today?" Mary asked. "Lydia called and said she couldn't make it tonight, and who could blame her after what she went through today."

"That was so terrifying," Phyllis agreed. "I saw the report on the five-o'clock news. Thank God that police detective showed up when he did. He saved Lydia and captured the sniper."

"And thank God that other officer who was shot is going to be all right."

"That is definitely good news," the others agreed.

"I'm going to give George a quick call, to see if he needs a ride or anything," Mary said.

She went out of the room to call him from the office phone. She returned a few moments later.

"There was no answer, so I guess something else came up. We'll go ahead and get started, then."

They covered the required material and then prayed before dismissing for the night. Among their closing prayers, they thanked God for all His blessings in their lives and for keeping Lydia safe from harm that day.

"If anybody sees or talks to George before I do, tell him we missed him."

"We will," they promised.

George was such a longtime, regular member of the prayer group that they were all a little concerned. It was very unusual for him not to attend or at least call if he couldn't make it. They all were hoping he was just out having fun somewhere and forgot to call.

George woke up from sleeping in his recliner chair and looked at the clock on the mantel. He couldn't believe it was after ten. He felt a moment of disorientation and panic as he tried to figure out where the time had gone. He'd been hurting at dinner time, so he'd taken a pain pill, wanting to make sure he felt better before it was time to go to prayer group—and now he'd slept through the whole thing.

Struggling to sit up straight in the recliner, George knew something was terribly, terribly wrong. He was weaker than he'd ever been in his entire life. He could barely muster the energy to push down the leg rest, let alone get up.

Disoriented and more than a little afraid, George realized he was in trouble. He'd come to know over the past few days that the end was near, and he had a feeling that he might be staring death in the face.

Once he managed to sit up straight, he paused for a moment to gather his strength, then pushed himself up out of the chair. He staggered to the door and unlocked it, then made his way weakly into the bedroom and all but collapsed on the bed.

Duchess knew something was wrong. She watched George carefully and stayed beside him as he moved. When he sprawled on the bed, she jumped on it and curled up next to him.

He was touched by her presence and managed to reach out and pet her.

"Good girl, Duchess. I need you, sweetheart."

She licked his hand and kept up her vigil.

George rested for a while, then summoned enough strength to pick up the bedside phone. He called Holy Family and entered Father Richards's extension.

"Father, this is George. I'm not feeling real well tonight, and I need to talk to you. If you could give me a call, I'd really appreciate it." He left his number and hung up.

He would wait for Father Richards's call.

There were still two important things he had to take care of.

Steve and Lydia sat together on the sofa in her living room, finishing the pizza he'd brought for dinner. They were enjoying the peace and solitude of their evening alone together.

Steve's investigation had taken far longer than he'd expected, and he hadn't arrived at Lydia's until almost nine. Since he'd been running so late, he'd picked up the pizza so they wouldn't have to go out. He wanted some time alone with her.

"You scared me today," Steve told her as he leaned back and looked over at her. "For a split second there, when I heard Gary's first gunshot, I was afraid something had happened to you. I was afraid I'd lost you."

Lydia knew it had taken a lot for Steve to admit that to her. She lifted one hand to touch his cheek adoringly. "I was never so glad to see anyone as I was to see you at that moment. I can't even imagine what would have happened if you hadn't gotten there in time."

Steve drew her to him and kissed her tenderly. "Don't even go there. You're safe now. That's all that matters."

"That's right. I'm safe and I'm here with you. It doesn't get any better than that."

They embraced again, a passionate kiss that spoke of desire and devotion. It was a long moment before they moved a bit apart.

"I know we haven't known each other all that long," Lydia began, "but I can't imagine my life without you now."

Steve smiled down at her. "I know. I feel the same way about you. I know we're still in the early stages of our relationship, but I'd like it to become more."

"I would, too, but there is one thing—one thing I need from you."

He couldn't imagine where she was going. "What?"

"Your faith. You have to go back to church with me."

"Lydia—" he started to protest, caught off guard by her request.

"Hear me out, Steve," she interrupted him. "God sent you to me. I know He did."

"How do you figure that?" Even as he argued with her, he remembered the quick prayer he'd offered up that Lydia would be safe when he'd heard Gary fire his first shot. He realized, thankfully now, that his prayer had been answered.

"Because God put you here in my life to save me, and you did."

"Lydia—"

"Steve—" she countered, smiling softly up at him. "I'm so glad you're in my life. I'm falling in love with you."

He looked down at her, seeing the truth of her emotions in the depths of her eyes. "I love you, too."

"Then you'll come back to church? You'll start going to Mass with me?" she asked, grinning up at him.

"All right. You win."

She threw herself into his arms and hugged him. "We can go in the morning."

"Tomorrow?"

"That's right. I usually go at least once during the week. I love attending seven-o'clock. It's a great way to start the day."

"We're going at seven a.m.?"

"Unless you'd like me to check at neighboring parishes to see if there's an earlier one," she teased.

"I'll pick you up at six forty-five," he promised.

Lydia looked up at him. "I am so blessed to have you in my life, Steve."

He was quiet for a moment before telling her, "I feel the same way about you."

Then he kissed her to show her just how he felt.

Father Richards saw that he had a message and checked it before retiring for the night. He listened to George's request and knew something was really wrong. He called him right back and was worried when the phone rang at least six times before George picked it up.

"Hello—" George's voice was terribly weak.

"George, this is Father Richards. Are you all right?"

"Father—I'm not good—not good at all. I need to see you. Could you come over? The front door's unlocked—" Just speaking exhausted him.

"I'm on my way, George. I'll be right there."

"Thanks." The line went dead.

Father Richards gathered what he needed for the Sacrament of the Anointing of the Sick and hurried to go to his friend.

Duchess met Father Richards at the front door and welcomed him warmly, yet she seemed anxious. He could tell that she sensed something was wrong, and he paused to pet her and try to ease her fears.

"It's all right, Duchess. Let's see how your master is doing," he told her as he started back toward the bedroom. "George?"

"Here, Father," came his barely audible reply.

Father Richards found him pale and weak on the bed. He quickly anointed him.

"I'm going to call an ambulance for you. We need to get you to the hospital."

"No—not yet," George said in a hoarse voice. "There are two things I need to take care of. Can you get me a pen and paper?"

"Right away."

Working with his pastor, George made his last wishes known.

"You'll take care of this for me?" he asked, looking at his longtime friend.

"Yes, George. I'll make sure this happens just as you've directed."

"Thanks." George closed his eyes as an overwhelming weariness consumed him.

Father Richards called for the ambulance.

# *Chapter Thirty*

The funeral Mass was crowded. The pews were filled with George's friends of all ages who wanted to say their final good-byes to a man they had loved and respected.

Teens from the youth group were there to honor him. They knew what a good friend George had been to them, and couldn't believe he was gone. Jim and Rob were there with their parents. The two teens knew they were going to miss George.

Lydia sat with her friends from the prayer group. Though they were all saddened by his passing, they realized he'd gone to a better place. George was no doubt happily in heaven now, reunited with his wife and son.

Irene and Ernie, along with Cheryl Hall and her children, were there to pay their respects, along with many others who'd known George and loved him.

It was truly a gathering of love, and many tears were shed as the funeral Mass came to an end.

Lydia walked slowly from the church into the greeting area, where she found Father Richards waiting for her.

"I need to speak with you a moment, Lydia, before I leave for the cemetery."

"What is it?"

"George called me the last night he was at home and asked me to take care of a few things for him. He wanted me to give you this." Father Richards handed Lydia an envelope.

She opened the letter and quickly read George's request. She was crying when she looked up at the priest. "I would be honored to take Duchess. Thank you, Father."

"I placed her in a kennel the night he passed away, so I can go with you later this afternoon, if you want, and we can pick her up."

"I'll be at home, so call me when you're ready."

"I'll do that. Thank you, Lydia. I know it meant a lot to George to be sure that Duchess would be taken care of."

Lydia moved on out of church.

Father Richards next sought out the Hunt family.

"Jim, could I speak with you and your parents for a moment?"

"Sure." Jim was surprised by his request. He couldn't imagine why the priest would want to talk to them.

Father Richards took them aside. "Jim, I have a note here for you from George."

"You do?" Jim was completely surprised.

"Yes. He asked me to give this to you with your parents' full knowledge and consent."

Belinda and Paul looked on in surprise as Jim opened the envelope and began to read:

*Dear Jim,*

*Your friendship and kindness has meant a lot to me these final days. You're a good boy. Please take care of the Mustang for me. I've made arrangements with Father to have the title transferred to your parents. I'm counting on you to keep her running. God bless you and keep you.*

George

Jim looked up at Father Richards with tears in his eyes. "I can't believe he did this."

"He cared about you, Jim. Make him proud of you," Father encouraged as he handed the keys over to Jim's dad.

"I will," Jim promised, and he meant it with all his heart.

Father Richards watched the Hunt family go, his heart filled with joy, knowing how George had managed to change so many lives for the better. He had been a rare man—a beloved man.

By the sheer power of his love, George had been a true miracle worker.

*Meanwhile, in a Hospital Across Town*

"All right, Rick," Dr. Hadley said. "Let's see how you're doing."

Rick, a thirty-five-year-old auto mechanic, had been burned by battery acid on the job and had lost his eyesight. Dr. Hadley had performed the cornea transplant with donated corneas, and they would now find out the results.

Rick blinked several times. A look of pure excitement and joy overtook him when he saw his beloved wife standing beside the doctor. He'd feared he was going to be blind forever—and now—

"Oh, my God!" Rick said with heartfelt emotion. "It's a miracle! I can see!"